the LONG mile

FORTHCOMING BY CLYDE W. FORD

Deuce's Wild

the Long mile

THE SHANGO MYSTERIES

Clyde W. Ford

Midnight Ink
Woodbury, Minnesota

First Edition
First Printing, 2005

Book design by Donna Burch
Cover design by Gavin Dayton Duffy
Cover photograph (Brooklyn Bridge) © 2004 by Kurt Scholz / SuperStock
Editing by Karin Simoneau

Midnight Ink, an imprint of Llewellyn Publications

Library of Congress Cataloging-in-Publication Data
Ford, Clyde W.
  The long mile / Clyde W. Ford
    p. cm.—(The Shango mysteries)
  ISBN 0-7387-0785-6
    1. Police—New York (State)—New York—Fiction. 2. African American
    police—Fiction. 3. New York (N.Y.)—Fiction. I. Title.

PS3606.O724L66 2005
813'.6—dc22   2005043768

Midnight Ink
Llewellyn Publications
2143 Wooddale Drive, Dept. 0-7387-0785-6
Woodbury, MN 55125-2989, U.S.A.
www.midnightinkbooks.com

Printed in the United States of America

To Chara:
Our long mile is love.

PROLOGUE

I PUSHED THROUGH THE turnstile, taking the long flight of stairs up from the subway two at a time, running fast, trying to keep one step ahead of the morbid images nipping at my heels: somber bagpipes playing over a sea of blue uniforms; a red-eyed widow in black clutching her child's hand in front of a flag-draped coffin. I've heard it said that one's soul is confused by sudden, violent death. That it flutters around the body like a bird over a downed mate, uncertain of what to do next.

I suppose every police officer has imagined the full-dress funeral that comes from falling in the line of duty. I envisioned myself futilely trying to get my wife Elizabeth's attention to tell her that I loved her, that I was sorry. And then trying my son, John Jr., believing he'd not outgrown such otherworldly communication. That he'd feel me as a breeze kissing his cheeks, raise his head, then press his hand to the air, as he pressed his hand to mine each night when we flexed our fingers against each other's three times in silence; three times for the words, "I love you."

I shook my head. I didn't like leaving my family to work nights, especially on a high-risk assignment.

On this humid, late summer evening, people strolled the Brooklyn streets with beach bags and towels under their arms. I made my way through a crowded Haitian neighborhood where the smell of fried food caused my stomach to growl. I had relatives from Haiti somewhere on my dad's side of the family.

By steady degrees, the streets emptied as I neared the river. I walked along the water's edge, while in the distance, Manhattan's lights flickered and the illuminated bridges spanning the East River appeared as huge strands of pearls strung across a dark, watery abyss.

I passed by hulking, abandoned buildings that were like dinosaurs frozen in space and time, relics of an industrial age long passed. The smell of stale urine greeted me at the entrance to the long tunnel that ran beneath these concrete and steel behemoths. The homeless sometimes used this tunnel, but so did our drug squad. These warehouses served as sets for our arranged drug deals, and this tunnel offered a means of slipping onstage and off unnoticed.

Tonight, Nicky Brooks' Harlem syndicate was making a big drug buy from a Columbian cartel. Bringing down Brooks' organization had been my operation, but the DEA planted one of their agents, Danny Rodrigues, inside the Columbian group. I wanted Brooks. DEA wanted the Columbians. I argued with Vincent Ciccarello, my superior, but ultimately the DEA got its way. They planned to let a four-million-dollar drug deal go through, just to get evidence for a federal case. I cared less about the federal case and more about taking several months' supply of crack off the streets. But then who listens to a detective? So the deal was set to go down tonight in one of these old warehouses, leaving surveillance and primary backup for Rodrigues to me.

I slipped into the tunnel and whispered into the darkness, "Radio check."

"Shannon, read you five by five." The response came through my ear bud. We also had a communications field team in a second abandoned warehouse overhead.

I switched on a small flashlight and counted rusting metal rungs traveling up from the tunnel. The first set led to a warehouse too close to the street and too exposed to the surrounding neighborhood. Engineers deemed the second warehouse structurally unstable. I gripped the rungs leading up to the third warehouse. Rust flaked off in my hand.

At the top, I switched off my flashlight and climbed out to the first floor. Dim outside light filtered in through the broken, dirt-caked windows, bathing the warehouse in an eerie glow. I hid behind the decaying remains of an elevator shaft and pulled my Browning 9mm out to check that I'd chambered a round. I also checked my watch. Nine o'clock. Liz was putting JJ to sleep, and he was pressing his fingers against the air. We'd made a pact that whenever I wasn't home by bedtime, we'd send each other our love this way. I raised my hand and flexed my fingers three times. Then I waited.

Suddenly, the huge bay doors of the warehouse rumbled open. A silver Mercedes and a dark blue BMW drove in. These weren't the traders, but the advance men on both sides, here to check the security of the warehouse for their bosses. I climbed back down the iron rungs and stepped into the tunnel. I heard heavy footsteps overhead and voices cursing the stench. I waited until the footsteps receded and then cautiously made my way back up. Two more cars pulled in—a limousine and a Lexus. Both cars left their headlights on. The Columbians were in the limo, while Brooks' men drove the Lexus. A battery-powered lantern set on top of the roof of the BMW sent a dazzling bright light throughout the space, and gave birth to a world of ominous, angular shadows.

Nicky wasn't here. He'd sent his lieutenants instead. A guy from the back of the limo and another from the back of the BMW got out and shook hands. The Columbian was a large man with a full head of jet-black hair tied back in a ponytail. The black guy working for Brooks had on a sweater and tennis shoes. He could have passed for a high school basketball coach except for the bulge under his left arm.

One of the Columbian bodyguards popped the limo's trunk and hauled out a wrapped brick of uncut cocaine about the size of a bread loaf. He placed it on the hood of the limo. Brooks' guy then waved to the Lexus, where a man stepped out. He pulled a test tube from a black bag he carried, dipped the tip of his knife into the package, and carefully extracted a blade of white powder, which he emptied into the tube. He added a few drops of liquid, shook the tube, then held it up to the light. He nodded his head and the Columbian smiled. Brooks' lead man reached into the Lexus and came out with a suitcase.

Suddenly, three guys jumped from the limo. Two from the BMW. I gripped my pistol and gritted my teeth.

I breathed into the mike. "Something's wrong. Deal looks like it's going south."

"We'll call in more backup."

But it was already too late for that. Rodrigues must have sensed trouble too. He ducked behind the BMW. And that's when all hell broke loose.

A Columbian raised his gun at Danny's head. Without thinking, I leaned against the metal cage, fired, and dropped him before he pulled the trigger. I thought the Columbians would turn their guns on Brooks' men, and vice versa, but they didn't. Instead, they all looked my way as though expecting to find me there. They fired at me with everything they had, pistols and automatic weapons.

"I need that backup, now!" I yelled into the mike.

I returned the fire, but I wasn't a match for them. Bullets pinged off metal and chuffed as they bit into old concrete. No backup had arrived, which meant the tunnel was my only hope. I thought I heard someone climbing the metal rungs. I remember thinking that one of the backup guys must have come in that way. But that was my last thought before my body jerked violently and a searing heat erupted in my chest. My pain spiked off-scale. I grabbed my chest and looked down to see blood oozing from between my fingers. "Hover above your body," I told myself. Then everything went blank.

I was surprised to wake up the next day with tubes plunged into most orifices. I barely made out a doctor holding a clipboard, hovering above me, uttering something about a bullet lodged next to my aorta. A few more millimeters over and I would never have awoken.

I struggled to raise my head and I looked past the foot of the bed. On the other side of a large window, Liz stood with JJ. Her eyes were red. JJ put his fingers to the window and flexed them three times. I tried to raise my hand but I couldn't. Both wrists were handcuffed to the bed.

Then a man in a suit stepped into the room and past the doctor. "John Shannon," he said, reading from a sheet of paper. "You're under arrest for the murder of Drug Enforcement Agent Daniel Rodrigues."

ONE

Two years later

"WE'RE ALL PRISONERS OF our minds."

Charles Promise liked to let the words hang in the air before he continued. "Doesn't matter which side of these cell bars you're on. The bars don't imprison you, your thoughts and feelings do. The bars won't set you free either, only your thoughts and feelings will. Someday you'll leave here. But when that day comes, will you step out of prison a free man?"

With a nerve-grating scrape of metal on metal, my cell door sliced open. I sat on the edge of my bunk mesmerized, unable to move, pondering Promise's words. After two years in prison, I was being set free. I was anxious to reclaim my life, yet from the pit of my stomach a hot swell of anger rose. I swallowed hard to keep it down. I'd served this time for murdering Danny Rodrigues. Now thanks to a smart lawyer I was temporarily free. I wanted to avenge Danny's murder and I wanted to vindicate myself, but I feared that this firestorm of anger would consume me first.

"Time, Shannon," a guard called out. He strummed the bars with his nightstick, beating out a one-note metallic dirge that ricocheted off the cellblock walls.

I stepped out of my cell. I nodded to the guard and then walked along slowly as he trailed me. We call this "walking the long mile." It's a term of honor, reserved for inmates taking their last steps down Death Row or their first steps toward freedom. A familiar musty smell hung in the air. Under my feet, the concrete felt hard and unforgiving. I walked past men standing silently in their cells. Our gazes met. Their eyes were fixed straight ahead, unflinching, an inmate's salute of defiance and respect.

I once worked as a NYPD detective. I never thought that I would earn the respect of convicted criminals, nor they mine. Now after two years in prison, I believe I knew why these men stood silently for me this morning. They saluted not the crimes for which we were convicted but the spirit within each of us that allowed us to survive in here day after day.

I slowed my pace and leaned over the railing for one last look down at the concrete floor four flights below. In my two years here, six men had taken this plunge. Some were pushed. Others jumped willingly. It's said that in the split seconds before hitting the floor, one has an unimaginable feeling of freedom.

"Move on, Shannon," the guard behind me growled, jabbing his nightstick into my back.

I stumbled forward but stopped at "the penthouse." I didn't care about the guard, or his nightstick. Neither could keep me from saying goodbye to my friend, Charles Promise. I reached through the cell bars and clasped Promise's hand. Our thumbs locked. Beneath his sagging flesh, I felt his bones.

"Thanks," I said.

"Wasn't nothing, John," he replied, looking me in the eyes, searching, not saluting.

Then his gaze softened. I let mine do the same. Promise and I stared at each other with our hands clasped. My palm grew warm.

In his early seventies, Promise's dark-brown skin was wrinkled, drawn at the corners of his eyes and lips. His light gray hair bordered on white. He had a prominent nose and deep, penetrating eyes. A serene smile always seemed to grace his lips.

Behind Promise, a thin blue light painted the early morning view from his barred window. On each level, the inmate closest to the stairs had a window, but only Promise, from his top-level cell, looked beyond the prison's walls.

The guard jabbed me harder, then barked, "Come on, Shannon."

I grit my teeth but I did not move.

"Ease up on him, Tom," Promise said, his voice floating like a feather from his darkened cell. "He's walking the long mile this morning. Let him walk it in his own time, in his own way."

Promise's voice had a hypnotic quality. The young white guard simply stared at the old black man. I'd witnessed this scene many times: a few quiet words from Promise calming an inmate or a guard. I believe Promise could do this because he'd been here in this same prison for so long. In some cases, he'd actually seen the fathers and grandfathers of inmates and guards come and go. His thin, ebony body was stooped now, though his arm muscles hinted of a once younger, robust man. He had an uncanny worldliness about him. In all his years inside prison, I bet he'd seen a lot more of life than the average person sees outside. I believe that Promise had found peace with his lifetime incarceration, and that gave him tremendous power over others on both sides of the cell bars who were seeking a similar peace in their lives. I dropped my hand and Promise pulled his inside.

"Been two years," he said, his voice still a whisper. "Walking out may shock your system."

"I'll manage," I said. "I get to see my wife . . . and my son. That'll help."

"That boy needs you," Promise said.

I smiled. "He's thirteen now. Bet he thinks he's grown and doesn't need anyone."

"I needed my father, and he wasn't there for me. You needed your father and he wasn't there for you. JJ needs his father, and you can be there for him now."

"I want to make up for lost time with him and with Liz."

"A man leaving prison doesn't always get a hero's welcome," Promise said. "Don't be surprised if JJ's angry 'cause you left him for two years."

"I didn't want to."

"It's his feelings that matter, not the facts."

I nodded.

"Don't be surprised if Liz's angry too."

"Because I left her?"

"Yes, and she's had a long time alone to think about what she really wants. Something's churning inside her or she wouldn't have sought a separation."

"Now that my conviction's been overturned, she and I can talk and set things straight between us. I want to start over," I said.

"May have less to do with your conviction than you think. It's her feelings that matter, not the facts," Promise said.

"But there are some facts that do matter," I said. "Like who killed Danny Rodrigues, and who framed me for his murder. Those facts I've got to discover."

"And I believe you will." Promise nodded. "But don't push the river. Let it come to you."

I nodded back.

"I'll come to see you," I said.

Promise's eyes brightened.

"I'd like that," he said.

I'm sure he'd heard similar promises from other inmates "walking the long mile." He fixed his gaze on me. His eyes moved slowly, deliberately, as though he was searching for something inside me. Maybe he already knew the truth of the promises I'd just made. Maybe he was searching for the truth in places within me I had yet to discover. The guard let us finish our exchange, and when Promise's smile widened, I knew he'd found what he'd been searching for.

"Whatever comes your way, you're gonna do just fine. I can see that," he said. "May not be easy, but you're gonna do just fine."

"Thanks," I said. I turned to leave, moving slower now. Whenever I walked away from Promise, I felt like I carried the added weight of his words.

The guard's heavy boots clunked on the metal steps as he walked down. Bedsprings squeaked as men flopped back onto their bunks. At the end of a long corridor illuminated with rows of fluorescent lights, we stopped in front of an office with a metal Dutch door. The guard shoved past me, then rapped his nightstick on the door, sending two dull thuds racing down the hallway and back. The top half of the door swung open.

"Shannon, John M," the guard on the other side said in a low monotone.

He pushed a paper my way. I signed for my possessions. He handed me a large envelope. But he held on. He set a cold piercing gaze in his eyes. The edges of his lips curled into a sneer.

"You lucky son-of-a-bitch," he said. "You kill another cop and then you beat the rap."

He sounded like a viper hissing. I tugged on the envelope, but the guard would not let go. His eyes said, "Go ahead. Rip it from my hands. Give me one last excuse to beat you." And I wanted to rip it from his hands. I wanted to rip my life from every hand that had stolen these two years from me.

"You'll be back," the guard said, adding a malevolent chuckle. "Just like homing pigeons, you black guys find your way back here."

I hardened my stare while the firestorm inside me grew. Then I remembered what Promise had done moments ago and what he'd told me many times: Not the eyes of a raging bull about to run into a matador's sword, but the eyes of a man steady within himself, who takes control by projecting quiet strength. I softened my gaze, still holding on to the envelope. Suddenly, the guard let go and then he slammed the upper half of the door in my face.

I opened the envelope and turned it on its end. I couldn't remember all the parts of me I'd given up when I stepped inside this prison. My wallet fell out, and it shocked me to see my photograph on an outdated driver's license. I wasn't bald then. I felt more items inside the envelope, but I decided to wait for a quiet moment away from here before rediscovering these lost pieces of myself.

Moments later, I walked the final steps of my "long mile," through the prison's front gate. I squinted, and when my eyes finally adjusted to the brilliant sunshine of this early October morning, I saw the rolling hills of upstate New York aflame in reds, yellows, and oranges against a cobalt-blue, cloudless sky. Early morning traffic whizzed by in both directions in front of the prison. Chilly air kissed my face and found its way through the weave of my sweater. I shivered slightly, but it felt invigorating and good.

A horn blew on the other side of the road.

"John."

I barely heard the muffled voice above the traffic. I looked across the road, hoping to see my wife and my son, but I saw a young white woman waving from the driver's window of her car. She stepped out. At first, I didn't recognize my lawyer, Nora Matthews. Until now, I'd only seen her across a thick glass partition, only spoken to her by prison telephone. After the separation decree, I knew that Liz might not be here to meet me. Still, I scanned Nora's car, hoping to see another door fly open and my son, John Jr., burst out.

But Nora stood alone.

A wall of traffic separated us. Winds rising from each passing vehicle swirled around me. While I waited for a break in the cars, I stared at Nora. She waved with wide sweeps of both arms, while her body bounced like a schoolgirl at a rock concert. I put her at five feet eight. She wore a full-length dress that was slit partially up one side and perfectly tailored to flow with the generous curves of her body. Its rust color also blended with the surrounding hills. But her smart outfit stood in sharp contrast to the fifteen-year-old Japanese import that she drove.

I stepped forward but misjudged the speed of an oncoming SUV. Nora rounded her lips and widened her eyes as I jumped back to my side of the road. I screwed up my face and shrugged. She laughed and put a hand out for me to wait. The yellow scarf fluttering around her neck gave her a carefree, untamed look.

Fed up with waiting, I sprinted through a gap in the traffic, racing across the two-lane roadway. My body flew through the crisp air, moving with an unfettered ease that I had nearly forgotten I possessed. Nora turned to face me. She reached her arms around my body. I pulled her into me, and she did not resist. Her soft, dark-brown hair brushed my chin. A subtle, fruity fragrance teased my nose. In the crisp fall air, I could feel heat rising from her body, carrying with it the unmistakable scent of a woman. She wrapped her arms tightly around me.

In part, I knew this was a victory hug. I'd let Innocence Watch take on my case after Nora and three other eager young white lawyers from the organization appeared at the prison. I'd already been in for six months. They said that Innocence Watch reviewed high-profile cases for breeches of the law. They only took on those that they thought they could win. They pointed out irregularities in the federal prosecution, and ineptitude in the way my attorney had handled the case. Nora led the team that successfully argued the appeal, resulting in my release.

She pressed her body further into me. My body responded. I started to lose myself in our embrace. I really wanted to. But then I stiffened and pushed away. A chill seized me. Nora was my lawyer not my lover. I wanted my wife here, and I couldn't pretend that Nora had taken her place.

"It's okay," Nora said.

But it wasn't okay.

"What happened to Liz and JJ?" I asked. "Did you hear from them? Is something wrong?"

"I don't know," she said. "I left messages. Liz never called back."

"Maybe she changed her mind," I said.

"Maybe," Nora said. "You can call her on my cell."

The caring I saw in her light-brown eyes told me she understood. She reached back in through the open window. I didn't want to face disappointment. Not yet. I put a hand on her shoulder. "I'll call on the drive back," I said.

A gust of wind caught Nora's yellow scarf, trailing it to one side of her neck. She grabbed my hand. "C'mon. We have a five-hour drive back to the city, and a lot to talk about on the way. You can stay at my place if you want. There's a hot bath, a great meal, and a comfortable couch."

A five-hour drive? Something inside of me snapped. I jerked my hand away from Nora. In prison, time is a commodity that you can possess more or less of. I could hear myself about to holler at Nora as though she'd just sentenced me to five hours. After two years in prison, even five hours in a car felt like too much time.

"Feds going to retry me?"

"They're still considering."

"Brooklyn D.A.?"

"Said he'd file no new charges until the feds decide."

"You believe him?"

"No. . . . Well, maybe."

"Maybe?"

Perhaps Nora could see the anguish in my face, or sense it in the way my body quivered. She grabbed my hand and squeezed tighter. "Don't worry," she said softly. "We'll get to the bottom of this together. We'll talk about it on the way home. One step at a time. We'll get there. One step at a time."

I traced the outline of Nora's vibrant red lips with my eyes as they formed each word slowly and deliberately. I searched her face. I desperately needed to believe her. She stared at me without blinking. "One step at a time." I repeated the words like a mantra. I also heard Promise tell me, "Don't push the river."

"Let's go," I said.

Nora smiled. She dropped my hand, opened the car door, and slipped into the driver's seat. I walked around toward the passenger's side. I heard honking overhead. I stopped and looked up. A flock of Canadian geese flew in chevron formation. Then, as if the order came from some unseen guiding hand, the entire flock pivoted in perfect harmony, heading off in a new direction.

I had just reached the trunk when I heard a set of brakes squeal. I whipped my head around. A car barreled toward me. I thought that a driver had gone off the road. I leapt out of the way. The tires kicked up a cloud of dust. The doors flung open and two men hopped out. I turned toward them. My body straightened.

A baby-faced, light-skinned black man approached me from the passenger's side, an older white male from behind the wheel. Both men wore a suit and a tie. Babyface walked with a swagger. The other man lagged a few feet behind.

I'm six foot three, and both of these men were at least as tall as me. If they wanted to fight, I felt pretty certain that I could take them. After two years in prison, my body was buff and rock hard. I saw Babyface look me over. Then I saw a slight bulge from beneath his armpit. He was carrying a weapon. I guessed the other one was carrying as well.

I wanted to jump Babyface before he had a chance to go for his gun, but Nora bolted from the car and came racing toward us. I stuck out my arm to hold her back. Simultaneously, both men reached into their pockets, whipped out thin wallets, and flashed badges at me.

"What the hell do you want?" I yelled.

"John Shannon," Babyface said, snapping like a bulldog. "NYPD. You're under arrest."

TWO

Babyface pulled out an all-black 9mm Walther and pointed it at me, but he stood so close I was sure I could take it from him before he got off a shot. My world began to move in slow motion. I could feel myself being split in two: a part of me ready to rush Babyface, another part screaming inside my head, "No!"

Nora must have sensed my inner standoff. "No," she said.

She pushed past me. She stood between the barrel of the Walther and me. Shock registered in Babyface's eyes. Nora's white skin flushed bright red.

"Who the hell are you?" Nora asked.

"Who the hell are you, lady?" Babyface replied.

"I'm his lawyer, dammit."

"Good. Then you can witness us reading him his rights. Now get outta my way." Babyface tried to sidestep Nora, but she moved with him like she was a championship guard and he was a basketball player trying to dribble around her.

Nora was in his face. "On what charges are you arresting him?" she asked.

"Manslaughter. Criminal negligence in the death of a federal agent. Interfering with a police investigation, for starters. It's all here," Babyface replied, yanking a crumpled sheet from his pocket and dangling it in front of Nora.

She snatched it from him. "Bullshit," she said, slapping the paper. "I demand that you wait here until I verify this arrest." She whipped out her cell phone.

Babyface's partner moved a few steps forward and pulled his semiautomatic pistol from its holster. It looked like an older-model Browning.

"Mommy's gone to make a call and find out what a bad boy her Johnny's been," he said in a taunting, singsong, childlike voice.

"Kiss my ass," I said.

He lunged at me, raising his gun as though ready to strike me. I stepped to one side, grabbed his arm, twisted it slightly, and then brought it down so the barrel of the pistol pointed at the ground. I held his arm there effortlessly while he grimaced and struggled against me. I smiled.

"Art, wait," Babyface said. He jerked his partner back.

I let go.

"Yeah Art," I said. "Junior has to muzzle his pit bull so it doesn't bite strangers."

Art glowered at me. I could feel myself breathing hard. From the cars whizzing by, exhaust fumes mingled with dust. The acrid mixture stung my eyes and burned my throat.

Whoever was on the other end of Nora's call got an earful. She shouted nonstop, stomped her feet in the dirt, and hurled epithets through the device. I cringed. It shocked me to hear such gutter language spewing from the lips of a beautiful woman. It must have shocked Babyface and Art too. But they laughed. She came back red-faced, near tears.

"I couldn't reach the Brooklyn D.A., only his assistant," she said. "But the bastard lied to me. I spoke with him right after the appellate court's ruling. He said that until the feds decided on a retrial, he'd agree to the terms of your release, and he wouldn't re-arrest you." Nora shook her head in disgust. "I'm so sorry." She blinked tears away. "It wasn't supposed to happen this way. Believe me, I didn't know."

She looked over to Babyface, and sneered. "Where are you booking him?"

"The Tombs," Babyface said.

"I'll be there before these two thugs have you there," she said. "I'll get you out again. I promise. In the meantime, don't resist."

Art chuckled.

"I guess this means no hot bath, good meal, and comfortable couch," I said.

Nora squinted at me. She cocked her head. Better to joke than to do something I'd later regret.

Art leaped to my side. He ripped the envelope with my belongings from my hand. Then in one smooth motion he twisted me around, threw me up against the trunk of Nora's car, and kicked my feet apart. He'd obviously done this many times. I felt like a rag doll. He put his hand on the back of my head and then pushed down. He jammed the side of my face painfully into the car, which flexed under my cheekbone, making a dimple in the trunk.

"Don't resist, Johnny," Art said, mocking Nora as he frisked me. "You heard what mommy said."

"You asshole," Nora said, tugging at Art's arm. "I'll have you up on charges of police brutality."

He brushed her aside. "And if you don't move out of my way, I'll haul you in for interfering with an arrest."

Art grabbed a handful of my sweater and then yanked me off the trunk. When he spun me around, Babyface snapped handcuffs on me and read me my rights. Nora jumped into her car and zoomed off. Babyface pushed me back toward their car. I stiffened against him. He pushed harder.

All the while I clung to the sound of Nora's engine fading in the distance, until I could no longer tease it apart from the clamor of traffic and the rustling of fallen leaves. I pulled my wrists against the cuffs and held them there, straining. The metal dug into my flesh but that didn't matter. The pain pulled me back from the edge of a dark abyss. Moments ago I'd walked out of the belly of a beast. Now it felt like that beast had opened its mouth and swallowed me whole again.

I put one foot into the unmarked police car. Babyface and Art pushed down hard on my shoulders, nearly folding me in two. They shoved me into the back seat and slammed the door shut. Sweat poured from my body. I forced myself to take slow, deep breaths. I closed my eyes and let my head fall back against the headrest. I tried to find Promise's voice in my mind. I worked hard to dampen the fiery vortex picking up speed as it whirled inside me.

———————

PROMISE LOVED MYTHOLOGY. He said that in ancient stories you could find truths for modern life. I remembered us walking the prison yard, talking about Sisyphus condemned in hell to forever push a boulder up a hill, only to have it roll back down again upon nearing the top.

After being convicted and sentenced for killing a DEA agent during a drug bust that went bad, I'd lived for two years at the bottom of Sisyphus' hill. Then, for a few moments this morning, I felt like I'd made it to the top of the hill with my boulder. Now, I imagined the Brooklyn D.A. sitting up there waiting for me, his face filled with glee, his foot on the boulder, ready to send it hurtling back down.

A stream of fall colors rushed past the windows. Through the partition, I saw my envelope perched above the dash. I strained against my cuffed hands, unable to take back anything that was mine. I tried to snap out of my funk by humming "'Round Midnight," but the plaintive sounds of Miles' horn only blew me deeper into a pit. I closed my eyes and started to doze off. The last thing I remember is Danny Rodrigues' face flashing across my mind.

Art hit the brakes, and our car came to halt, throwing me forward, catapulting me from my dreamy thoughts. We'd stopped at a toll plaza. Art whipped out his badge to get us through. We were less than an hour out of New York City now, traveling across the winding expanse of the Tappan Zee Bridge. Below us, the Hudson River threw off sunlight in thousands of tiny diamond flashes set against a backdrop of shimmering liquid green. Ahead, it looked like a painter had set a fiery autumn brush to the cliffs on the far side of the river. A few cumulus clouds hovered in the sky. Further south, a brownish haze encased New York City.

We entered Manhattan as the sun began to slump low in the sky, casting the shadows of tall skyscrapers over the roadway and the East River. The windows of buildings in Queens and Brooklyn, to my left across the river, glittered in the afternoon light. Sunlight struck the East River bridges midway. I fantasized about walking across a bridge, past the shadows, and then turning back to feel the sun's rays on my face.

We got off at Canal Street and headed west. As we crossed Bowery Street, I saw the twin towers of "The Tombs," as every cop and criminal called the Manhattan Detention Center.

I searched among the pedestrians for Nora. I looked for her car along the street, even though I knew she'd probably pulled into an underground garage. I needed the comfort of something familiar, something safe. Then our car blew right past Centre Street. I spun my head around, watching the towers glide by as though they held out some unknown promise now lost to me forever.

"Hey." I banged on the partition, pointing out the window with an almost prayerful gesture of my cuffed hands. "The Tombs are that way."

Neither man turned around. The muscles in my gut tightened. A sudden bilious taste arose in my mouth. Convicted of killing a federal agent, I was the scum of the scum to Babyface and Art; looked down upon by my former brothers and sisters in blue as a pariah, a bug they'd just as well squash. Thoughts of being dropped out of the car in an abandoned Brooklyn lot, told to run, and then shot, crossed my mind. I talked fast to myself. If that was the plan, these two were the stupidest cops on the force. They'd apprehended me in front of my lawyer. Besides, this wasn't the way to Brooklyn.

"Where are you taking me?" I yelled, banging on the partition again.

Art and Babyface looked at each other several times, but never at me. The car moved slowly along the traffic-clogged street. I continued yelling. I'm sure my muted voice was lost amidst the furious soundscape of the city, as my life's present drama was certainly lost to the throng of people walking by.

The car turned left onto Broadway. Ten blocks later we pulled into an underground parking lot at City Hall. Art rolled down his window. A security guard poked his head out of a small white booth. He looked at Art and Babyface, and then scowled at me. He stuck his head back inside. A moment later the yellow barrier in front of us rose, and the guard waved our car through. Art drove down several ramps to a secluded section with only a few parked cars, most of them the kind of limousines that carried city officials. City Hall? It didn't make sense. No one books an arrest here. Suddenly, Babyface and Art jumped out without a word, disappearing through a door.

Sitting alone, handcuffed, I felt like I'd been thrown into solitary. No. In solitary, at least you knew to expect three meals a day. I didn't know what to expect here. I stared at the car door and thought about ramming it with my shoulder then kicking at the opposite window with all my strength until my muscles ached. I knew better. I'd driven cars like this before. The window would only resound with dull thuds. I'd never break it. I took some deep breaths and let my head fall back into the seat.

Everything happened so quickly after Danny Rodrigues' murder. It seemed as though I'd barely recovered from being shot when I was on trial, then in prison. The judge denied me bail. I was in custody from the moment I was taken to the hospital until my release today. I never had a chance to get back on the streets to find out who set me up, and why. I'd waited two years for that opportunity, and here it was being taken from me again, and again I didn't know by whom or why. Living with unanswered questions can be the cruelest punishment.

Twenty minutes later, the door that Babyface and Art disappeared through opened. Two new guys in suits headed for the car. Young, white, tall, clean-cut, they certainly didn't work for NYPD. One was blonde, the other dark haired. They looked like they'd been cut from the same Midwest cloth, like they both had just stepped off an Ivy League campus and ought to be working a few more blocks downtown in a Wall Street banking firm. From the slight bulge under their armpits, I knew they were packing. FBI was my first thought, DEA my second. Damn. Were these guys coming after me because they thought that I'd killed Danny Rodrigues?

One suit opened the door. The other stood back, guarding against my escape. "Mr. Shannon," the one reaching for my arm said calmly, "please follow us, sir."

Something inside me let go.

"Fuck you!" I yelled, pulling my arm from his and sliding farther back into the car. "I'm not going anywhere."

The second guy rushed around to the other door and opened it. He stuck his head in and I butted him in the face with the back of my head, hard. He yelped. I must have hit his nose. It sprung a leak and started bleeding.

"Damn you, Shannon," I heard the first guy say. He reached in and grabbed my left leg with both his arms. My ankles had not been cuffed, so I sent the heel of my right shoe into his face. He reeled back holding his mouth with both hands.

All I had to fight with were my legs and my head, but I wasn't going without a fight, even though I knew I couldn't win. I inched my body along the back seat and squirmed out the door. The guy I'd kicked in the face was reaching inside his jacket. I kneed him in the groin and he went down groaning. I knew I'd better look out for the other stockbroker. I turned around and then ducked quickly as he swung at me. I caught him in the stomach with my shoulder and flipped him to the ground. I went back for the first guy, struggling to get to his feet. I kicked him in the chest and he moaned.

I spun around for the other man, when suddenly cold metal exploded against the back of my head. I tried to reach for my head with my cuffed hands but I couldn't. The pain in my head skyrocketed. A warm sticky trickle oozed from my skull. My knees buckled under me. The world around me slipped away.

THREE

ONE NICE THING ABOUT waking up from being knocked unconscious is the first few moments of euphoria. Groggy, but thankful to be alive, it's like being born again. I've often wondered if we wake up in a similar state after death. Promise said that in traditional African beliefs, death is a journey underground or underwater to a world that is a mirror image of the world of the living, only upside down. I blinked my eyes open, and when the fuzzy double images settled down, my world was upside down.

I sat up. The room I was in spun like a carousel. After the ride ended, I looked around, expecting to find myself inside a holding cell or a small sparse interrogation room. Instead, I sat on a soft leather couch in an office full of books. A man stood in front of me, leaning against the edge of a heavy wooden desk. A hint of his cologne floated my way. My vision drifted in and out of focus, finally stabilizing enough for me to bring him into focus.

This man must have been in his late fifties, and was dressed in an expensive dark-blue woolen pinstriped suit with a bold red tie and a matching red silk handkerchief folded so that two points stuck out of his breast pocket. A high gloss shone from the toes of his maroon oxfords. I placed him only an inch or two shorter than me. He filled out his suit in a way that suggested a sturdy, in-shape body. I could easily picture him in sweat-stained clothes on a racquetball court at the New York Athletic Club. He had black hair, graying at the temples, and chiseled facial features. A deep furrow angled prominently across both cheeks, which were tinted a subtle shade of blue. This guy needed to shave twice a day.

We eyed each other for a few seconds. I had the feeling he was sizing up how much of a threat I posed. My head ached. When I reached my fingers behind me, they found their way to a chestnut-sized lump protruding from the back of my skull. The lump was cold. On the couch beside me, I saw an ice pack wrapped in a bloodstained towel.

"Ken Tucker, John," the man said. "I apologize for the manner in which you were brought here."

The handcuffs were off but my wrists still burned. I rubbed them. "Really?" I said. "Suppose I jumped up and punched you out, then apologized when you came to?" I stared at Tucker while a drumfire of pain beat inside my head.

"You wouldn't make it more than a few inches off the couch," Tucker said impassively. "But I can understand why you'd like to try."

"Who the hell are you?" I asked. "Why did you have me brought here?" I couldn't tell if I was still in City Hall. Tucker's office must have been on an upper floor. Out of his window, I only saw blue sky and the tops of other buildings. The sky was still light. I must have been out for less than an hour.

"I'm the head of the Mayor's Office of Municipal Security," he said.

MOMS. I ran the acronym through my mind. I laughed. "Bullshit."

"I worked at the CIA for thirty years," Tucker said. "The mayor's an old friend. When he took office, he asked me to leave my position as Director of Counterintelligence to set up the Office of Municipal Security here in New York. He wants the city to be out in front of Washington on homeland security. He thought New York needed to coordinate intelligence gathering, law enforcement, and threat assessment through one office."

Tucker stood up and walked to the wall behind his desk. I stayed seated, blinking my eyes a couple times to get them to stay in focus. I reached for the ice pack and put it to my head. The cold numbed the pain. It angered me that I probably couldn't have made it more than a few inches off the couch if I'd gone after Tucker. I wanted to believe it was because I had been knocked unconscious, though from his relaxed demeanor I knew Tucker felt that he could take me in a fight. His disjointed nose, which appeared to have been broken more than once, suggested that he was no stranger to violence.

A purple glass vase with fresh yellow flowers sat on Tucker's desk, alongside family photos in a silver frame. A telephone, a water pitcher, and a glass were the only other items I noticed. No papers cluttered his desktop. Photographs of him shaking hands with three presidents adorned the walls. From a spot next to the picture of him shaking hands with Clinton, Tucker plucked a silver-plated letter and handed it to me. In it, the mayor welcomed him to his new post as Director of the Office of Municipal Security. I wasn't impressed. "Does all this attention mean you're about to re-arrest me as a terrorist and strip me of my constitutional rights?"

He chuckled. "No. It means I want to offer you a job."

"Hell of a recruitment campaign you have here. Kidnap prospective employees, knock them unconscious, and then throw them on a couch in the director's office for their first interview. What do you do if an employee shows up late for work? Send out a SWAT team?"

"It needed to look like an actual arrest. If you hadn't resisted, no one would have gotten hurt."

"And if you had gone about things in a normal way—"

"I don't go about things in a normal way."

"Apparently not. Anyway, the answer is no. Even if I was looking for a job, I think I'd choose an employer with a little less enthusiastic recruitment style. Now if the employment interview is over, I'll be leaving." I stood up and handed the silver letter back to Tucker. Gravity took its toll. My head pounded harder with each inch farther away from the ground. I felt woozy and collapsed back onto the couch.

As I slumped, Tucker rose, straightening his body, pushing himself away from the edge of his desk in a calculated, choreographed dance of physical intimidation. After proving his point, he leaned on the desk again.

"Since you're in no shape to leave, you might as well hear me out," Tucker said. "One of my conditions was that I be given complete authority to recruit and hire the best of the best in law enforcement across any department of the city."

"What? Are you kidding? I thought intelligence was your game. Haven't you heard? I was convicted of murdering a DEA agent. I'd hardly qualify as 'the best of the best.'"

"Evidentiary discrepancies. Eyewitness inconsistencies. Generally poor defense counsel. You weren't convicted. You were probably framed, although by amateurs. I've toppled governments with less evidence than the prosecutors had in your case. Someone got sloppy. They didn't figure on Innocence Watch. You're out. But Justice may retry. The Brooklyn D.A. may file new charges. So you're not free."

"Gee, sounds like you know more about my case than my lawyer. Tell me, who really killed Danny Rodrigues?"

"I wish I knew," Tucker answered.

"Bullshit." It hurt my head to yell. "I step out of prison. You snatch me off the side of the road. Offer me a job. Cut the crap. Stop playing games with me. Ex-cons make great informers. Is that what you're looking for? Someone with connections inside the federal prison system? If it is, I'm not interested."

Tucker smiled. "No. Nothing trivial like that. I'm looking for Office of Municipal Security agents. Terrorism's on the rise, and the terrorists want to bring it to America. New York City is America as far as they're concerned. The city has the biggest defense and intelligence budget outside of the federal government. Post 9/11, the city spends more money in this one area than many small countries. And I'm the guy everyone loves to hate. Under one umbrella, I'm supposed to bring together agencies that have for decades staked out turf here and jealously guarded it—police, fire, emergency services, FBI, Coast Guard, to name a few. My department is a mini-replica of the Department of Homeland Security. I coordinate federal, local, and state agencies with "old boy" networks based on favors, family, and friendships, sometimes legal, sometimes not. I come along, appointed by the mayor, and these agencies are told to work with me, to share the information and resources that have been the life-blood of their power. Suddenly I'm the enemy. You saw what happened when the Department of Homeland Security was established."

"No, I didn't. I was sitting on the sidelines for that."

"Coast Guard, FEMA, INS, transportation, the same agencies we have at the local level had to come together nationally," Tucker continued. His baritone voice reminded me of a radio announcer. "All fought to maintain power. Same thing happened in the city. You want to crack a network, you either plant friendlies inside or find friendlies who've been inside."

"What makes you think I'm a friendly?"

"You've got an enemy out there who framed you for murder." Tucker pointed out the window. The sleeve of his jacket rose with the motion, exposing a gold cufflink. "An enemy possibly within the NYPD. And if I were you, I'd be champing at the bit to find out who and why."

"What makes you think that I have an enemy inside NYPD?"

"Thirty years of reading tea leaves."

"So you don't think I'm guilty?"

"I think you were a smart cop with a great record. You stretched the rules when you could, and broke them when you had to. I like people who think and act outside the box."

"As long as they're kept inside of your box."

Tucker turned his back on me. He stared out the window, which faced west. Deep orange tinged the edges of the evening sky, fading fast to indigo.

"I need someone who knows how NYPD works, but with no allegiance to the force," he said.

"In case you also have an enemy inside NYPD?"

He turned around, stared at me, and said bluntly, "The enemy of my enemy is my friend. Especially given that my liaison at NYPD is Vincent Ciccarello."

My head snapped back and a sharp pain shot down my neck upon hearing the name. Tucker simply stared at me without flinching.

"I don't understand," I said. "Vincent Ciccarello's head of the Brooklyn and Manhattan Narcotics Unit. I served under him before I was convicted and sent to prison."

"*Was* head of BMNU," Tucker said. "After 9/11, he was appointed to head NYPD Intelligence."

I laughed even though it hurt. "Now there's a double oxymoron."

"What?" Tucker asked.

"NYPD intelligence for starters. Vincent Ciccarello as its head."

"I'm not sure what to make of the man and his two-thousand-dollar suits," Tucker said. "But I checked his record. That's how I stumbled upon you. He damaged your case with his testimony. Why? You had the best record of all of his narcotics detectives. Why would he turn on you?"

Tucker knew how to burrow into his opponent's weaknesses. He knew that I'd asked myself that same question many times in the last two years. "It's not like we were ever friends," I said.

"Is he dirty?"

"Don't know."

"Does he have something to hide?"

"Don't know that either."

"That's what bothers me," Tucker said. "I don't like it when I don't know. At the Agency, I worked for twenty years beside a man whom I thought I knew. We were friends. Our kids played together. Our wives shopped together. We went to the same church. Turns out he'd been a Soviet double agent all that time. Even his wife didn't know. He did untold damage, exposing our assets in Eastern Europe, many of whom were executed. I'm an outsider coming into this job. I've got to have people around me that I can trust."

"If your recruitment style doesn't change, you'll have a hard time finding any. You don't know me. Why trust me?"

"I don't know you, but I've known many men like you. And I don't trust you. What I trust is how you'll respond to the pressures you're put under."

"Like an experimental rat navigating an electrified maze?"

"Depends."

"On what?"

"How sadistic the experimenter is."

Tucker bent over a vase on his desk. He caught the stem of a yellow flower between his fingers. He sniffed it. "Even if Ciccarello is

31

squeaky clean, I can't take at face value what comes out of his office. Drugs, terrorism, organized crime. The information is too important. I need my own agents out there, agents with no ties to NYPD independently verifying the intel that I receive. That's how we played the game at the Agency, and that's the way I'll play it here."

"Spy versus spy versus spy?"

Tucker laughed. "Yes," he said.

"No thanks. The job description doesn't sound appealing."

"You'll answer only to me. I answer only to the mayor."

"And who answers to their conscience?" I asked.

He looked at me quizzically, as if that question had never crossed his mind.

"I don't care how short the chain of command is," I said. "The last time I trusted it, a link broke and I ended up being convicted of murder. Frankly, I'd rather be self-employed."

"Doing what?" He laughed.

"Finding out who framed me, for starters."

"How are you going to manage that? Your name's been smeared over the front page of every New York newspaper; every policeman in the city believes you gunned down a DEA agent; you can't even carry a gun for your own protection; your wife's ready to divorce you; you're at the mercy of a district attorney who hates you and a starry-eyed lawyer who's taken you on as her *cause du jour*. Not a world-class beginning to an investigation."

"You know my shoe size, as well?"

"Thirteen," Tucker said without hesitation.

"Go to hell."

Woozy or not, I got up to leave. Tucker beat me to the door, put his hand on the doorknob, and blocked my way out. His cologne was strong. The steely look in his blue eyes was even stronger. He seemed capable of staring at me forever without looking away. I stared back.

"You never belonged with the NYPD. You were too smart. I've seen your college transcripts. Graduated with honors from City College in History. Applied to doctoral programs at NYU and Rutgers. Got accepted at both places, then wrote to the admissions officers and told them you'd have to postpone your entry because of your mother's sudden illness. You needed to find work to support her. Tragically, your mother died, but you never made it back to grad school. Dreams like that may be deferred but they don't die. You wanted to be more than a cop. Deep down you probably still do."

"What? You've got a degree in psychotherapy too?"

"No, but I make a point of running psychological profiles on prospective employees. You've got the mind of a scholar and the heart of a warrior. Your marks at the police academy were superior. If you'd applied for a job at the Agency, I'd have hired you in a heartbeat. And we'd have found a way for you to get that advanced degree. It may not be too late. NYU's still a great school. You could enroll there and work here. I'm sure I can figure out a way for this office to help with tuition."

"I'm flattered, but I'm still not interested."

"If you want to find out who framed you for Rodrigues' murder, I can help. If you work for me, you'll be licensed to carry. You'll have unsurpassed access to information and resources. I've got friends in the government. I'll see about quashing a new federal trial. I'll talk to the mayor. He'll talk to the Brooklyn D.A. . . . . Shannon, I'm offering you a chance to have your life back."

"No. You're offering to play god with my life."

Tucker was not easily deterred. "I'm sure you want to see your boy. He could look up to you as more than just an ex-con."

"You leave JJ out of this." I pushed his arm aside and reached for the doorknob.

But Tucker grabbed my wrist and pried my hand from the door. He pushed me back. From the look in his eyes, I wasn't sure what he was going to do next, or if he even knew. He relaxed his grip. I was thankful because I was too weak to fight him off.

"I have two boys, grown now, but I still remember the swell in my chest when I'd see that look in their eyes that said, 'That's my dad, and I'm proud of him.' Look, if you change your mind, give me a call." Tucker stuffed his business card into my pants pocket.

"If I change my mind, I'll sue you for false arrest and imprisonment."

"Don't make a decision you'll regret."

"Is that a threat?"

He answered with his silence.

FOUR

I YANKED TUCKER'S DOOR open and burst through the outer door
into the hallway. The elevator bell dinged and the doors slid open.
Several people were waiting to step on. If I hustled I could make it
too. But a woman's voice called out from inside Tucker's office as the
door swung shut. "Mr. Shannon, wait. I have something for you."

I twirled around too quickly. I stumbled back to Tucker's office. I
groped for the door handle. I held on to it while the hallway spun.
When things settled down, I pulled the door open. A killer pair of
hazel eyes looked up at me from behind a desk. I don't know how I
missed her before. Tucker's secretary must have been in her mid to
late thirties. She had on a sweater the color of her eyes, with a matching necklace and earrings. From her honey-colored skin, thick dark
hair, high cheekbones, and full, fleshy lips, she could have been
African American, Native American, or even Polynesian. Bottom line:
she'd stop traffic crossing a street.

"Do you need to sit down?" she asked.

"No." I waved her off.

"Mr. Tucker wanted you to have this before you left." She reached into her desk drawer and came out with the envelope I had taken from prison. I'd forgotten all about it. I let go of the door and walked back into the office. A wave of embarrassment swept through me. I must have looked a mess, with a bloody knot on my head.

"My name is Charlene," she said. She handed me the envelope, then she lowered her voice, which only turned up her charm. "This one too," she said. She pulled a smaller white envelope from her desk.

"John Shannon," I replied.

"I know," she said.

I took both envelopes from her. I reached out to shake her hand. Her skin felt soft and silky smooth. I'd gone two years without holding or touching a woman. I held Charlene's hand longer than I should have, but she didn't pull away. I could have held it all day. Finally, I let it go and turned to leave.

"I hope I see you soon," she said.

"That would be my pleasure."

"Take care of your head," she said.

She smiled at me, which was worth at least two Tylenol. I wanted to say more to her, but out of the corner of my eye I saw Ken Tucker watching from behind the blinds of his office. I wondered if she also figured in his recruitment scheme, which made my headache return.

I walked through the main door and stood on the red carpet in front of the elevator. I leaned into the "down" button. The lighted numbers above the elevator doors showed that the cars were in the twenties and going down. I'd be here for a while. I slipped my finger under the flap of the small envelope and opened it. My head jerked back. A thick wad of twenty-dollar bills was tucked inside. Blood pounded in my gut. My head started throbbing again. I wanted to burst through both of Tucker's doors and stuff the money down his throat. Instead, I walked back through the first door, smiled at Charlene, and said, "I'm back."

She smiled. "So soon."

"Tell Mr. Tucker thanks, but I won't be needing this." I handed the envelope with the bills to Charlene. She frowned. I made a point of staring in the direction of Tucker's office, in case he was still watching.

When I walked out of the office again, the doors of an elevator car were beginning to close. I picked up my pace, thrusting my hand between them. The doors backed open and I stepped in. The elevator dropped and my stomach with it. An image lingered of Ken Tucker delicately holding the stem of a yellow flower between his fingers. Give him twenty more years and he'd perfectly fit the bill for an eccentric spymaster. I felt invaded, the same way I felt invaded in prison, where guards had the right to know everything about you, including your shoe size. Regardless of what Tucker offered, working for him would be like stepping into a menagerie of manipulation. My freedom was worth more to me than that.

It must have been rush hour. The elevator seemed to stop at every floor. People packed the car. I stared at the back of a man's head, his thinning, brown hair barely covering a bald spot. I followed the contours of a woman's neckline as it appeared from beneath the gentle waves of her hair and disappeared into her blouse. Freedom brings small rewards. People-watching could get you killed in prison.

Tucker's mention of Ciccarello surprised me. Ciccarello and I clashed from the moment he was promoted to head my narcotics unit. He allowed the DEA to take over my investigation of a major drug deal between a Colombian group and a drug lord in Harlem named Nicky Brooks. That deal resulted in the death of Danny Rodrigues and my conviction for his murder. And Ciccarello was number one on my hit parade of who set me up. I wondered what more

Tucker knew about him. A company man like Tucker never plays all of his cards on the first hand.

The elevator bounced softly at the lobby. The doors slid back and I was swept out with a mass of people. I'd get back to Tucker and Ciccarello. Right now, what I wanted—what I needed—was to see my wife and my son. But I looked a mess. I couldn't show up on their doorstep like this.

Outside, the sun set low in the sky. The city was a shadowed maze of asphalt canyons. I hunched my body against the chilly fall air. I tucked my prison envelope under my arm. From the bulge in it, it felt like a box or book was inside. I hailed a cab on the first try. I slid into the back seat. The driver had a full beard and wore a dark blue turban. The name on his license read "Abdullah Hajji." Abdullah's static-filled voice came over a small speaker.

"Where to?" he asked. His *w* sounded more like a *v*. "Hospital?"

"What?"

"Don't look so good," Abdullah said.

"I hit my head. I need to go home, clean up. Go to 232 West 138th Street," I said.

"Striver's Row?" he said. "Must be a rich man."

I realized I'd given him my home address without thinking. My home? Well, according to the separation papers, Liz's now. "No, make that 125th Street and Malcolm X Boulevard," I said. "State Office Building."

"Ahh, going to see President Clinton?" He made the *i* in Clinton's name sound like a long *e*. "Must be a powerful man." He chuckled and then pushed a button to start the cab's meter.

"It's rush hour, and I've only got forty dollars on me," I said.

Abdullah shook his head. "Neither rich nor powerful. Might have to get out at 86th Street and walk from there." He laughed, zooming off in the direction of the Hudson River.

We crawled through rush hour traffic until we reached the Westside Drive. I rubbed the bruised spot on the back of my head and winced. At 86th street, the meter read just over twenty-seven dollars. I did a quick mental calculation. With a tip, I'd just about make it to the State Office Building. Nora had her office there. I couldn't think of another place to go.

I turned the envelope over, then turned it back the other way again. The back of a taxi was not the right place to reopen my past. We got off the West Side Drive at 125th Street. Bright store lights illuminated the street. I strained to see out the window, hardly recognizing Harlem after two years of being away. Old Navy, The Disney Store, Foot Locker, Starbucks, Staples, and Marshalls. The Disney Store on 125th Street? Black America's main street looked ever more like a Middle American shopping mall.

Abdullah must have sensed my dismay. "You know IHOP has taken over Small's," he said. "But they left the front of the old building standing."

"And I'm sure they'll name a pancake after Bessie Smith and Duke Ellington, maybe a waffle after Count Basie."

I don't think Abdullah knew whom I was talking about, but he did understand what I meant. "See, 9/11 changed things a little," he said, bringing his thumb and index finger together. "Money changes things a lot." He gestured along 125th Street.

"Be careful what kind of equality you fight for," Promise liked to say. "Do you really want to be equal in the materialism, greed, and avarice of this society? Or do you want equality of opportunity to live your life by more authentic, humane values?"

The New York State Office Building loomed massive and lonely ahead of us across Malcolm X Boulevard. I wondered how many other tall buildings and chain stores would join it in fifty or one hundred years, engulfing Harlem. Perhaps a visitor then might find a small plaque inside the lobby of one of these steel and glass behemoths that testified to a time when Harlem was the soul of Black America.

We waited for a light at Malcolm X Boulevard. I looked over to the southeast corner of the intersection. Malcolm once preached from a soapbox in front of the Hotel Theresa there. I always identified with that corner. I was born a few years after Malcolm's murder. John Malcolm Shannon. My father claimed he named me after the man.

The light changed, but by the time we crawled to the intersection, it had changed back to red again. Abdullah checked the meter and pushed a button. It stopped ticking. I reached for the doorknob to get out.

"No. No," he said. He held up his hand. "I take you to the door. You give my regards to President Clinton when you see him. Clinton, good man. Not so much bad at home or abroad when he was president." He pointed to his turban. "Especially for us Muslims."

Abdullah sped through the intersection on the next green light. The tires of the cab screeched as he made a sweeping U-turn, which placed us directly in front of the State Office Building's plaza. I handed him two twenties. He handed me a receipt. I got out.

Above me, west-facing windows on a few of the upper floors still glowed with a deep orange, like the myriad eyes of a fly reflecting the dying rays of the sun. In the large plate glass windows on the bottom floor, I caught a glimpse of myself walking toward the revolving doors. I looked ragged. I tugged my sweater off, sending bursts of shivering pain through my body as the sweater slid over the knot on my head. I found a bloodstain on the back of my sweater. I wondered if blood had soaked through to my shirt as well. I didn't see any in front. I didn't want to think about what I might find on the back.

The revolving doors ejected me inside. Two burly guards eyed me suspiciously as I walked through the metal detector. It beeped, and one guard leapt at me. I left my watch in a tray and stepped through the detector again. I cleared without a beep, but he still swept my body with a wand.

"Who you here to see?" he asked.

"Innocence Watch."

"Twelfth floor."

I checked the building's registry anyway, located behind massive glass frames on one of the highly polished granite walls. It was hard to miss Clinton's entry. "Office of the President of the United States, William Jefferson Clinton. Penthouse." Under *I*, I found Innocence Watch on the twelfth floor.

I waited for an elevator. Clinton had guts to locate his office here in the middle of Harlem. I respected him for that, even if I didn't like all that he'd done in office. At least he was the first president who really appeared comfortable around African Americans. He seemed to enjoy, even understand us. He hadn't appointed lightweights to important positions, either, or placed blacks in his cabinet, then undercut their authority. Most of all, I liked Clinton because he was smart. He spoke eloquently and intelligibly. The current guy in office didn't do much for me.

Nora had guts too, taking on my case. She was a woman who took charge. She did most of the talking the day Innocence Watch visited me in prison. Fire leapt into her eyes. She seemed like she was on a crusade. She told me that one of the organization's interns discovered that the FBI Crime Labs handled evidence from my case during a period when a whistleblower exposed widespread problems there. The intern followed the evidence trail back to NYPD, and found a discrepancy there.

"Your 9mm Browning, the weapon that fired two bullets into agent Danny Rodrigues' body, was bagged at the warehouse with four rounds still in the gun," Nora said.

"The FBI Crime Labs also logged the gun in with four rounds," I said.

"But the ballistics report from the Crime Labs said that all four rounds were in the magazine." She gave me a wholesome smile.

"Which would mean that someone reloaded my magazine but forgot to chamber a round," I said.

"Or didn't have time to chamber it," Nora said. "And whoever did that probably shot and killed Danny Rodrigues, or at least knows who did."

"And there I was with a bullet in my chest, blood all over me. I probably looked dead already."

"Or the backup team could have gotten there and this mystery man had to escape back into the tunnel. Whatever the reason, we don't have to produce the killer. All we have to do is show beyond reasonable doubt that you didn't kill Rodrigues."

I remembered Nora, with her never-say-die determination and a slightly incongruous Midwest twang, saying to me, "We want to take on your case. I want to be your lawyer. I know I can win."

I also remembered how quickly I tempered my elation. Prison teaches you not to have great expectations. Promise believed that wasn't all bad. "Make no appointments, you'll have no disappointments," he'd say. "Just accept life as it comes, good or bad."

In front of me, the elevator door slid open. A sea of people flooded out, sweeping me backward with them. I fought upstream, then stepped alone into the empty car. I pressed "twelve." The doors closed and I looked up at the convex mirror tucked into a corner of the car, where I saw a grotesquely distorted image of myself with a huge bald head and a tiny, truncated body. The elevator jerked as it rose.

When I stepped off the elevator at the twelfth floor, I followed the numbers and the nut-brown carpet to 1284. The sign on the tall light-oak door read "Innocence Watch." I pushed down on the tubular metal door handle and walked inside. A sweet, fruity smell greeted me as I entered. A young man sat behind a light oak desk in the reception area. He raised his head and looked at me as though he'd been awaiting my arrival. It surprised me to find a male receptionist.

"Hi," he said, stretching the word into a one-note song. He held out his hand without standing. "I'm Brendan." The name oozed from his lips.

Brendan had a bantamweight handshake. I pulled up on mine, fearing that I'd crush him. "I'm John Shannon," I said.

"Oh, my word," he gushed. "Nora was worried to death about you. When she didn't find you at The Tombs, she had me call every precinct in Manhattan. Honey, is she going to be glad you're alright." He pulled his hand slowly from my grasp, then slapped the air gracefully. "She didn't tell me you were bald. I think bald men are so sexy."

His comment surprised me. Obviously, Brendan wasn't bashful about speaking his mind.

I gave Brendan a quick rundown of what happened after Babyface and Art delivered me to City Hall. Brendan's eyes bounced from side to side, as though he was visually following each of my words. He had smooth alabaster skin and fine features. His dark-brown hair was slicked back and parted in the middle. He wore a teal, collarless linen shirt. A gold bracelet hung from his left wrist and several rings graced his long, slender fingers. His fingernails glistened, as though he had nail polish on. A small gold stud pierced his left earlobe, and the sweet smell in the air was his cologne, though it would have complemented Nora well.

"Is she here?" I asked, pointing toward an oak door with her name on it.

Brendan's eyes ran the length of my body, which made me a little uncomfortable. We had a saying in prison: "It's okay to window shop as long as you don't try to enter the store."

"She's in with another client." He squinted. "Don't you want to freshen up before you see her?"

He swiveled around in his chair and stood up without waiting for an answer. I followed the scent of his cologne as he strolled over to a closet on the far side of his desk. He swung the door open and stuck his head in, flipped through several racks of clothes, and emerged holding a hanger upon which a sweater had been neatly folded over a pair of trousers.

"You can change there." His arm rose gracefully from his side, and he tapped the air lightly with his index finger in the direction of a door on the other side of the room. "Do you need help dressing?" He smiled mischievously.

I shook my head. "I think I can manage."

"When you leave, there's a nice coat for you to wear." He pointed to the wooden coat rack by the door. "I'll hang it there."

Once inside the office bathroom, I discovered not just a sweater and trousers, but underwear and an undershirt as well. I stood in front of the mirror in my new silk boxers. I chuckled. It must have been a lucky guess. Unless Nora had spoken with Ken Tucker, she couldn't have known that I preferred boxers.

In almost two years, I hadn't taken a long hard look at myself. The crow's feet around my eyes had deepened. The furrows across my brow were more permanent. I traced the outlines of my upper body muscles. I clenched my fists and flexed my arms. The two heads of my biceps popped out. I pulled my elbows into my sides and squeezed. My pecs swelled, pushing my nipples forward.

My gaze dropped just below my collarbone, and I shrank from the sight. I approached it again, timidly, with morbid fascination. On the right side of my chest, I had a circular scar from the .44 round that I'd taken the night that Danny Rodrigues was killed.

Proud flesh. What a strange name to call a wound. I ran my fingers over the smooth hairless mound at least as large as a half-dollar coin, and darker than my already dark skin. Its edges were tapered, giving the appearance of a huge third eye staring back at me in the mirror. "Anger or wisdom. You can choose how to view your wound," Promise once said. "You can become consumed with a need for vengeance, or look at it as an opening to bring you greater insight into yourself."

Outside the bathroom, doors opened and closed. It sounded like Nora's client had left. I slipped the off-white mock turtleneck sweater gently over my head and stepped into the brown woolen trousers. A gentle knock on the door followed. I cracked the door open to see Brendan smiling.

"I thought you might need these." A pair of shoes dangled from his hands.

"Thanks," I said.

I took the shoes, closed the bathroom door, and checked the size. Thirteen. Damn. Maybe Nora *had* talked with Tucker.

When I stepped from the bathroom, Brendan looked up from his desk and whistled. "My, don't you look handsome," he said. He pressed a button on his telephone, then trolled, "Nora, darling, he's here . . . and looking mighty good."

Several doors with hand-carved nameplates surrounded the reception area. One read, "Nora Daniels." Nora's door burst open and she flew out. She rushed over and grabbed my hand.

"Where did they take you? I waited for you at The Tombs." She dragged me toward her office. "When you didn't show up there, I called the Brooklyn D.A.'s office again. He swore he knew nothing about an arrest warrant issued for you today."

We were about to enter her office when Brendan called out, "Nora, sweetie."

We both turned around.

"I'm going home for the night. Ta ta."

He waved good-bye and strolled out of the office.

I turned to Nora. "Ta ta?"

She smiled. "He dances to a different beat."

"Something about Brendan I like," I said. "Even if he did check me out."

"Big, tall, muscular," she said. "You're his type." Nora looked me over, then smiled. "He's right. You do look handsome in those clothes."

"As long as he only window shops."

"What?" Nora asked.

I explained the meaning of the term.

I stepped into Nora's office. She slammed the door closed, standing in front me, not allowing me to move. She grabbed my hand, squeezed it. I don't know if she realized that she'd pinned me against the door. I wondered what she might do next. I told her what happened with Babyface, Art, the suits, and Tucker. Her gaze hardened. She dropped my hand and paced over to her large wooden desk. She banged her fist on the desktop.

"Just throw away the Fourth and Fifth Amendments. The government cries 'terrorism' and then suspends individual rights. They bring in people like Tucker, and turn a blind eye to his methods. He's probably having the time of his life doing whatever he wants without regard for the Constitution." She walked behind her desk and fell into her leather chair.

I gently touched the welt on my head. She saw me flinch.

"Turn around," she said. She gasped.

"Who gave you that?"

"Tucker's crew."

"They ask you not to resist?"

"Uh huh."

"And you resisted?"

"Uh huh."

Nora shook her head. "You worry me. You don't know when to yield."

"I don't yield to intimidation."

"And that's how you wind up hurt or in jail."

"Are you suggesting that I roll over?"

"No. I'm suggesting that you pick battles that you can win. Do you need to get that looked at?"

"No." I took a seat in one of the burgundy leather chairs in front of her desk.

Nora lowered her head into her hands.

"Tucker offered me a job," I said.

She snapped her head up. "Doing what?"

"Spying on the spies."

She exhaled deeply. Her nostrils flared. "A lot of money?"

"Don't know. I turned him down before we got that far."

"Good, because I wanted you to work here."

"Doing what?"

"Spying on the spies." She laughed sarcastically. "Innocence Watch needs a trained investigator."

Out of the darkened window to Nora's right, a column of red and white lights marched slowly along the streets. Next to the window, an L-shaped bookcase held row after row of the leather-bound legal volumes you'd expect to find in a lawyer's office. But Nora's walls were lavender and the rug a plush beige pile. A large painting of a flower hung on the wall behind her desk, a reproduction of a Georgia O'Keeffe work.

"Right now, I couldn't even get a P.I. license," I said. "Besides, I want to see Liz and JJ and then I want to get busy finding out who set me up. I also want to know more about the federal and local cases that might be brought against me."

"I know I jumped the gun," Nora said. "But I wanted to put in my bid before someone else snapped you up."

I liked the mischievous smile she gave me.

Nora continued, "I just got the results of your second lie detector test in the mail today. Even though you passed the first round of testing in my opinion, I'm glad we went for another." She shuffled through a stack of papers on her desk, and waved an envelope at me.

FIVE

Nora pulled a sheet of paper from the envelope. "This guy put the questions to you in an even more provocative way," she said. "When asked if you ever contemplated harming Danny Rodrigues, you said no. The test confirmed it. Were you working for either the Harlem buyers or the Colombian sellers in the drug deal? You said no to both questions. Confirmed. Were you angry about not being promoted? Yes. Confirmed. Did you blame Ciccarello for blocking your promotion? Yes. Confirmed. Did you see Danny Rodrigues as a roadblock to your promotion? No. Confirmed. Did you believe that you were denied the promotion because of your race? Yes. Confirmed. Did you fire the shot that killed Danny Rodrigues? No. Confirmed."

I sighed. "But you can't use the results of a lie detector test in a trial."

"No. But our job now is to prevent a federal retrial on the same charges or the Brooklyn D.A. from trying you on new charges. I can put these new lie detector results in my motion for dismissal. I can show it to the federal prosecutors or the Brooklyn D.A. It's a bell. Once I ring it, it can't be unrung. They'll have to deal with it."

Nora checked her watch. "There's more. I want to review with you how we'll be handling your case from here on out. But you look beat, and I have to teach an evening class. We'll go over all this tomorrow. You want to read the lie detector results yourself?" She held the paper out to me.

"No," I said. "I knew all along that I was telling the truth."

Nora opened a drawer and pulled out a set of keys. They tinkled as she dangled them in front of me. "Address is 300 Central Park West, South Tower, apartment 25G," she said. She put the keys on top of a small white envelope and slid both across the desk.

I slipped the keys into my pocket. "The El Dorado?"

"You know the building?"

"Ritzy."

She looked away from me as though embarrassed. "Are you allergic to cats?"

"Nope."

"Good. Because I've got one. There's a couple hundred dollars in the envelope. Consider it an advance."

"Against what?"

"Don't know yet. I'll think of something."

Nora laughed. I did too. I stuffed the bills into my wallet.

"Thanks," I said.

"Make yourself at home. It was Guinness, right? That story about you, a beer, a bartender, your last name, and how you got that nickname 'Irish?'"

"Uh huh."

She threw a carefree laugh my way. "There's a six-pack in the fridge." Nora appeared to be studying my face. She shook her head. "Don't let your hair grow back," she said.

I smiled. "I went bald in prison as a symbolic protest over being convicted and sentenced for a crime I didn't commit." I ran my hand over the top of my head. "I always said I'd let my hair grow back once I finally got out to signify regaining my freedom. But I've grown accustomed to being bald and I'm thinking about staying that way."

"It makes you look older and wiser. And . . ." She paused. "Well, it might impress a jury if we ever have to go back to trial."

"Brendan seemed to think that bald men were sexy."

"Brendan has good taste." Nora laughed. "My class is over by nine thirty. I'll be home by ten."

"After I grab a shower, I'm thinking about—"

Nora's telephone rang. She started for it, then turned toward the door. She waved the call off. "Let the answering service get it."

The phone quieted, but a moment later it rang again.

"Someone wants you," I said.

"Someone always wants me," she said, then huffed. She set her briefcase down before grabbing the phone.

Nora rolled her eyes. "Yeah," she said. "Who?"

She listened, then squinted, then raised her voice. "What the hell do you want with him now?"

She looked at me and mouthed silently, "Tucker."

"Well he's not here." She smiled slyly.

"What?" Nora's mouth hung open. "His son?"

My head snapped back. I snatched the phone from Nora.

"You bastard. What'd you do to JJ?"

"Maybe you'd better get uptown," Tucker said. "I just got word that your wife filed a missing-persons report. JJ hasn't been seen since early this morning."

A knot tightened in the pit of my stomach. I saw JJ's face in my mind and my arms ached to hold him. Then that knot sunk even lower, into my gut. I held the phone without speaking. I hadn't been there to protect my son; hadn't been there when he needed me. My body flushed with a wave of guilt. But that knot rose again. I hammered my fist into Nora's table and yelled into the phone. "Damn you. If I find that you had anything to do with JJ going missing, I'll come after you. I don't care who you work for."

"I'm sorry, Shannon," Tucker said. "Call if you need help."

Nora grabbed my hand. "Maybe you shouldn't go up there right now."

I stripped my hand away. "What? My son's missing and you're telling me to stay away from my home?"

"At least call Liz first. It's in the separation decree. You have to call before you visit."

"Bullshit. It's my son we're talking about. I don't give a damn about a separation decree. I'm going up there to find out what happened."

"I'll go with you."

I pushed past Nora and jerked her office door open.

"Wait." She leapt in front of me and jammed her palm hard into my chest.

"I don't need a lawyer," I said. "I need answers."

"You're angry and scared," Nora said. "I'd be too, if it was my son. Please John, cool down first. If you violate the separation order Liz can have you arrested. That's all we need—JJ missing and you back behind bars."

Nora dropped her hand and I stormed through her door.

"John." She called to me loudly across the outer office and I turned around. "Come back to my apartment the minute you're finished at Liz's."

I saw the worry in Nora's eyes and I sighed, "Would you take this home with you?" I handed her my prison envelope. I tried to sound calm, to allay her fears, but in the pit of my belly, embers smoldered.

I stripped the dark-brown trenchcoat from the office coat rack and stormed out the door.

———————

WHEN I STEPPED FROM Nora's building, clouds of my breath, tinged orange by the sodium streetlights, floated up and away against the darkness. A chill settled onto my scalp. I turned to walk toward the subway, then turned again toward the street looking for a taxi, then turned once more, blew a warm breath into my hands, and poked each hand into a pocket. I'd take a brisk walk to Striver's Row. Nora was right: I needed to cool down.

I walked over to Malcolm X Boulevard, then headed north. I'd always thought of Striver's Row as an enclave within Harlem rather than a neighborhood. Sugar Hill, Edgecombe, Morningside Heights, these are Harlem neighborhoods with fluid, porous boundaries that blend seamlessly into each other. But Striver's Row, with its massive nineteenth-century townhouses designed by world-famous architects like Stanford White, and with signs that still read "Tie Horsedrawn Carts Here," stands apart from Harlem.

Striver's Row, 137th and 138th Streets between Malcolm X and Adam Clayton Powell Boulevards, could not have been named better. Generations of upperclass African Americans—doctors, lawyers, politicians, and musicians—strove to get there. And even those Harlemites who would never live in Striver's Row could still point to it with pride or contempt as a symbol of what to strive for.

I married into Striver's Row. According to some, I married above myself to get there. Elizabeth's family, the Winsteads, had lived in the Row for several generations. Old man Arthur Winstead, Liz's great-great-grandfather, was reportedly the first licensed black doctor in the entire city. She'd inherited the family home and also the family profession. Like her, many of the Winsteads prided themselves on being physicians.

The Winsteads also prided themselves on being light-skinned. "High yellow" is what they'd say. Marry light, marry right. Marry yellow, marry mellow. Marry brown, marry down. Marry black, marry back. That's how the ditty went. With chestnut-colored skin, that left me somewhere between "down" and "back" among the older Winsteads. For the younger and more tolerant generation, green was the preferred color. But when you compared my detective's salary with what Liz made as an obstetrician and gynecologist, that still put me somewhere between "down" and "back."

By the time I'd reached 132nd Street, I noticed a car moving behind me. I listened to the sound of the same engine for several blocks. I picked up the glare of headlights in the windows of the parked cars I passed. It wasn't a blue-and-white, although it could have been an unmarked NYPD car. After I crossed 135th Street, the car narrowed the gap, although it still trailed behind me.

When I crossed 137th Street it was as though I'd stepped over an invisible barrier. Two short whoops from the car's siren blasted me. A throbbing blue light pulsed into the night. The car's engine roared as it zoomed around the corner ahead of me. It angled between a parked car and a fire hydrant, coming to a screeching halt with one tire up over the curb. Doors flew open. Two large African-American men hopped out, breathing hard, vapor escaping from their mouths as if they were dragons guarding a lair.

"We help you?" the driver said in a low gravelly voice.

He leaned menacingly against his open door. A holstered pistol slung low over his bulging midriff.

"Man's talkin' to you," the other fellow said. He was thinner than the driver. His voice was high-pitched. "You deaf?"

Something clicked. "Al? Shorty?"

The driver squinted at me. "Irish? That you? Damn, Shorty," he said, turning to his partner who was standing on the other side of the car. "It's John Shannon." He turned back to me. "Irish, I'm sorry. Man, I'm sorry. I didn't recognize you."

Al reached into the car and turned off the pulsing blue light. "Man, you the last person I'd expect to see here. I mean . . . well . . . any word about your son?"

"That's why I'm here."

"You want a ride to the house?"

"Thanks, Al. It's only a block away."

"Anything I can do Irish, just let me know."

I walked around the front of the patrol car. Al gripped me by the shoulder as I passed. "Glad to see you out, man. Never thought you was guilty in the first place."

SIX

Rounding 138th Street, I saw a row of squad cars in front of our house, blue and red lights flailing at the night. Most of the inside lights were on. Many of the neighbors' lights were on too. I rushed up the front stairs. A policeman held out his hand to block my way.

"Friend of the family?" he asked.

"Father." I pushed past him.

A sergeant stood in the hallway, scribbling notes on a small pad. He leaned on a highly-polished French colonial desk that some said old doctor Winstead used when he wrote prescriptions. I entered the living room and paused at the strange scene. Liz sat on the living room couch, a nineteenth-century piece with an oval back and red velvet cushions. She held a wadded tissue in one hand. Tearstains ran down her cheeks. In the antique setting, she looked a grieving heroine on the set of a black-and-white silent movie. She had on a long skirt and a blouse with ruffled sleeves and collar, which only added to the illusion. The young policewoman next to her looked up when I walked in. Liz raised her head halfway. I crouched in front of Liz.

"What happened to JJ?"

"And you are, sir?" the policewoman asked.

Liz's eyes were red.

"When did you last see him?" I asked.

"Sir, I asked—"

"Father." I waved the officer away.

"Last night he wanted to drive upstate to meet you this morning," Liz said. She sucked in her words. "But this morning he was angry. He kept asking me if you would come back to live in this house and if we would be a family again. Then he insisted that he needed to go to school rather than take the day off to pick you up. So I let him go to school. Claudine called me from the school at ten. He never arrived there. I thought maybe he'd played hooky. He's due home by six. That's the rule. Sometimes he hangs with his friends or plays ball in the park. When he wasn't home by seven, I found the security guards that patrol the neighborhood and we went out looking for him. We checked all the places we could think of—playgrounds, basketball courts, rec centers. Then I came home and called a few parents of boys he knew. They hadn't seen him either."

Liz started to cry. "When he wasn't home by eight, I called the police."

"You did the right thing, ma'am," the policewoman chimed in.

I narrowed my eyes at her. "Officer—?"

"McBride, sir," she answered smartly.

"Well, Officer McBride, Elizabeth and I appreciate you being here. I take it you have enough information for a preliminary report, like physical description, photograph, description of clothing, time and place JJ was last seen, known places he frequents?" I raised my arm to check my watch. "If you do, then you can write up your report, distribute his image by computer, and have a hard copy ready for the morning shift."

"Sir, who do you think you are, barging in here and telling me how to do my job? I haven't taken a statement from you."

"Maybe you didn't hear me. I'm the boy's father, and you won't be getting a statement from me tonight," I said. "What are you? Fifty-first Precinct? I'll come by the stationhouse in the morning to file a report."

McBride jumped up from the couch. She had a stocky body with brunette hair tied in a bun and tucked up under her hat. She stood about five feet six and looked scrappy, like the kind of woman who'd grown up roughhousing with older brothers.

"Sir, would you step over here please?"

"John, don't make a scene. Not now," Liz said.

Still kneeling, I held my palm out to the officer and then said to Liz, "I just want them out of here. There's nothing more to be gained from them being around."

"Sir, I asked you to step over here," McBride said in the assertive voice I'm sure she'd learned in the academy.

I'd gone to the academy too. "Look Officer McBride," I said in an equally assertive voice. "We would very much appreciate it if you left us alone right now."

With more insistence, she said, "I asked you to step over here."

Then she moved toward me. I stood up. At six foot three, I looked down on her. She shrunk back a pace. I smiled. She appeared to be contemplating her options.

"Mac," a voice called out. A hand shot forth to pull her away.

The sergeant, an older man, tugged McBride over to the fireplace. They whispered, and occasionally McBride cast a foul glance my way. After their huddle, she sauntered over to me.

"I don't care if you were on the force once or if this is your son who's missing," she said, pointing her nightstick at me. "Don't ever interfere with my investigation again."

McBride and the sergeant walked toward the front door. I followed them. The sergeant pulled the door open and a blast of chilly air rushed in. He stepped outside, then turned around.

"Look, Shannon," he said gruffly. "It must be hard to step out of jail only to find that your son's missing. But if you ever treat one of my officers that way again," he wagged his finger in my face, "I'll make you lick the dirt off of her shoes."

"Good night, Sergeant," I said, closing the door behind him.

I rushed back to Liz. She'd buried her head in her hands.

"You didn't have to treat her like that," Liz said without raising her head. "She was only trying to help."

"Like hell," I said. "I don't care about the NYPD. I want to know what happened to our son."

Liz seemed unable to speak. I stood in front of her, unsure of whether to sit beside her or put my arm around her. I wanted to comfort her but I didn't know if I should or could. She'd let her hair grow since I last saw her. It now reached down to her shoulders, where it curled up like the bottom branches of a weeping willow frightened to touch the water. She didn't have on lipstick, and, frankly, I never thought she needed it. Her brown, fleshy lips stood out so marvelously and sensually against her tawny skin, and if you followed a path up from the edges of her lips to her high cheekbones then to her eyes, you'd also find that her lips and eyes were the same brown color.

I recalled how brown accented tan along the length of Liz's svelte body, from her nipples and the circle of dark skin around them to the boundaries of her other secret places. Blood rushed through me.

Finally, she raised her head and dabbed the corner of both eyes with the frayed tissue.

"What happened to our son?" she said, sniffing back tears. "You waltz into this house after two years in prison and ask me what happened to our son?"

Her tears erupted again. "You were convicted of murder and sent to prison. That's what happened to our son."

So much for a hero's welcome. Promise knew.

"May I sit down?"

"Of course."

I turned to face Liz. "But I wasn't guilty in the first place," I said. "Now my conviction's been overturned."

"So what? I believe that you didn't kill that agent. But that's not what the jury believed. That's not what every newspaper headline screamed. That's not what JJ heard at school."

"Now the newspapers will have to write a new story. And JJ can hear about how his father was set up for a crime he didn't commit."

"The damage has already been done."

"To whom?"

"To me. To JJ."

I pointed at my chest. "To me. I'm the one falsely convicted of murdering Danny Rodrigues. I spent two years in prison away from my family. Now we can start over. A new beginning for JJ, you, and me."

"What new beginning? I've spoken to Nora. You may be out of prison but you're not out of jeopardy. You're facing a possible retrial by the federal government or a new trial by the city. After that, there's still the possibility of a civil suit against you. How long will this hang over your head? Years? And what if another criminal jury convicts you and you're sent to prison? You can't be a husband or a father behind bars. I know because JJ and I have spent the last two years without you."

"You make it sound as though it's my fault that I was convicted of murdering Rodrigues."

"In some way it was."

"What?" Liz's words sent me reeling.

"It was your anger more than anything else that landed you in prison," she said. "I was at the trial. I saw that federal prosecutor paint a picture of you as an angry man, a rogue cop. And it worked. The jury bought it."

"The jury bought it because—"

"'I know that angry man.'" Liz cut me off. "That's what I sat in court thinking. I've heard him rail at home about how his superiors let the DEA take over his investigation. I've heard his anger about being treated unfairly because he was black. You even accused my family of that. I've listened to you talk about cutting corners to get a search warrant because you knew someone was guilty and you didn't give a damn about the system and its rules. You got angry over being denied promotions that you thought you deserved, or angry over little things between us, like how JJ should be disciplined. I just saw you unleash your anger at an officer doing her job here tonight. You're quick to point the finger of blame, quick to act on your anger. It was a button easily pushed."

I caught myself about to pound the soft leather couch, but I held back and only tapped it with my clenched fist. "JJ's missing, and you're talking about my trial and my anger."

"Did it ever occur to you that they're related?"

"What?" Her words hit me hard again.

"You don't get it, do you?" Liz shook her head. A watery film covered her eyes. "That's the reason I wanted a separation."

"What's the reason?"

"Your anger."

I swallowed hard. I tried not to react. I tried to hold on to Promise's voice reminding me that what mattered were Liz's feelings and not the facts. It wasn't easy.

Liz continued. "At first I was scared of living alone with you in prison and no possibility of parole for twenty-five years. Truthfully, I didn't think I could do that, but I told myself I'd try. Then I saw what was happening to JJ. That scared me far more, convincing me that separation was the right thing. He needed a new beginning. He needed to start over apart from you."

"What do you mean, what was happening to JJ?"

"I saw his anger, just like I'd seen yours. I was afraid for him."

"You never told me anything was wrong."

"For months after you were convicted, JJ said, 'Sometimes Dad has to kill bad guys but he didn't kill that man, did he? That man wasn't a bad guy. Why do people think that Dad killed him?' The kids at school and in the neighborhood constantly harassed him. Called him the 'son of a cop killer.' I told him you had difficulty controlling your anger, and sometimes took it out on other people even if you didn't mean to."

I clenched my fist tighter. "But I never took my anger out on him or on you. I promised you that I wouldn't repeat with our family what happened in mine."

"And you didn't. You never took your anger out on JJ. But you've lived so long with anger and violence that I don't think you realize how much they're a part of your makeup; how quickly your anger turns into violence. JJ read newspapers. He overheard you talking about what you had to do during a bust or an arrest. He thought of you as a god, and he grew up wanting to be like you. And that's what I started to see: JJ acting like you, his anger turning into violence. It scared me. About two or three months ago, JJ stopped being the butt of other kids' jokes. He started bragging to some of the boys in gangs about his dad 'poppin' a cop.'"

"No." I finally pounded the couch.

"It gave him status and suddenly he became popular with the gangbangers. He started hanging out with them. I tried to talk with him, but he ignored me."

"No." I shook my head. "JJ was hanging out with gangbangers?"

Liz grimaced. "Yes."

"Who? Where? Which gang was he with? I won't let them take him. I'll go out after them right now."

Liz hung her head. "You see? You're ready to go after someone. That's why I was scared that JJ would grow up to be like you—angry and ready to take it out on someone else. I deliver babies. What do I know about gangs?"

"Why didn't you bring him to see me? I could have talked to him, set him straight."

"His grades plummeted. He started dressing in baggy clothes. He had a foul mouth. He wanted to see you, but I didn't want you to see him. Not like that. You couldn't change anything from your prison cell. So I kept him away and I did my best. Besides, Nora was in the midst of your appeal and I didn't want to burden you with anything else."

"You didn't want to burden me?" I heard myself yell, so I thrust my palm toward Liz, gesturing for her to stop. Then I took some slow deep breaths and let Promise's calming voice float into my mind. I swallowed hard before I continued.

"Prison is exactly the place JJ should have come, if only so I could instill fear in him, so he could see where he'd end up if he didn't straighten up. I've dealt with gangs. I know how gangbangers think. I could have helped JJ find his way out of whatever mess he'd gotten himself into. Dammit, I'm his father. I'm supposed to be there for this kind of thing."

"But you weren't. When JJ needed you, you weren't there. You were in prison. You can't parent a child from behind bars. You can't be a parent for a few hours once or twice a month across a glass partition." Liz's voice dropped. She sniffed back tears. "I wasn't sure what was right. I did the best I could. Maybe I could have done something differently. Maybe seeing you in prison would have helped."

"Did it ever occur to you that JJ was acting out because of the separation? He hadn't done any of this before, unless you're not telling me everything."

"I tried talking with him about my reasons for wanting a separation."

"Your facts. His feelings. Hurt. Anger. Betrayal. He's feeling it in his body, in his gut, and he doesn't have the tools to deal with it."

Liz turned to me. "And suddenly you do?"

"Prison helped."

"Not with Officer McBride."

"Now he's afraid of losing face," I said.

"What?" she asked.

"If JJ was bragging about his father 'poppin' a cop,' then he was better off if I was a legend hidden away in the hills of upstate New York like Rip Van Winkle. And that worked fine until my conviction was overturned and I was released from prison. He couldn't brag about me anymore. He'd lose status and face in the gang. And he might do something to reclaim what he'd lost. He's split. One part of him wants me out of prison; the other part needs me to stay in. I've got to get out there and find him."

Liz put her hand on top of mine, sending an electric current racing through my body. She was on the verge of more tears. "That's what's so damn confusing," she said.

"What?" I asked. "About JJ and the gangs? It's basic street—"

"No." She cut me off, squeezing my hand tighter. "Not about JJ. About you. One minute you're acting like a brute about to tear off this poor woman's head." Liz pointed to where Officer McBride had been sitting. "The next minute you're talking about what's going on inside of our son like a gifted therapist. When you came home from work, I never knew who was going to walk through the door. I still don't."

"I want my life back. I want to know who set me up for a murder I didn't commit. I want my wife back because I never stopped loving her. I want to give our marriage another chance." I stared into Liz's eyes. "And most of all, I want JJ back. Maybe my anger had something to do with his disappearance and our problems. If so, I'll deal with that once he's back and he's safe. Right now, if something's happened to our son, I'm going to find out what. If someone's done something to him, I'm going to find out who. I'm going to bring JJ home whatever it takes."

A tear slowly worked its way over the edge of Liz's upper lip. Without thinking, I began to lean forward and kiss it away, but I caught myself and pulled back.

"You're just out of prison. Let the police do their job. Let them find JJ. You're no longer a detective. You don't carry a gun. I'm afraid if you go out looking for JJ this angry, you'll only wind up getting yourself hurt."

"In a missing-persons case, the first twenty-four hours are crucial. The police won't get serious about finding JJ for at least another day, maybe two. It's all the more reason for me to get busy looking for him now. They'll want to know that he's not just another runaway."

"Do you think he is?"

"A runaway? No," I said. "If he's angry he'll go find his homeboys. Whoever's top dog in the gang will sense where JJ's at and seize upon his weakness, probably try to force him to do something bold to prove he's still got the right stuff to hang with the gang. That's why I need to find him before he does anything stupid."

"He's our baby, John, and I'm scared for him."

Liz squeezed the tissue in her hand. Her arm trembled from the pressure. And then the floodgates let go. She sobbed. Propriety be damned. I reached for my wife, pulled her into my body. Each time her chest heaved, a shock wave passed through me. The tissue fluttered from her hand. She pulled away and fell back against the couch. I reached down and scooped her tissue off the floor. Then I got up and plucked two new ones from a box resting on the mantle.

I paused to stare at the pictures there: Our wedding photograph with Liz in a flowing white gown and me in a tuxedo; one from our annual vacation with JJ to the Winstead's summer cottage in Martha's Vineyard; and another showing JJ with his first fish caught on our first fishing trip into Long Island Sound.

I turned around, crouched low, and handed the tissues to Liz. She blew her nose with one, and with the other she wiped her face and eyes. I put my hand on her knee.

"I'm glad that we can talk," I said. "Even if it's about our problems, about JJ. It's been a long time."

She blew her nose again. "Two people in a relationship need time. Once you got promoted to the Narcotics Unit it seemed like we had less and less time for us."

I wanted to say something about working hard to further my career. I also wanted to remind Liz of the years she'd spent working the late shift as an ER doc. Instead, I said, "I know something about time now. I know how important time is."

"I guess you do," she said. Liz rounded her mouth and relaxed it. The ridge on her upper lip stood out. I remember her making this face when she played with JJ as a baby, and when we made love. "I didn't like it at first but it's growing on me."

"What? Time?"

"No. Your bare head," she said.

I didn't question how we got here. I just went with the flow. "You think it makes me look sexy?" I grinned.

Liz managed a weak smile. "Kinda."

After two years of forced celibacy, I didn't need much to feel sexy, especially around Liz. It didn't take much to follow the contours of her body beneath her skirt and blouse, both of which she filled out nicely. Then a sudden flash of pain shot through me. I reached for the back of my head.

"Turn around," Liz said. "You have a contusion? How'd you get that so soon?"

"Employment interview," I said.

"You need some ice?"

I was about to say yes when the front door chimes went off. I jumped up and ran to the door. Liz wasn't far behind. I knew we were praying for the same thing. I slid the deadbolts back and yanked the door open, expecting to see JJ's face.

"Shannon," the well-dressed man said.

Vincent Ciccarello stood in the doorway.

SEVEN

Ciccarello was a short, thin man. A smell of sweet cologne rose from his body and mixed with the foul odor of cigarettes on his breath. His ashen skin lay partially hidden in the shadows of the night. With a long overcoat draped around his shoulders like a cape, he reminded me of a diminutive Phantom of the Opera.

"Evening, Elizabeth," he said, nodding slightly to Liz as she stuck her head around from behind the door. "I'm very sorry to hear about the disappearance of your son. Believe me, the NYPD will do everything in its power to bring him home safely."

Liz stuck her head back inside without speaking. She liked Ciccarello about as much as I did.

"Can we talk?" Ciccarello asked.

I hadn't taken off my coat, so I stepped outside. In front of the house, a black limousine waited with its engine running. Ciccarello slipped his arms into his coat and we walked slowly down 138th Street. His shoulders swung forward with each step, as though he was trying to push away invisible weights that he carried there. He lit a cigarette, and a cloud of blue smoke encircled us. His limousine moved slowly beside us with its headlights off, like a panther stalking in tall grass.

"Nice neighborhood," he said. "Didn't know you blacks had anything like this in Harlem." Ciccarello blew out a thin stream of smoke. He looked around as though he'd just stepped from a tour bus.

"Long way at a late hour for you whites to go sight-seeing. Bet you're not here to get a missing-persons report either."

"Always a funny guy." He chuckled but it turned into a cough. In the midst of struggling to recover his breath, he took a long drag on his cigarette and coughed more. "I see prison didn't change you much."

"You'd be surprised," I said. "Heard you got bumped upstairs."

"Yeah, you heard right." He wheezed. "I'm head of NYPD intelligence."

I stifled a laugh.

"So isn't missing persons a little outside of your field?"

"Nothing's outside of my field now," Ciccarello said. He spoke with a gruff Brooklyn brogue and gesticulated by moving his shoulders and hands. "The moment you were released you were placed on a watch list."

"I thought that was reserved for terrorists."

"For anyone considered a potential threat."

"Like me?"

"Don't know," Ciccarello said. "But I didn't take a chance. Guess it depends on how you act now that you're out. So far you haven't gotten off to such a good start. You harass an officer doing her duty at your house. Her sergeant files a report by computer from his car. Our central computer matches your name against the names on the watch list. Bim. Bam. Boom." Ciccarello slapped his palm with the back of his hand. He pulled the cigarette from his mouth, lifted his head, and blew out a thin line of smoke. "I'm on my way home. After a nice dinner in Little Italy—at the home of the city's best gelato, I might add—my cell phone rings. Someone tells me there's a hit on your name. Since I'm so close by, I swing off the highway to pay you a visit. Bim. Bam. Boom." He slapped his palm again. "Modern technology's something, isn't it?"

"Especially for those who were never good at police work to begin with."

Ciccarello glared at me. We stopped at the corner. So did the limo.

"You were a good cop once, a good detective. I thought that deep down maybe I'd still find that good cop."

This didn't sound like the Ciccarello I knew. The man we called "Napoleon" or "the Little General" came across a bit too charming. Frankly, I didn't trust him, not for a minute.

"At my trial you seemed unable to find anything but the 'rogue cop' spinning out of control despite your best efforts to rein him in."

"Well time changes things, don't it?"

"Depends on what you do with the time," I said.

"I realize that through friends and contacts made in prison, someone like you just might hear and remember certain things," Ciccarello said. "Things that would prove useful to those of us on the outside."

"Like what things?" I was beginning to get the picture but I played along.

"Tips, confessions, plans, rumors, scuttlebutt."

"Lot of that going around a penitentiary," I said.

"That's what I mean. And if that kind of intelligence was made available to those of us who could analyze it and do something with it. . . . Well, let's just say that certain other things might go easier for you now that you're out."

Ciccarello was at best a bumbling salesman. "Like what certain other things?" I asked.

"Things at the Brooklyn D.A.'s office regarding your case," he said.

He didn't know the basics of closing a deal. If he peddled shoes, a lot of people would be walking the streets of New York barefoot.

"So you're proposing a quid pro quo?" I asked.

"What the hell is that?"

"What for what? That's what the hell it is."

"Huh?"

Ciccarello was already in over his head.

"Quid pro quo means 'what for what' in Latin. Kinda like you scratch my back, I'll scratch yours."

"Whatever." Ciccarello puffed on his cigarette and scratched his head. "You got information, maybe we can deal. We'd still like to nail Nicky Brooks. He got away from that warehouse deal clean."

"What?" I caught myself again. I took some more deep breaths. I didn't respond with my first impulse. "Of course he got away clean from the warehouse because the prosecution used his guys to testify against me. You probably made a deal with Brooks in exchange for their testimony. What, he get slapped on the wrist? Lose a few of his key players for a while? I got a fifty-five-year sentence, with no parole for twenty-five."

"Don't remember any deal," Ciccarello said.

"You wanna deal with me?" I asked. "Okay, let's try this. You tell me who really killed Danny Rodrigues. Then I'll tell you the latest sophistry from cellblock C."

"You bastard, now you're screwing around with me." He didn't like my quo.

"Not nearly as bad as you screwed around with me." But then I hadn't liked his quid.

He sucked in a lungful of smoke. "I was trying to be nice, maybe help you out. But understand one thing. I don't care what technicality got you out of prison. I made a mistake with you once and a federal agent was killed. I'm not gonna make a mistake with you again." He blew out the smoke and coughed.

Now this was the Ciccarello I knew.

Al and Shorty cruised by. They slowed as they reached the corner. Shorty leaned out the window. "Everything all right, Irish?"

I looked over and waved them on. Then I turned back to Ciccarello. "The technicality that got me out of prison was the truth. Now that I'm out, I will find out who set me up for Danny Rodrigues' murder, and I'll follow that trail wherever, and to whomever, it leads."

"Now that you're out?" Ciccarello took another deep drag. "Hell, O.J. walked because of a smart lawyer too. Word is that the Brooklyn D.A.'s gonna issue an arrest warrant for you and file new charges. And he won't screw up like the feds did. So you'd better enjoy these few days of freedom." He blew smoke my way.

"What are you trying to do, play 'good cop, bad cop' all by yourself? One minute you offer me a deal, the next minute you threaten me with new charges."

In the darkness I couldn't clearly see the expression in Ciccarello's eyes, but coldness permeated the air between us. Steam rose from both of our noses.

Express. Repress. Observe. Three ways to handle emotions. I heard Promise's voice in my mind. It's good to express them, but not always safe. Repress them and they eat you up from inside. You can always observe them, watching what emotions do inside your body. Notice that whatever physical sensation accompanies an emotion ultimately changes. Neither the sensations nor the emotions stay the same forever. Observe emotions and they pass through you like waves passing through water. Then you can use them as the guides they're meant to be, and not the rulers we let them become.

So I observed. Even in the cold night, I felt heat rising in the core of my body, tension spreading through my arms and legs.

"You want NYPD to find your kid, then you play by my rules. You understand? My rules." Ciccarello ripped the cigarette from his mouth, holding it between two fingers as he jabbed the air toward me.

Napoleon didn't intimidate me, but his presence in the Row had me wondering. "You showed up on my doorstep pretty damn quick. You know anything about JJ's disappearance?" I asked.

Ciccarello reared back. His eyes got big. He yelled. "You questioning me? Some goddamn nerve. Buddy, you got no badge, no gun, and no goddamn authority anywhere in my city. You so much as look wrong at another NYPD officer and I won't wait for the D.A.'s arrest warrant. I'll issue my own and I'll haul your ass in my damn self. I don't want you anywhere near this investigation. You understand? You're caught snooping around and it's an immediate arrest for obstruction. I can put you under twenty-four-seven surveillance anytime I want."

"And you don't need to report to Ken Tucker why you'd devote the city's precious resources to monitoring me?"

"Tucker?" Ciccarello's body stiffened. His voice rose an octave. "What? So you tried to make a deal with him already? Thinks he can whip people into shape just because he worked for the CIA. He don't mean shit to me. Forget him. You remember what I said. You stay clear of this investigation, and clear of the NYPD. You got that?"

I stared at Ciccarello and watched what happened in my body. The heat spread up from the center of my chest and down my arms, and as it did, it dissipated to a warm glow.

"Is that clear?" He yelled. A cloud of breath and tobacco smoke gushed from his mouth.

What was clear was that Ciccarello never answered my question. I kept staring at him and observing myself.

"Is that clear?" he screamed.

Even in the subdued light, his face turned red. My arms relaxed, and a comforting warmth settled in my belly.

"You smug motherfucker."

Ciccarello swung at me, sending a puny right cross my way. I side-stepped the punch without raising a hand. He stumbled forward, and instantly the front door of his limo popped open. A beefy man in plain clothes sprung out, leaping between us.

"Problem, Cap'n?" The man asked in a gruff voice.

"No, Bobby. I'm just sayin' goodnight to Mr. Shannon." Ciccarello tugged on the lapels of his overcoat, straightening it on his body. The man called Bobby rushed to the back door and held it open. Ciccarello let his cigarette butt drop, then he stomped it, twisting his foot back and forth and grinding it into the sidewalk. As he ducked inside the limo, he turned to me and said, "Shannon, just remember you're garbage in this city as far as I'm concerned. And when I come across a piece of garbage, I call the Sanitation Department to clean it up." He slammed the door.

I walked back to Liz's house and up the stairs. I didn't buy that Ciccarello had driven all this way just to deliver a message to stay away from investigating JJ's disappearance. Where Tucker was smooth like silk, Ciccarello was rough and crude like sandpaper. My release from prison came with conditions. I couldn't carry a weapon, be out after midnight, drive a car, or travel outside of New York City. If Ciccarello and the Brooklyn D.A. wanted to nail me, then they'd set the perfect trap. They must have known that I'd do everything in my power to get JJ back. Even if that meant violating every term of my release.

I gazed at the doorbell and thought about walking back down the stairs. I stomped my feet against the chill and jabbed the doorbell with my finger. Moments later I heard light footsteps shuffling across the wooden floors. It sounded like Elizabeth didn't have shoes on. Through the thick glass of the front doors, behind the thin, knitted curtains, I saw her walking toward me. My heartbeat quickened with each of her steps. She parted the curtains and stuck her head through. She had a puzzled expression, and the curtains and glass framed her face like the Mona Lisa of Striver's Row.

The curtains snapped closed. Liz didn't immediately open the door. I felt the night's chill seeping back into my body. Again, I thought about leaving. Then I heard the metallic clunk of the deadbolt. The door creaked open a few inches until a heavy brass chain stiffened, holding Liz back from opening it more. Her eyes and lips filled the gap. She'd changed into the slim, white, silk nightgown I'd given her one Christmas. Her breath escaped in a plume of steam out the door.

"What was that all about?" she asked.

"A warning not to investigate JJ's disappearance."

"Are you going to listen to him?"

"No. Not as long as JJ's out there."

I thought I saw her about to close the door. But she didn't.

"It's late. Do you need a place to sleep tonight?"

I thought I saw her skin darken against the white silk, as though the offer caught her by surprise as well.

"No. Not as long as JJ's out there."

EIGHT

"No!" I cried out.

I didn't care who heard me. Only now, walking away from Striver's Row, did the impact of JJ's disappearance fully hit me. It felt as though someone had reached into my chest and ripped out my heart. JJ brought such happiness and joy and meaning into my life. I'd worked missing-child cases before, delivered the crushing news to parents. I'd seen firsthand the depravity and brutality visited upon children. I'd felt the devastation wrought when I returned to tell those parents that their child would never be coming home again. I wouldn't let this happen to JJ. Not if I could help it. That meant I'd have to go after his gang and find out what they knew.

Gangs don't have mailing addresses, but they do stake out turf. Like bats, they come out at night, which is the best time to hunt them. I didn't know if JJ's disappearance was connected to a gang, but it was a good bet that whatever gang he fell in with knew something about why he'd never showed up at school. I needed to know where he hung out. Liz couldn't help much, but I had a good idea who could: her workout buddy, Dr. Claudine Johnson, the director of the DuBois School, which JJ attended.

I didn't think that Liz would have appreciated me disturbing Claudine this late at night, so I didn't bother asking her for Claudine's number. I walked out of the Row and stopped at the first telephone booth I came to. I was surprised to find that the phone book, dangling from a coiled cord, had not been stolen. The heavy book smelled like urine. Guess that's why it was still there. The white pages were now yellow, but not the kind I wanted my fingers to walk through. I pulled the taxi receipt from my pocket and used it to pry back the pages until I came to "Johnson."

Claudine lived somewhere nearby, but I'd never been to her house. I ran the receipt down the list of names and found her. She lived at 150th Street and Riverside Drive, only a ten-minute walk away. It was after eleven o'clock, and it would have been polite to call first, but I decided that I had a better chance of success if I simply showed up at her door. I stepped out of the phone booth and headed toward Riverside Drive.

I crossed Amsterdam Avenue at 147th Street. Late night exposed the underbelly of Harlem, as it did in any community. Drunken men and those high on drugs tottered down the street, their arms and legs periodically frozen in bizarre poses. Cars with bass thumping loudly rumbled by. A hooker walked past me in short pants so tight they molded to every curve and crevice of her body.

"You got time for me, honey?" she asked.

Her eyes were bloodshot and glazed. I don't even think she heard me say no.

Claudine Johnson directed the DuBois School. Semi-private, run in conjunction with Columbia University, it catered to African-American students from nearby Harlem, and JJ had been there since kindergarten. I felt truant. DuBois demanded parent participation. In two years, I'd missed at least a dozen parent conferences and failed to sign an equal number of report cards. But beyond that, I felt truant because I no longer knew JJ. In two years, the little guy I used to take fishing had grown into a troubled young man wrestling with the allure of the streets.

When I reached Claudine's apartment building, I pushed through the double-pane glass doors, walked over to the building's registry, and then slid my index finger along the list of names. She lived in apartment 17D. I mashed the button next to her name with my thumb, and waited. Nothing happened. I tried it again. . . . Same thing. It looked like I'd have to visit the Dubois School in the morning.

But as I turned to leave, a raspy, static-filled voice come over the speaker.

"Yes."

I picked up the handset. "Claudine, this is John Shannon. I'm very sorry to trouble you this late, but I need to talk to you about JJ's disappearance."

In the long silence that followed, a troupe of images danced across my mind. I knew nothing about Claudine's personal life in the last two years. Before I went to prison she was single, something I'd always found hard to believe. She might be married now or have a lover. I had no idea what I might be barging in on at this late hour. Finally, the speaker squealed.

"Sorry," Claudine said. "I'm having trouble waking up. I'll buzz you in. I'm in 17D."

"Thank you," I said.

I pushed the front door open when Claudine buzzed. I hit the elevator button. A motor whined, and I heard cables moving behind the closed doors, but the elevator took forever to get to the lobby. At this hour, maybe it was having trouble waking up too.

Claudine opened the door to her apartment with a yawn, then a smile, wearing gray baggy sweatpants and a matching oversized sweatshirt. In her early thirties, she still had her hair as I remembered it, in tiny braids that sprouted over her head. My mother would have described Claudine's skin as "dark and sweet as a Hershey's kiss." In her slippers, she rose to the top of my chest.

"You're not wearing glasses," I said, stepping into her hallway. While her thick frames gave her a schoolmistress' exterior, I always believed they hid a lioness' soul.

"Contacts." She pointed to her eyes. "And you're not wearing hair," she said pointing to me. Claudine's words rolled from her mouth with a lyrical West Indian sound.

We both laughed and I remembered how much I liked her easygoing manner. She showed me into the living room, which had a commanding view of the Hudson River. A large red light moved slowly downstream to my left, and I could barely make out the dark hulk of a ship sliding by. To my right, the lights of the George Washington Bridge stretched across the river to the dark New Jersey palisades like a string of jewels. I took a seat on the sofa. Claudine sat across from me in an easy chair.

She had reproductions of famous paintings by African-American artists on her walls. A series of works by Jacob Lawrence told the story of black folks migrating north in bold reds, yellows, and blues. And a larger painting by Romare Bearden moved with the energy of an evening crowd listening to jazz at a Harlem club.

"I'm really sorry about John Jr.," she said, letting her chin rest on her clasped hands. "I spoke to Liz earlier. She was pretty upset. How's she holding up?"

"She's scared," I said. "Are you two still working out together?"

"No," Claudine frowned and shook her head. "Liz's into yoga now. Takes two classes each week. She also takes a meditation class."

"Liz?"

"Uh huh. I tried. It's not for me."

"Cute instructor?"

"Black woman named Daya, been teaching yoga for decades. She's pushing seventy. Looks forty. Very spiritual. Liz says it's helping her find herself." Claudine yawned. "But you didn't come over to talk about her."

"No. I hate to bother you this late, but I need to find out all I can about JJ."

"It's not a bother." Claudine rubbed her eyes. "He's been going through a tough time. He hasn't been the same child in the last few months. Some of it no doubt attributable to being a teen. JJ's grown tall like you. He's also developed a tough exterior. Seems he's constantly looking for a fight with other students, even with teachers. He was an *A* student. Now he skates by with *C*s. We gave him extra attention, and special instruction. But we can't compete with that." Claudine pointed toward her kitchen, but I understood she meant the streets. "Most of our children walk to school, which means they have to cross a wasteland to reach our oasis. JJ got stuck in the wasteland. Bit by bit we lost him. I talked with Elizabeth. She tried her best. She'd drive him to school and pick him up when she could. But the school isn't a prison, and we can't keep our students locked in all day." She lowered her gaze.

"Liz told me that JJ was hanging with a gang, but she didn't know where. Do you?"

A pained look came over Claudine. "I'm an educator not a police officer, but I heard from one of the teachers that JJ had fallen in with a gang around 117th or 118th Street near Malcolm X. I don't know if that helps."

"A lot," I said.

"Is there anything you can do?"

"Maybe." I didn't really have a plan. "I'll start by seeing if I can find the gang and then have a talk with them."

"Are you . . . I mean did they reinstate—"

"No, I'm not back on the force. I was just released from prison today."

"What an awful thing to come home to. I read that your conviction was overturned. It can't be easy doing the work that you did. The split-second decisions you have to make must be painfully hard. I'm glad that you're back for JJ's sake. You find him and together we'll turn him around."

"Thanks," I said. I rose to leave. Claudine stood up as well. My gaze fixed on the wall behind me where she'd hung a print of an old black man giving a young boy sitting on his knee a banjo lesson. Claudine must have seen me staring at the image.

"Henry Ossawa Tanner painted that in 1893," she said. "It's called 'The Banjo Lesson' and the original hangs in the Hampton University Library where I went to school. I like sitting in this chair, looking out the window at the river. But I also wanted that painting where I would see it often, as a reminder of why I became a teacher. That old man is passing along his knowledge. And that's why I'm the director of the DuBois School. We can save our kids, but we have to start by passing our knowledge along."

I searched Tanner's painting, which appeared to be set in the sparse surroundings of a cabin or a shack.

"From the old man's hands I get the feeling he'd labored hard and known pain, perhaps he'd once been a slave. Playing the banjo became his way of coping." I pointed to the painting. "I can almost hear him whispering gentle words of guidance and encouragement in the child's ear. Maybe it was his grandchild. It could have been his son." As I spoke, pressure built behind my eyes, a slight tension in my chest. I missed my dad. I missed my son. And I also missed my friend Promise.

I USED TO KNOW a gang just by knowing its turf, but territory and alliances shift rapidly. Two years off the streets is far too long to rely on prior knowledge. It would be like trying to drive across the country today using a map from the Lewis and Clark expedition. So I wandered up and down the streets from 125th to 116th Street between Malcolm X and Adam Clayton Powell Boulevards—twenty blocks from Striver's Row, but light years away.

In this part of Harlem, heaven and hell might be only a block apart. On some blocks, scaffolding covered the façades of old brownstones. I imagined that during the day, workers threw bricks and plaster out of upstairs windows into the long wooden troughs that emptied into the huge green dumpsters sprawled along the sidewalks, while outside, young white men in blue jeans with pencils stuck behind their ears and cell phones in their hands conversed with other men in hardhats. I passed a vacant lot where once kids played during the day and gangs fought at night. Now it had a sign behind a barbed wire fence advertising condominiums soon to come. Where did those who couldn't afford condominiums move?

I needed no imagination in the adjacent blocks. Young men periodically darted from rundown buildings, slipping between parked cars to the Benzes, BMWs, and Lexuses that cruised by slowly. Tinted windows whined as they lowered. White hands extended from inside the cars. Black hands previously stuck in jacket pockets reached out to greet them, not in brotherhood but in a quick exchange of money for a small vial or an envelope; an exchange that could have passed for a handshake, when in reality it was the grip of death. But the teens emerging from the shadows to work the streets were too high up on the food chain of Harlem's predators to be of interest to me right now. I was looking for the younger wannabees waiting in the wings, those who knew the brevity of life in these alternate blocks, who knew that soon they'd get their turn and simply marked time until that day.

A fenced-in basketball court sat in the middle of the next block I turned down. The gate had been padlocked and chained, but the bottom of the fence had been bent back. I slipped under the fence. A single streetlamp cast a bright orange glow over the court, giving the appearance of daylight.

Small patches of grass grew from between the cracks on the asphalt surface where pavement Picassos had their spray-can artwork on display. A lone backboard sat atop a metal post. Its hoop had been bent at least a foot or two lower than normal so that maybe even the smallest player might rise above these surroundings in a shining moment and pull off a slam dunk.

A row of young boys sat huddled together on the edge of the basketball court, their backs against the fence, some with runny noses, all underdressed for the cold. Even though it was well after midnight, they were waiting to get into the game—not the one on the court because no one was playing, but the one on the streets I'd just left.

They eyed me warily as I walked up.

"You a cop?" one kid said.

"Used to be."

"What you mean used to be? Either you is or you ain't. No 'used to be' 'bout it."

"Means I used to work for the NYPD but now I don't," I said.

"You got fired from NYPD?" a kid laughed.

"He ain't got fired," another kid said. "He did time upstate. Don't you know who that is?"

"Like you do?" a third kid chimed in.

"Hell, man, call him Irish. He's the one that wasted a cop."

"Yo, like you wasted a cop?" a boy asked.

"He's JoJo's old man," another kid said.

"You mean JJ?" I asked.

The kid looked at me, his eyes bloodshot and crusty. "No, I mean JoJo. What kind of name is JJ?" He wagged his head as he spoke. "Reminds me of that goofy guy on rerun TV. JoJo. That's what he call himself now."

"Have you seen him lately?" I asked.

"'Bout time we got to bed, don't you think?" a kid blurted out. The others snickered but they all got up to leave. Not one boy appeared to be over thirteen. Their baggy pants swept the ground with each swaggering step they took. They looked like a squad of drunken sailors tottering down the deck of a pitching ship.

"Yo," I called out to the one who'd said "JoJo." "I asked if you'd seen my son."

One of the other boys whispered something to him. He didn't turn around. I walked quickly to him, reached out and grabbed him by the collar of his faded red jacket.

"Man, you'd better turn me loose." He tried to shake out of my grip but I dragged him back to the basketball post. I pushed him up against it.

"Son, I asked if you'd seen my boy."

The child shook under my grip. Out of the corner of my eye, I saw the other boys running down the block.

"Man, what you doin'? You tryin' to get me killed? Even if I did know sumun' 'bout JoJo I couldn't tell you. They kill me if I did."

"Who'd kill you?"

"Kill me if I tell you that too. Now if I was you, I'd let me go and get your ass outta here real quick. Where you think my homeboys went?" he asked with an arrogant shake of his head.

"Well, let's you and I stay here until they return or until you tell me about JoJo."

"Ain't tellin' you nothin'." He tried to shake away from me again. "You ain't no cop, probably don't even have a gun on you. You one crazy dude come around here with no piece dissing me and my homeys."

A few minutes later I heard his homeys coming back. They were dragging an older kid, who looked about fifteen, behind them. Once the older boy saw me, he brushed the younger boys off and began to strut. His hand dipped into his jacket pocket. He had a weapon there.

He sauntered up to me, a hand in one pocket, the other pocket bulging as well, not with a gun but with drugs and money. This teen wore baggy pants also. He had on a red jacket that looked brand new and tennis shoes sporting a designer's logo. When he opened his mouth, I saw one tooth missing from his upper row. He had a scar that ran from just under his right ear down to the corner of his mouth.

"You think you the man? Come 'round here and mess with my boys?" the older kid asked.

The other boys lined up behind this kid, a drug dealer who lived a level above them on the food chain. Someone for them to idolize or die trying.

"I was asking this young man about my son." I moved my body slowly around to the other side of the post. The drug dealer and the other boys mirrored my movements.

"I didn't say nothin' to him, Slide. Nothin'."

The young kid tried to squirm away from me but I held on to his collar tightly. I could see Slide was sizing up how and when he could take his best shot. Right now this young kid was all that stood between a bullet and me.

"Aww-right," Slide said. "It goes down like this. You let my home-boy go, and you walk outta here alive. You got that?"

"I don't think so," I said. "Let me tell you how it goes down. You tell me what happened to JoJo and I let you walk outta here alive."

"Man you one stupid clown." Slide whipped the pistol out of his pocket and pointed it at me. I recognized the 9mm Smith & Wesson. I once carried the same model.

A wave of glee washed over the other boys' faces. Their bodies bounced behind Slide with anticipation, like a chorus behind a lead singer. Slide took a wide stance and held the gun at a ninety-degree angle to a normal shooting position.

"Let my homeboy go," he said.

He stuck the gun out in front and swayed his body back and forth. If he were on MTV he might look cool whipping around a gun like that, but this was the real world, and he obviously didn't know the first thing about accurately firing a pistol.

"I let your homeboy go when you tell me what happened to JoJo," I said.

"Fuck you, man," Slide yelled. "You interruptin' the evenin's bid-ness. I ain't got time for your bullshit. Now you let my homeboy go or I'll shoot your ass dead."

"You can't shoot me with your homeboy between us." I picked up the squirming kid. He was as light as a feather. I held him up to my chest.

"Don't shoot. Don't shoot, Slide." The kid in my arms started crying.

"Move outta m'way," Slide yelled at the other boys. They backed up to the entrance of the court.

"No one has to get hurt," I said to Slide. "Tell me where JoJo is. Everybody walks outta here. You go back to work."

"I'm holdin' the gun. Means I'm givin' the orders," he said. Slide was moving slowly to my left, his body crouched low to the ground, trying to get around behind me where he could take a clean shot. He waved the gun back and forth. But you can't focus on shooting someone if you're busy acting like you're onstage. I eyed him and turned with him. I tracked his every movement, while still holding on to the writhing young boy. Even with a novice shooter, you can't afford to be cocky when you're facing his loaded gun. Sweat had worked its way onto my forehead and under my arms.

"You play basketball, Slide?" I asked, watching the arc of the pistol as he swung it left and right.

He said nothing. His eyes were fixed on me. His body was tense. His movements were slow and calculated. But I don't think he realized that we'd danced around to the point where the fence was almost against his back. The next time Slide's gun reached the end of its arc, I took a step toward him. He suddenly backed into the fence, faltering for an instant.

"Catch," I said. I tossed the kid at him. Both boys bounced off the fence. Slide's pistol fired. The young boy screamed, "I'm shot! I'm shot!"

NINE

I pounced on Slide, grabbed his wrist, pushed it down hard and then scraped it along the top of the asphalt, which was littered with small bits of glass. He screamed, but his hand opened and I yanked the weapon from him. I patted him down quickly, and pulled a large knife from the small of his back.

"Face down on the ground, hands behind your back. Do it now," I said.

Slide shook. The other boys had long since scattered. I kept my knee and the full weight of my body in Slide's back while pointing the pistol at the young boy.

"Get up son," I said. "You're not shot."

He looked at me wide-eyed, then staggered to his feet. His baggy pants were ripped. Blood oozed from a skinned knee. His face lit up. For a moment, I thought he was about to thank me. But he quickly regained his scowl and hobbled from the court.

"Okay, Slide," I said. "Now it's just you and me. I figure you got maybe five grand or so in your pocket. If you don't turn it over to your accountant, that young boy I let go will walk in your shoes to-morrow night. And you won't be walking again. So here's how it goes down. You tell me what happened to JoJo and I let you walk with your earnings. You got that?"

Slide's body trembled. I pressed down harder with my knee and dug the barrel of the pistol into the back of his head. When I was this age, my mother only needed a switch.

"Juke," he whispered.

"What did you say?"

"Man, Juke. Come 'round here yesterday and said that JoJo, Poonie, Tank, and Snoop were gone. And we'd better make like nothing happened. Like they was never here."

"Who does Juke work for?"

Slide said nothing. I stuck my hand in his pocket and pulled out a thick wad of bills.

"Man, that's my take."

"Who does Juke work for?" I pushed Slide's face back down into the asphalt.

He struggled to speak so I eased up on him a little.

"Fryer," he said in a choked voice, barely a whisper. "Man works for Fryer."

My time away showed. I hadn't heard his name either. "Okay, Slide, let's work our way up the chain of command. Whom does Fryer work for?"

"Don't know that."

I leaned my knee into him harder. He squirmed under the weight.

"Shoot me, muthafucka," he said. His voice sounded airy and thin, as though he was on the verge of tears. "Get it over with and shoot me," Slide said. "'Cause I don't know who Fryer works for. I'm too low down. Don't tell a street soldier them things."

"If you're lying to me, I'll come back for you, and next time there won't be any deals struck. Do you understand?"

I could feel him trying to nod his head under my weight. I reached my hand into his other pocket and pulled out a fistful of small glass vials filled with hardened crystals and glassine envelopes so thin you could hardly tell they contained white powder. I threw the wad of bills a few feet away and stood up. I kept the gun pointed at Slide as he rose.

"Get up slowly," I said. "Then pick up your money and walk out of here."

Slide crawled over to the bills and stuffed them in his pocket. Then he stood to face me.

"Man, you gonna give me back my merchandise?"

I dropped the vials and the envelopes to the ground, smashing them with my heels, then grinding them into the asphalt.

"No," I said.

Slide moaned. "That's thousands of dollars you wasted, man." He threw his hands up in the air.

"But think about all the lives I saved. Now, when you go back to your source you tell him that Irish wants to see Fryer. Tonight. And the longer Fryer waits, the more of his merchandise will be liquidated."

Slide shook his head. "How 'bout my *S* and *W*?" he asked, pointing to the pistol.

"Get the hell outta here," I said, "while I'm still feeling charitable."

"Damn." Slide shook his head again and then sidled off the court.

He pulled a bandana from his pocket and wrapped it around his scraped wrist. When he was gone, I tucked his 9mm into the small of my back. I walked off the court and slid back under the fence. I made a mental note of what block Slide turned down. Then I turned and went the other way.

THE LAST I KNEW, only a handful of organizations controlled the Harlem trade. Fryer might be an underling acting on the orders of a larger drug boss like Nicky Brooks, or he could be working for a smalltime player who wanted to break into the big leagues by sending a message that he could make a move on a larger player's turf. I hustled past a row of brownstones with scaffolds, chutes, and large green dumpsters out in front.

A couple of things plagued me. Even though four boys were snatched off the street, I couldn't escape the fact that it happened on the day I was released. The message may have been meant for me. I pounded a fist into my thigh. Mostly, I was having a hard time accepting that JJ hung out on these streets.

Once my father beat me so hard that my eye swelled closed, and he left a large welt on the side of my face. He blamed me for stealing fifty dollars from my mother's purse, when in fact during a drunken stupor he had taken the money for booze. The bruises hurt, but the betrayal cut like a sharp knife through the soft marrow of my young soul. I'd wondered if JJ felt something similar when I was convicted of murder and sent to prison. I wouldn't know until I found him. I wouldn't find him until I worked my way up this drug-infested chain of command.

I turned down the next street I came to. Slide had taken this street from the other end. A black BMW cruised slowly behind me. I tracked the car through the sideview mirrors I passed. It pulled to a stop ahead of me. I reached behind me for the 9mm. The BMW's window slowly lowered. On cue, a door creaked open from a broken down tenement and a young boy with his hands in both pockets jogged down the front steps and over to the driver.

In the cold night air, tiny vapor plumes shot between the driver and the dealer as they exchanged a few words. Then the boy reached into his right pocket, which meant he was a left-handed shooter. I moved quickly.

I dashed to the car, grabbed the boy's left hand, and jerked it hard behind his back. Inside, the driver's pudgy face changed from white to red. I slammed the dealer into the hood of the car and then I pointed my gun at the driver. I brought out my best police voice.

"Sir," I said to the driver. "NYPD. Please turn off your car. Then step out and hand me your keys."

"Oh my god. My god," the man said. He moaned. "You can't be serious. I have a family, a wife and a child."

I could have rammed the 9mm down his throat. I yelled, "Step out now, sir. I will not ask you again."

When I heard the engine wind down, I turned back to the dealer. "Spread 'em," I said. I frisked him quickly. I jammed my hand into his left pocket and pulled out a small caliber semiautomatic Colt and stuck it into my pocket. From his other pocket, I pulled a roll of bills and a handful of vials and envelopes.

The dealer complained. "That's my stuff. Man, you ain't got no right to search me."

"You're right," I said. "I don't got no right. And since that statement's a double negative I guess it means it's okay." I stuffed the money back into his pocket, spun him around, and jabbed the muzzle of the 9mm into the soft flesh under his chin. Then I dumped the envelopes and vials on the ground, pressing my foot into them and crushing them on the street. The dealer's eyes got big. "You tell Fryer that Irish needs to talk," I said. I peeled him off the hood of the car and threw him down the street. He ran. He looked back, dazed, as if he was a seal that had just escaped a shark's jaws.

"What'd you let him go for?" The pudgy man asked. "He's just as guilty as I am."

"Like hell he is. If you didn't want it, he wouldn't sell it. Capitalism. You look like a man who understands the laws of supply and demand."

The man actually looked disheveled. His shirt stuck out of his pants. His pants were unzipped. He didn't have on a suit jacket. Out of the corner of my eye I thought I saw a head move down in the passenger's seat. I strolled over to the window.

"Sweetheart, you get out here too," I said, motioning with my gun.

The passenger's door swung open. A dark-skinned African-American woman taller than me in her boots sashayed around to the front of the car. She wore a very short, tightly-fitted red dress cut so low in the front that if she moved too quickly her merchandise might spill out. Her straightened hair, or wig, fell over one shoulder in front. Underneath the orange streetlamps, the sheen from her lipstick glistened. The two of them stood there with smoke rising from their nostrils. Both of them looked cold, but only the man shivered.

"Honey, the meter in my cab's still runnin'," the woman said. "Whether we got to where you wanted to get off or not."

I wanted to laugh, but instead I climbed into the car, rolled up the window, and drove off. In the rearview mirror, I saw the prostitute with her hand out toward the man. He kicked the pavement and shook his fist in my direction. He'd have a lot of explaining to do to his wife and child in the morning.

I didn't know how wide an area Fryer controlled, so I drove a few blocks over, then slowed down and cruised up the street. I stopped in the middle of the block and the scene repeated itself like the rerun of a bad movie, only this time the boy emerging from the shadows kept one hand in his right pocket. He did business with his left.

"Rock or powder?" he said.

I raised the door lock, lifted the handle, and shouldered open the door with all the force I could muster. The boy went down on the ground, and before he could reach for his gun I was out with mine in his face. I liquidated his merchandise, confiscated his gun, and sent him off with the same message for Fryer. I repeated my performance three more times in the surrounding blocks. It's like casting bloody chum over the water, then waiting for the arrival of sharks.

Dorsal fins surfaced in the next block.

I stopped but no teen scurried to serve me. Ahead, a parked car pulled in front of me. I threw the BMW into reverse, but another car pulled into the street to block my way. The sharks had arrived, and I only had a rough plan of how I'd reel in the big one.

I jumped out of the car and ran to the sidewalk. The doors of the other two cars opened and then slammed closed. Two men came strutting down the block toward me from the front. I turned around. Another two came at me from behind. I ran in the direction of the first two men, scanning the buildings that I passed. One had no front door and broken first-floor windows. It looked like a vacant slum.

A low murmur of voices escaped from the broken windows. A man staggered out and down the front steps. Good bet that this was a crack house, if only for the night. I took the front steps two at a time and as I crossed the threshold, the pungent aroma of burning cocaine and marijuana smoke filled my nostrils. I knew that the crunching sound under my feet was not fallen leaves but discarded crack vials and used syringes. When I looked over my shoulder, I saw four men converging on the stairs.

The only light inside the building came from candles. I raced to the back of the first floor, stepping over two men sprawled out, one with a belt still wrapped around his biceps, the other's eyes rolled back in his head. I entered a room strewn with mattresses that reeked of urine and a cocktail of other body fluids. The dim light silhouetted dark forms draped lifelessly on some mattresses, while on others, couples grunted and groaned as their bodies moved up and down against each other. In one corner of the room a man stood against the wall while a woman kneeled with her head buried in his groin. I found an empty mattress and tumbled onto it head down. I coughed from the thick smoke.

I peeked at the entrance to the room. Two of the men entered, coughing. They covered their noses with handkerchiefs and walked around, but they passed right by me. I struggled to my feet and staggered toward the door, bent over and tottering as though I were high. Then I twirled through the doorway and when I came to the first man outside, I fell slowly into him without ever raising my head. I draped my arms around his waist like a junkie about to fall over. He tried to throw me off but I punched him hard in the abdomen and then elbowed him in his throat. He doubled over. Now he looked like a junkie. The second man put his hand on my shoulder, pulling me back. I spun around and knocked him to ground with a single punch to his face.

By now, the two men who had walked inside the drug den were headed toward the hall. I stepped to the side of the doorway and waited until the second man stepped out. Then I brought the full weight of my pistol butt down into the angle between his neck and shoulders. He moaned and the first man turned around. I threw a quick combination punch to his mid-section, then his jaw, before racing outside.

A shiver rippled through my body as my sweat met the chilly air. I ducked low, using the parked cars for cover. I opened the back door of the car that had pulled in front of the crack house. I stuck my gun into the base of the driver's head and got in.

"Put both hands on the steering wheel," I said. "If either of them leaves, the last sound you'll hear is the click of this trigger. Do you understand? Now go!"

The driver shook his head, started the car, and then pulled away.

"Where to?" he asked. His voice trembled as he spoke.

"Riverside Drive," I said. "I like the view of the Hudson."

He sat in the shadows of the front seat. All I saw of his face were two bloodshot eyes in the rearview mirror. "Are you Fryer?" I asked.

He nodded his head again. "How'd you know?"

"You're high enough up so that others do your dirty work, but not high enough to rate a chauffeur." Fryer stopped at a red light. My body lurched forward. My gun jammed further into his skull. "Four boys were snatched off the streets yesterday. Why?"

"Don't know," he said.

My patience gave out. I cracked him in the back of his head with my gun barrel. Not hard enough to render him unconscious, but hard enough to hurt. He screamed and tried to reach back.

"Both hands on the wheel," I said, slapping his hand away with the gun.

A trickle of blood oozed from the back of Fryer's head.

"Drive," I said. I reached around his neck and into his jacket, emerging with a Glock that he'd stuffed into a shoulder holster. The mostly plastic gun was as light as a feather.

We stopped at another red light.

"Look, man, I don't know who the hell you are, but I do as I'm told," Fryer said. "And I was told to notify my dealers that four kids were snatched and they'd better be quiet about it."

"Who gave you the orders," I asked.

Fryer said nothing. I caught his neck in a chokehold between my forearms. He coughed. I squeezed tighter. The light changed to green.

Behind us, drivers honked their horns. I held on until he raised both hands in the air, then I eased up a little.

"Nicky told me to do it."

"You work for Nicky Brooks?" I asked.

Fryer nodded.

Drivers behind us furiously blew their horns. I hit Fryer again, this time with the butt of the gun, as hard as I could. He slumped over the wheel. I reached over the seat and turned off the engine. When I looked up, the light had turned back to red. I opened the door and got out. I turned to the line of traffic behind me and shrugged my shoulders. I didn't need to ask Fryer why Nicky Brooks had given those orders. I'd ask Nicky Brooks myself.

TEN

DURING THE GOLDEN AGE of Harlem, the Emperor's Club on 132nd Street just off Malcolm X Boulevard was the place to hear the finest jazz and blues, where zoot suits reigned and regal black women strutted their stuff. Even in the club today, you could find faded photographs of Ella's lips wrapped around a note, Duke's fingers tickling a keyboard, Coltrane's eyes staring deep into polyphonic inner space, and Cab Calloway smiling so wide you'd swear the decades-old echoes of "Hi-De-Ho" still bounced off the grease-stained walls.

But nowadays, the only jazz at the Emperor's Club came from the bartender's CD player. Today the club was not home to the greatest names of Harlem's jazz scene but the greatest names of Harlem's drug scene. Nicky "Fat Daddy" Brooks owned the Emperor's Club. He called it his castle.

I walked in and took a seat at the bar. Behind me, a dark stage bore silent witness to all those who'd ever made music here. Nicky boasted of one day bringing back the golden days of jazz to the Emperor's Club, but the Kings and Queens, Princes and Priestesses, Earls and First Ladies, Dukes and Counts, Sultans and Monks of jazz would never hold court on this stage again. Those days had long since passed with the deaths of jazz royalty and the changing landscape of their once great black kingdom here in Harlem.

"Guinness," I said to Earl, the bartender.

He was a rotund man who'd worked at the club for as long as I could remember. He barely raised his head. He growled, "Don't you know black folks don't drink Irish beer?"

I stood up from my barstool. "Name's John Shannon," I said. "Shannon is an Irish name and I like Irish beer. The darker the better."

Earl snapped his head up. He let out a belly laugh. "Goddamn. If it ain't Irish."

The Emperor's Club is where I got the name "Irish" years ago, after a similar exchange with Earl.

Earl insisted on shaking my hand before letting me sit down. "How you doin', man? First, I heard they put you away for a long time, and then talk was you'd worked some magic to get out. Damn, Irish. Go on with your bald head. You lookin' mighty good for a man who's done time. You come around for a job? I'm sure Fat Daddy has a place for you seein' as how you have inside information about the dangers involved in his line of work." Earl grinned.

"No, Earl. I'm not looking to work for Fat Daddy."

"You'd be surprised, Irish. Fat Daddy's come a long way. Irish, what you drinkin' these days?"

"Guinness," I said.

Earl laughed.

"But I'll take a whiskey on the rocks . . . Irish whiskey."

Earl laughed again. "Comin' up," he said. "You get a taste for hard liquor in the pen?"

Working the streets for any length of time you develop a strange relationship with the very people you're out to apprehend. A good cop could probably find a dozen reasons to close down the Emperor's Club right now, but rousting a bigtime player like Nicky Brooks for petty violations of the law only made it more difficult to nail him for really serious crimes.

So during my years in Narcotics, I frequented the Emperor's Club off-duty and on, just to keep tabs on my quarry. Earl was Nicky Brooks' first line of defense. Somewhere behind the bar lay a gun, but far more important than that, somewhere behind the bar lay a buzzer that Earl could use to alert Nicky to trouble and allow him to escape.

A "threshold guardian." I believe that's the name Promise gave to a person in Earl's position, like a troll in a fairy tale. And I also remember Promise saying there were two ways to get around the troll under the bridge—outfight him or outsmart him.

Earl slapped the glass of whiskey in front of me.

"Be right back," I said.

I got up and headed for the men's room. When I finished, I pretended to make a telephone call on a pay phone outside the men's room door. I watched Earl out of the corner of my eye. He went to the far end of the bar with his back to me. I gently set the headset in the cradle and slipped into the kitchen. I'd made it past troll number one.

I nearly gagged on the smell of the boiling grease used to fry the chicken and ribs. The short-order cooks stepped out of my way as I moved quickly between a large butcher-block table and the stove. I opened a door beside the walk-in freezer and entered a dimly lit hall. At the end of the hallway, two men stood on either side of a door with their hands in front, clasping their wrists like a matching pair of gargoyles. Both were larger than me. Both had bulges on the left side of their chests.

"Earl sent me back to see Mr. Brooks," I said. I held up both hands. "He told me I'd have to be frisked."

The two guards seemed dumbfounded. I walked toward them with my arms in the air. One stepped forward to meet me. He patted down my sides. As he reached around to my back, I kneed him hard in the groin. I reached inside his jacket as he slumped to ground. I had his gun out and pointed at the other guard before that man had his weapon pointed at me.

"Bring it out slowly," I said. "With two fingers, then drop it on the floor and kick it over here."

He did that. I picked up his gun, stuffing it in my coat pocket, but the guy with the sore testicles tried to rise to his knees. I hit him on the back of his head with the handle of his weapon. He crumpled back down. Then the other guard bent over toward his ankle for a gun or the knife he kept there. I caught him bent over. He looked up at me with a stupid grin on his face.

"That one too," I said. "Two fingers and kick it over."

He gently pulled a snub-nosed .38 revolver from an ankle holster. I didn't think anyone used them anymore. I put that pistol into my coat pocket as well. At the rate I was going, I'd soon be ready to open a small arms factory. I kicked the ankles of the other guard sprawled on the floor but felt nothing there.

"Now turn around, knock on the door, open it, and tell Mr. Brooks that Irish is here to see him," I said to the guard still standing.

He pounded on the door, but he got no reply so he pushed it open.

"What the hell are you doing?" a voice screamed at him from the other side.

The guard flinched. "Cat named Irish says he's here to see you."

I grabbed the guard's arm and wrenched it around, back and up his spine. Simultaneously, I jammed my pistol into his temple and pushed him into the room. This was the kind of greeting Nicky Brooks understood. Brooks looked up, his eyes wide, his mouth still chewing his food. He had a leg of fried chicken in one hand. His other hand disappeared up the panties of a woman sitting on his lap. She had nothing else on.

Brooks seemed at a loss for words. Two boyish eyes twinkled above his high, prominent cheekbones. A thin moustache lined his upper lip. His hair was slicked back. If this were the Golden Age of Harlem, then Nicky Brooks would have been the one in the pinstriped zoot suit and wide-brimmed hat. Tonight, he had on a blue open-collar shirt with a subtle floral pattern, and I'm sure the sweet scent in the air came from his cologne, not his companion's perfume.

"Sorry to interrupt your meal," I said. "I'm only here to talk."

Brooks pushed the woman from his lap and then smacked her buttocks. "Go," he ordered.

She grabbed a robe and clutched it around her. Consternation and humiliation mixed equally in her eyes. She sidestepped me as she fled from the room.

"What you want, Irish?" Brooks asked. He dabbed the corners of his mouth with a napkin.

"Stand up, put your hands in the air, and keep them there."

Brooks stood up hesitantly.

"Now. You call off your linebackers. Then just you and I talk. Deal?"

Brooks looked at me askew. He rubbed his eyes. "Man, what's to stop me from bringing a goddamn army in here and blowing your ass away?"

"Me," I said. " 'Cause I'm angry." I pointed my gun at his groin. "And you value Fat Daddy too much. Now step out from behind the desk." I waved Nicky toward me. "Have a seat in that chair and put both hands on top of your legs. And do it quickly or the deal's off and your girlfriend won't find you of much use after tonight." I ratcheted the bodyguard's arm farther up his back. The man muttered something under his breath. I'm sure he wasn't complimenting Nora's taste in clothes.

"Okay," Brooks mumbled.

I let the bodyguard go but I backed a few feet away and kept my gun pointed at him.

"What the hell do I pay you for?" Brooks said to the man. "Take Willie or Nillie or whatever his name is and both of you get your sorry asses off my premises. You s'pose to protect me, not let some cowboy like this in here."

The man slunk out the door. I sat on the edge of the desk. Brooks looked at me and turned on his charm.

"Irish, you looking good. I like that bald thing. Seein' as how you now outta prison, you want a job? Man, after a performance like that I'll make you head of my security detail. You know, kinda like the Secret Service protects the president. Pay you more money than you've ever seen."

"What president have you been taking lessons from? Clinton?"

"That's funny. You a real funny man, Irish." Only Brooks wasn't laughing.

"Let's see, that's the third or fourth job offer I've had today, depending on how I do the counting. If I'd known going to prison was such a good career move I would have gone sooner. Don't call me about the job; I'll call you. In the meantime, you're going to tell me all about what happened to my son."

"Don't know nothin' 'bout your son."

I stood up calmly and then unloaded a punch into Brooks' solar plexus. He moaned. Then he doubled over in pain, holding his stomach with both hands.

"Wrong answer," I said. Then I yelled, "I thought I told you to keep both hands on top of your legs."

Brooks, still bent over, slid his hands back on top of his thighs. I walked around behind him, hooked his throat in the crook of my arm, yanked his head back, and jammed the muzzle of the pistol into his skull. He winced.

"Think before you answer this time." I flexed my arm quickly, crushing his throat for an instant before I backed off. He coughed, tried to raise a hand to his throat, but I slammed the pistol into his forearm. "Top of your leg." His arm dropped back down. "Yesterday, four kids were swept off the street and everyone else was told to make like nothing happened. My son was among those kids. Now you tell me what the hell happened, or I'll go after Fat Daddy next." I pointed the pistol down between his legs and tightened my hold on his throat.

"Look, Irish," he said in a high-pitched, labored whisper. I eased up on his throat. "I didn't have nothin' to do with those kids disappearance."

"It happened on your turf, Nicky. Nothing happens on your turf that you don't know about. If you didn't do it, who did?"

"Mafia."

"Bullshit." I jabbed the pistol back into his temple and flexed my arm. Only this time I held it there, choking Brooks. "You got to level with me, brother. It's my son we're talking about and I'm not in a mood to be jerked around."

Brooks started sweating. His hands went up in the air, clawing at my arm. He was fighting for a breath but I continued to choke him. When I felt the fight slip from him, I let go of my chokehold, but I kept my arm around his throat. He coughed violently, then held both hands in the air as though trying to surrender.

"No bullshit, Irish," he said in a hoarse, barely audible voice. "I didn't have nothin' to do with them kids being picked up. At least not directly. Look, Harlem's changing. Long time ago, the Mob ran drugs in Harlem. Then the brothers moved in. Now white folks moving back into Harlem. Mob wants back in the game. I said no. They kidnapped some low-level players to make a point. I gave the order to keep quiet about it. Didn't want the word out. Only brings more vultures out of the woods."

"Thought you were king of the flock."

"And Fat Daddy intends to stay king." Even in a chokehold, bravado infused his words.

"Are you trying to tell me that this is all about the mob trying to muscle its way back into Harlem?"

"That's what I'm sayin'."

"My boy dealin' for you?" I tightened my arm on Brooks' throat and jammed the gun harder into his head. "If you lie to me and I find out, I'll be back and I won't knock next time."

I eased off of his throat. "Nah, he ain't dealin', Irish," Brooks squeaked. "He's a wannabee. You know, he hangs around with some young punks and asks if he can do favors for them. S'pose he thinks it's cool."

"While we're on the subject of drug deals, one last question." I tightened my hold on his throat again. "Who killed the DEA agent in that drug deal, then framed me?"

Brooks' body squirmed. From his face, I could tell he was laughing, but it sounded more like a gurgle. I loosened my hold.

"Why you asking me, Irish? You the one convicted of the crime."

Without moving my arm, I squeezed my fist together. That tightened my biceps, choking off Brooks' windpipe more. I jabbed the gun harder into his skull. " 'Cause your boys were making the deal, and when I shot to protect Danny Rodrigues, your boys and the Colombians didn't fire on each other. They all turned to fire on me, like they expected I'd be there."

"Must be psychics," Brooks said in a thin, hoarse voice.

I was considering whether to hit him when a buzzer went off somewhere behind his desk. Two short tones repeated several times. Brooks' eyes flashed open.

"What's that signal?" I asked. I squeezed harder on his throat.

Brooks tried to smile, though he grimaced with pain. "Police," he said, his voice still no more than a murmur.

I smashed the barrel of my pistol into the side of Brooks' head. He cried out and then slumped down silently in his chair, like a man who'd had too much to drink. I raced from his office. I shouldered open the back door to the club. I expected to be met by a cop, but no one was there.

When I walked from the alley back to 132nd Street, I saw that two unmarked cars had pulled onto the curb in front of the club. Pulsing red beams from portable lights on their roofs dueled in the chilly night air. Whoever those detectives were, they hadn't busted the Emperor's Club before. We always planted someone at the back door prior to going in.

———————

I DIDN'T LIKE WHAT I heard from Nicky Brooks, especially since it involved JJ being kidnapped in a drug land feud. But I didn't trust what I heard from Nicky Brooks either. Although pain is a persuasive tool for extracting the truth, his story about the Mafia rediscovering Harlem sounded far-fetched, and I needed some independent verification. I laughed. I was starting to sound like Ken Tucker. I stopped at a phone booth, dropped some coins in, and called Curtis Wilson. I checked my watch as the phone rang. It was just after three a.m., but a thirty-year veteran of NYPD is unfazed by such an early morning call, and Curt was one of the few detectives I knew I could trust.

"Yeah," Curt answered in a sleepy, husky voice.

"Curt, man, it's Shannon. I need your help. Is the Mafia trying to work its way back into the Harlem drug trade?"

"Am I dreaming? I heard you were about to be released. But you sound like you're back working the late shift. What time is it anyway?" I heard him fumble for his clock.

"Seriously, man. Is the Mafia trying to muscle its way back into the Harlem drug scene?"

"Uh huh."

"Is there a war going on between Nicky Brooks and the Mob?"

"Why?"

"JJ's disappeared and I think it might have something to do with a drug war in Harlem."

I heard Curt yawn. "Damn," he said. "Meet me for coffee at seven at Anna's." He hung up.

I called Nora next. She refused to say anything other than I'd better get to her place soon. A half hour later a taxi deposited me in front of her building.

"Where the hell were you?" she asked as I walked through the front door. She sounded like an angry mother. "You're out after midnight. You've already violated the terms of your release."

Nora stood in the hallway in a nightgown, cradling her cat and stroking it. She didn't sound like a woman who'd just woken up. She cornered me. The cat looked up as if to ask why I'd even bothered to come. Before I could get my coat off, I told Nora more about JJ's disappearance; about Liz and Claudine; and about my one-man romp through drug land.

"Is that why Tucker called here?" she asked.

"What?"

"He said he had some information he thought you might want to know—about the Mafia, drugs, and a kidnapping in Harlem."

"Damn." I slammed the heel of my hand into the wall. Maybe he's behind JJ's disappearance as a way of trying to get to me."

Nora started to say something, but I took off my coat. She saw the gun tucked into the small of my back and she screamed. "Where the hell did you get that? And what are you doing carrying a gun? Are you crazy? Do you want to go back to prison? If you're caught with a firearm the Brooklyn D.A. will have a field day."

"I couldn't walk into the Emperor's Club unarmed."

I gently eased my coat onto a hanger, trying not to rattle the weapons cache still in my pockets.

"Believe me, if you're caught with a gun you will walk into prison unarmed and there'll be little I can do."

I pulled Slide's weapon from my belt. "Someone's got my son." I brandished the weapon. "And this is the only language they understand."

"Violence?"

"Uh huh."

"You don't like someone . . . kill them. It's the way the men who run this government think and act. So why shouldn't others do the same?" Nora's voice dripped with sarcasm. "When I worked in the public defender's office, I dealt with shooters every day of the week. Some as young as seven. All males. Guns and penises," she sighed, storming down the hallway. "They're two parts of male anatomy that I'll never understand."

"And most women who commit violence use a knife or some other intimate means. Knives and vaginas don't make the crime any less vicious. It's not anatomy, it's violence that's the problem."

Nora turned around. "You're out of prison. Don't you want to stop living your life by the rules of the jungle?"

"I want my son back, even if it means playing by those rules."

Nora shook her head disapprovingly. "There're blankets on the couch," she said. "When you're through with Tucker tomorrow, come by my office. I'll be there all afternoon. We need to discuss your case."

She was about to step into her room when I asked, "Does your cat have a name?"

"Madame Meow," she said.

"Madame Meow?"

The cat raised its head and looked dismissively at me. Nora swallowed a laugh. She stroked Madame Meow and the cat purred loudly. Then Nora stepped into her room and pulled the door behind her. It closed hard, sending a small blast of air my way. A moment later, the door opened again.

"I'm sorry for what happened to JJ," Nora said.

"Thanks," I said.

She closed her bedroom door softly this time. I stared at the door. Nora looked good. Really good. She had a great body. I tried to remember the last time I made love with a woman. That was more than two years ago with Liz. Then today's events coalesced into a throbbing yearning for comfort, a desire to feel the warmth of another human being pressed close to my body. And I fought back the urge to knock on Nora's bedroom door.

I unfolded the blankets and threw them on the couch. Then I stripped down to my underwear, tossing my clothes on her recliner. I sat on the edge of the couch. I didn't want to go to sleep. I wanted to walk out the door and keep looking for JJ, even though I knew there was nothing I could or should do until I talked to Curt. I forced myself to get up and turn off the light.

But on the end table, I saw the envelope I'd left prison with. I picked it up and slipped my fingers under the flap, then inside. They found their way over the pages of a book, which surprised me. I hadn't brought a book with me into prison. I pulled it out. *Keepers of the*

Flame: African Myths and Sacred Wisdom. A crack ran down its spine. I smiled. Then I thumbed through the first of the many dog-eared pages until I came to the inscription: "John, this book changed my life. You might enjoy it too. Regards, Promise."

I remembered Promise carrying this book. He once asked me, "What's the myth you're living?" Not the lie, he explained, but the deeper story of your life. "Discover that and you'll understand the journey you're meant to follow, and where you thought you would be traveling in the outside world, you will really be venturing into the depths of your own soul."

Sometimes I swore that unrehearsed poetry flowed from Promise's lips. I wondered how many lives would have been changed if he'd found his way into a classroom instead of a cellblock. But then I'm glad he was in that cellblock when I got there. Promise seemed to be waiting for me with his uncommon wisdom and his subtle but powerful presence. Sometimes I felt fortunate to have gone to prison because I met him there. I know I'm a different person for the time I spent with Promise, even if I couldn't name all the ways how. I just hoped I wouldn't forget all that I learned from the man.

I laid the book in my lap, then spread the envelope open with my fingers. Promise had also placed a card inside. I reached for it. When I opened it, a silver chain dropped out, dangling in space. A hand-made silver pendant at the other end was Scotch-taped to one side of the card. About the size of a quarter, the pendant looked like a butterfly with convex wings. On the opposite side of the card, Promise wrote:

A double-headed axe is the symbol of the African god, Shango. One blade represents wisdom, justice, and enlightenment; the other, anger, retribution, and ignorance. Both blades are powerful. Which one you fight with depends upon how you wield the axe. Wear it well. Promise.

I peeled the pendant off the card. It gleamed under the lamp. I slipped the chain around my neck and tucked it into my undershirt. I shivered momentarily as the cold metal hit my skin. When it warmed up, I felt the comforting touch of a friend.

Promise had left a bookmark sticking out of the book. I wasn't sure it was for me, but I flipped to the page anyway.

ELEVEN

PROMISE HAD BOOKMARKED A myth about the orisha Shango, the Yoruba god of thunder and lightning. When angry, one look from the god was enough to burst a person into flames. But Shango apparently had uncontrollable, violent outbursts, and sometimes burned the wrong people. He was addicted to violence, even though it revolted him. Like an addict, violence was this god's drug. As I read, I thought about the men and boys that I'd burned tonight. Violence is not only a drug, it's also a muscle. The more you use it, the stronger it gets and the easier it is to use. I remembered my conversation with Liz. Was I also addicted to violence like this god?

I fell asleep before I finished Shango's story. I didn't sleep long, or well. I had a recurring nightmare that had begun shortly after my conviction. JJ and I are out fishing from a chartered boat. A fog bank suddenly moves in, and just as suddenly, I'm alone in a dinghy, looking over to JJ on the fishing boat's stern. I row furiously to the larger boat, but it motors away just outside of my reach. "Dad," I hear him call out repeatedly. But the fog envelops the fishing boat and JJ disappears from my sight.

I awoke to small footsteps on my chest and a sandpaper tongue on my cheek. Apparently, Madame Meow had a change of heart overnight. I smelled coffee but I didn't see or hear Nora. Maybe Madame Meow was being felicitous because Nora had already gone and I was the only one left to pet her. Always an easy mark for felicitous females, I obliged her.

I cradled the cat while standing in front of Nora's living room window, which faced Central Park, where early morning joggers looked like ants as they circled the huge reservoir.

Sunlight streamed in, setting the butterscotch-colored leather couch and matching loveseat ablaze. The plush white carpet dazzled in the light. A large oil painting of a reclining female nude hung prominently over Nora's mantle. A wrought-iron rack of several hundred CDs covered a portion of one wall and next to them she had a high-end stereo system. I questioned where her money came from. Certainly not from pro bono work with Innocence Watch.

On the mantle, a framed picture showed an older man with his arm around Nora. They had the same broad smile and stood in front of a red brick building. Above them, a large sign read "Law Offices of Matthews, Robinson, and Haney. Serving Minnesotans Since 1892." Question answered.

Nora left two small stacks of clothes for me on a chair in her living room. I thumbed through the silk boxers and undershirts, pulled off tags, and dressed. I slipped into my coat, stooped to pet the Madame of the house once more, then left the building and hopped on a downtown local for 23rd Street.

ANNA'S CAFÉ IS A dive in Chelsea run by a Greek family. Curt and I had met there for breakfast many times. Inside, Anna's looks like a diner from the 1950s with barstools at a counter and booths along the sidewalls. The Andropolos family had probably painted the walls in this garish yellow after acquiring the place in the 1970s and then never bothered to repaint the now smoke-stained walls again. I swung into a booth and plopped down on the worn red leather seat.

At the counter, two teenage schoolgirls in blue plaid uniforms sat with a pile of books on their laps and a plate of Greek pastries in front of them. At a booth across from me, a man held the *Wall Street Journal* in front of his face like a shield. His hand would emerge from the paper periodically, and then a coffee cup would disappear behind the market quotes.

"I like. I like," Sophia, the proprietor's plump, eldest daughter said. She held a coffee cup in one hand and ran her other hand back and forth in the air above her head.

My baldness appeared to be a big hit across gender lines.

She set my coffee down. I took a sip. It was even more bitter than I remembered. I ordered breakfast: two eggs sunny-side up with hash browns. It came about as fast as the coffee. The egg whites were still runny; not my idea of sunny-side up. Great service, lousy food. Reminded me of the mess hall in prison.

I'd just broken the surface of one egg when Curt strolled in. He had closely cropped salt-and-pepper hair, a broad nose, and wide, full lips. A network of small lines and crevices traversed his sepia-toned face. A slight paunch hung out above his belt. Curt had never progressed much beyond a 1960s look in clothes. He favored polyester slacks, a sports jacket that sometimes matched, and on a crisp, fall day, a sweater over his button-down blue cotton shirt and a thin tie—all of which he had on today. Curt was a lieutenant, although he could have made captain or inspector long ago. He turned down the opportunities, claiming too much desk time would surely kill him. He'd been my mentor, welcoming me into the ranks when I made detective, showing me the ropes. Most of all, Curt had been my friend. He even visited me a couple of times in prison.

Sophia had a cup of her magic elixir waiting for Curt too.

I stood up. Curt and I locked thumbs, shook hands, and then pulled each other in for a hug. He pushed back and looked me up and down.

"Man, you looking mighty good for a fellow's spent two years behind bars. Designer clothes. Got that bald thing going. All you need now is pair of wraparound sunglasses. Then you'll look just like Hawk." Curt laughed.

"Who?"

"You know, the baldheaded brother on that television series back in the 1980s, *Spenser for Hire*. Didn't he go on to do *Star Trek*, or something like that?"

"Uh huh." I dropped my voice low.

Curt didn't pay me any attention. He slid into the seat across from me. I don't think my impersonation of Hawk impressed him.

I sopped up some egg with a wedge of toast and took a bite.

"Breakfast any good?" Curt asked.

"Nope."

"Least it hasn't changed since we last ate here."

"Yep."

Sophia came over to our table. She didn't say anything. She held her small green pad and pencil out in front. She hovered over Curt.

"Think I'll pass," he said.

Without comment, Sophia glided back behind the counter, grabbed the coffee pot, and went looking for her next customer.

"Good idea," I said. I went back to my eggs.

"Now what's all this about JJ missing?"

Between bites, I told Curt what happened last night at Striver's Row with Slide, Fryer, and Nicky Brooks.

"Hmmm." He took a sip of coffee and then grimaced. "Don't like it."

"You mean, same day I come out, JJ disappears?"

"Uh huh. Too much coincidence for me," Curt said.

"Me too. He was hanging with a gang on the fringe of Nicky's drug operation, using my murder conviction as a means of status. I thought he might have been upset about the overturn of my conviction."

"Loss of status. Loss of face," Curt said.

"Exactly."

"'Cept there's more going on than you know," he said.

"Like what?"

"Like the overturn of your conviction rattled some cages up and down the command."

"Ciccarello's?"

"For starters. But there were others."

"Who?"

"Don't know. Tried to find out. But everything about your case was kept under tight wraps. Still is. I'm a thirty-year veteran, and I still can't sign out the evidence box for your case."

"You know why?" I asked.

"No," Curt answered.

"'Cause that's where one of the major holes in the government's case existed." I told Curt about the discrepancy between the FBI and NYPD evidence logs.

He shook his head and sipped more coffee. "Don't like it."

"Someone else fired my gun, then loaded it with more rounds but bungled the coverup by forgetting to chamber one. One possibility is that they know I'm out and looking for them, so they kidnap JJ, make it look like a drug land feud. I go after JJ and that takes the heat off them."

"That's a possibility," Curt said. "Bet you walked into Nicky's with a piece."

"Uh huh."

"Already violated the terms of your release?"

"Uh huh."

"So now you get arrested for carrying and bounced right back to prison."

"Without passing Go and collecting any money."

"One angry ex-cop out of the way," Curt said.

"And one coverup remains covered up," I said.

"But who's the someone who fired the shot? Who's the one covering up?" Curt asked.

"Don't know," I said. "Do know that detectives raided the Emperor's Club while I was there."

"Damn. Raid doesn't just happen. Takes some planning. I work at the 51st. Okay, so I'm in the Organized Crime Unit. But still, how come I didn't hear about it? They usually let OCU know about any pending busts, so we don't get our wires crossed." Curt shook his head. He frowned. "Don't like it."

"What about this story Fat Daddy gave me? The Mafia trying to move back into Harlem."

"Now that's the only thing you've said so far that makes sense. Gentrification, you know? White folks in the suburbs now want to move back into the inner city, displacing black folks and other people of color out into the suburbs."

"Translated another way," I said. "Powdered cocaine comes back into the city, rock cocaine goes out into the suburbs."

"Uh huh," Curt said.

"It's a whole different culture and a whole different color of people around powdered cocaine. Wall Street bankers do powder. Harlem junkies do crack. Now the Mafia sees a chance to get back into a lucrative market, only people like Nicky Brooks stand in the way."

"Always the smart kid in the class, weren't you? But it doesn't stop there," Curt said. "Folks in Narcotics tell me that in the last couple of years Nicky has expanded his operation. Harlem's not enough. He's bought out or shot dead his competitors to the point that he's now the major player in Manhattan, the Bronx, Brooklyn, and Queens."

"Staten Island?"

"Nope," Curt said. "Nicky must not like ferries."

"Mob wouldn't like a big organization like that around," I said. "Think there's any chance that JJ and the other boys were kidnapped by the Mob to send a message to Brooks?"

"Maybe," Curt said.

"Before Rodrigues was shot I worked on Brooks' connection with a Colombian seller. Ciccarello yanked me off the case when the DEA inserted Rodrigues undercover into the Colombian ring. I think I was getting close to something that Ciccarello didn't want me close to— like him on someone's payroll."

"Brooks' payroll?" Curt asked.

"Didn't know you blacks had a place like this in Harlem." I did my impersonation of Ciccarello on Striver's Row last night.

This time Curt laughed. "Man does not like black folks," he said.

"If Ciccarello's behind JJ's disappearance, he's trying to keep me from digging up dirty laundry that would jeopardize his career. And if Brooks is behind it, he's trying to keep me from disrupting his city-wide expansion plans. Brooks blamed it on the Mob. But Ciccarello could have easily planted that rumor on Brooks' turf."

Curt put his hand up as if to stop me from saying anything more. "You ever worry about thinking too much?" he asked.

"'Bout all you have time for in prison."

"Guess so. But out here, I let others take the load when I can. I've got informants. I'll find out for sure if the Mob's behind this before the end of the day," Curt said. "Think you can stay out of trouble until then?"

"I'll try."

"I'll contact you. You got a cell phone?"

"No," I said. "I can score one on the street."

"Nah. Don't bother," Curt said. "I'll figure something out."

"You can contact me through my lawyer's office," I said. I grabbed a napkin and scribbled Nora's office number.

"Her phone's probably tapped too. Give me the address."

"Easy," I said. "She works with Clinton."

"State Office Building?"

"Uh huh."

"Used to be that white folks were scared to death of Harlem. Now they can't get enough. . . . By the way, did you give a statement to the police last night?"

"No."

"Good. Better not to have them ask questions you don't want to answer." Curt smiled. "I'll write up the statement I took from you over breakfast. That way no one'll bother you about it."

"Thanks," I said. "Do you know a man named Ken Tucker?"

"Yeah." Curt narrowed his eyes. "What's Tucker got to do with this?"

"I'm trying to figure that out too."

I told Curt the story of being picked up outside of prison and brought to Tucker's office. I also told him of Tucker's call to Nora's last night.

"You think he had something to do with JJ?" Curt asked.

"I don't know what to think, or even how to think about all this," I answered.

"City's changed a lot since you went to prison. And not all for the better if you ask me. Since 9/11, New York's really become a police state. I don't like it. And I'm the police. There's now a high-security office in the basement of City Hall, looks like something from a Hollywood movie. Twenty-four-seven they've got people behind huge computer screens analyzing satellite imagery of the city. Man simply clicks a button and zooms in. They can read a license plate. See you and me walking down the street. Folks at the other desks are plugged into earphones, staring at computer monitors typing away furiously. Above the desks are little labels: NYPD, NYFD, Emergency Services, CIA, DIA, CG, FEMA, Customs, Immigration.

Alphabet soup of fear. That's what I call it. And then, at the back of the room, there are two guys in army uniforms who sit next to a red telephone all day, stone-faced, without saying a word. It's a hotline directly into the Oval Office. Fear, that's what it is if you ask me. Government creates it, manipulates it, and folks like Ken Tucker manage it. With a background like his, who knows what he could be involved in. I hope you're not into something that's over your head."

"Me too."

"With Ciccarello now head of NYPD intelligence, I wouldn't put it past his little 'designer suit' ass if he was involved with JJ's disappearance," Curt said. "He'd probably love nothing better than to put you away. Trouble with Ciccarello is that he's got too much unchecked power since he became head of NYPD intelligence. He can wiretap anyone he damn pleases. And he's got a squad of detectives that report directly to him.

Like I said before. Fear. Keep people scared, and men like Ciccarello step in to take greater power. Listen to me talking. I sound like some left-wing radical, don't I? But I've seen it up close since 9/11. People in this country are willing to give up their rights faster than those in power can take them away. Why? 'Cause they're scared, and someone's told them that nipping away a little at the Fourth Amendment here and the First Amendment there will make them safer. And they buy that lie hook, line, and sinker.

It's not what I got into police work for. Nine months more and I'm laying down my badge and picking up my pole. Dorothy and I are moving to Montana to retire. We got a place near a stream that's loaded with trout. You should come out and fish with me. But then you like that open ocean stuff don't you? Makes me seasick."

"Sure, I'll come out," I said. "They've got grizzly bears in Montana."

"Hell, they got armor-piercing ammo in New York. 'Sides, the bears fish just like humans. There's plenty of fish to go around. If you don't bother them, they won't bother you."

"Got those White Supremacists out there too."

"I said put down my badge, not my gun." Curt chuckled. "Look, you hang tight. I'll get in touch with you through your lawyer later today. We'll find JJ. And we'll get him back."

Curt finished his coffee. I finished my eggs and hash browns. Then we both left Anna's Café. I headed to City Hall for a second visit with Ken Tucker.

WHETHER OR NOT TUCKER had anything to do with JJ's disappearance, he was using it to get at me. That didn't sit well. I barged into his office without an appointment. Charlene had a big smile. I didn't smile back or stop to talk to her. She looked hurt. "Mr. Tucker said you might be here first thing this morning." She looked down at her phone. "He's on a call right now but he'll be with you very soon."

Taking others for granted seemed a skill that Ken Tucker had honed to perfection. Five minutes later, his door swung open.

"Morning, John," he said, making a grand sweeping gesture for me to enter.

Tucker wore the same attire as before, only in different colors; today he was in a brown suit, a pale yellow button-down shirt with a gold and red paisley tie, and a matching handkerchief in his jacket pocket, folded to one point instead of two. I smelled the same cologne as before too. About the only thing different was my head. It wasn't hurting so badly.

"My lawyer said you had some information for me. Something about drug wars and a kidnapping in Harlem," I said, walking into his office.

Tucker slowed the tempo. He leaned on the edge of his desk. "My offer still stands. Have you thought about it any further?"

"Is this my second interview, or do you really have some information to pass along?"

"I'm sure you understand that a lot of very sensitive information comes through this office. Information that's not for public consumption."

"John," I mocked Tucker's proper voice. "If you come to work for me I can share information with you that may lead to the discovery of your son. It's called quid pro quo."

"Your Latin's good," Tucker laughed.

"Your tact isn't."

"I know you're out there looking for your son. I'd be doing the same thing. Intel says there's a turf war going on in Harlem. Mafia wants to move back in—not only to run retail, but to be the middlemen as well. They buy directly from South America or even Afghanistan now."

"Tell me something I don't already know. What's this got to do with JJ?"

"There's been some tit-for-tat kidnappings of dealers; some young boys were taken off the streets of Harlem yesterday. It's possible he was among them."

"Possible? Or you know that for a fact?"

"All intelligence is just a possibility, rendered more likely only by the degree to which it is confirmed."

"Spare me the theory. I'm interested in my boy."

"I know. By now, so does whoever took him. Makes you vulnerable even if he wasn't kidnapped for that purpose. You're more easily subject to manipulation."

"Could be you pulling the strings."

"Could be."

Tucker stepped behind his desk and opened a drawer. He pulled out a wallet, laying it open on the desktop so I could see the OMS identification card and gold badge. Then he withdrew a semiautomatic Smith & Wesson, placing it alongside the wallet.

"No legal weapon. No license to carry one. NYPD waiting for you to make a mistake. You'll get eaten up alive out there. Come in. I'll take care of you. You have my word. We want these guys as badly as you do. Drugs and terrorism are linked. A network that can move drugs is easily recruited to move other things. Drug money funds more than haciendas outside of Bogota or villas in upstate New York. We've got assets to go after them—you can't even imagine. Assets that would be very useful in locating JJ. And I can use any means at my disposal."

"What exactly do you want from me?"

Tucker smiled. "If you worked for me, I'd expect you to question every piece of intel from Ciccarello. If it smells funny, you go out and investigate it yourself. If he's jerking me around, I want his chain jerked hard. You'll have special-agent status. Go anywhere. Run down any lead. Look into anything. You get your life back. You get a gun and a badge back. You get your son back."

"For the low, low price of one soul, eh, Mephistopheles?" I stared at the gun and the badge on the desk. I thought about the resources he could bring to bear searching for JJ. "Why do I get the feeling that I'm being used as a pawn in your chess game?"

"Because intelligence is a chess game," Tucker said, "and the smarter you are the more likely it is that you'll win."

"So you and Ciccarello are playing chess with me and my son."

Tucker dismissed my remark with a backhand flick of his wrist. "He plays checkers. I play chess." He pointed to himself.

"I'm not playing either," I said. I moved toward the door.

"Before you leave," Tucker said nonchalantly, "there's someone in the building I thought you might like to see. Might help change your mind."

"You've been holding JJ here all this time?"

"No, not your son," he said. "Your friend, Charles Promise."

"Promise, here?"

"Check," Tucker said, pretending to pick up a chess piece and move it through the air.

TWELVE

A TALL MAN IN a blue blazer and chinos met me as I walked out of Tucker's office. Once we stepped into the elevator, he rifled through a set of keys, selecting one that he inserted into a switch on the elevator's control panel. He twisted the key and then pressed an unmarked button. The doors closed and the car lurched downward. We made no stops and the lighted floor numbers plummeted like the countdown to a launch. The car sped past the lobby and came to a jerking halt somewhere in the basement. I followed the tall man down a corridor with security cameras discreetly placed along the juncture of the ceiling and walls. We stopped and he motioned at the door in front of us.

"Knock when you're through," he said.

He stepped to one side of the door, stood at attention, and held his wrist in front of his body. I reached for the doorknob, and a tremor rippled through me. It had only been a day since I'd last seen Promise, and yet I had a sudden flash of fear that I'd forgotten what he looked like, forgotten what his voice sounded like. I pushed the door open.

"Hi, John."

When I heard his soft voice and saw his wizened face, I realized that my fear wasn't over forgetting the man, but forgetting what I'd learned from him.

"Hi," I said.

I reached out with my hand. Promise stood up. We locked thumbs in a handshake and then we hugged. Feeling his hand clasped in mine brought back good memories of the time I'd spent in prison. He was still dressed in blue jeans and a light blue denim shirt. It did look as though Tucker had simply plucked him from upstate and moved him down here as one lifts a bishop from a square then moves it along an open diagonal on a chessboard.

Promise took his seat on the other side of a small table. "Sit," he said.

The windowless room had cinderblock walls and only this small metal table with two chairs. Fluorescent lights hung overhead. I looked but I didn't see an obvious camera in the room. I swept my hand underneath the table and the chair, feeling nothing there. Even though Tucker said our conversation would not be monitored, I didn't trust him. And I suppose there could have been microphones embedded in the walls.

"Sit," Promise said again, waving off my search. "Doesn't matter if someone's listening. You know the New York Public Library on 42nd Street? Got those two huge stone lions on either side of the stairs. Symbolic guardians of the truth. Anyone can walk up stairs, go through a door, pick up a book, or listen to words spoken. But not everyone will encounter the truth. It doesn't matter what you hear or see from the outside. What matters is your capacity for hearing and seeing within." He touched his chest.

I sat. Promise clasped his hands on the table and stared at me with a penetrating look, nonetheless unnerving for all its familiarity.

"I'm glad to see you, but I'm sorry about all this," I said.

"Sorry about what?"

"For rousing you early this morning, forcing you to take a five hour ride."

"Way I understand it, you didn't force me. Fellow named Tucker did."

"He thinks this display of power will impress me. He brought you here to convince me to work for him."

I gave Promise a brief rundown on Ken Tucker.

"Shoot, if that's why he brought me here, I could have saved him some gas money. I've known you for two years. You're too strong-willed to be convinced of anything." Promise chuckled.

"Still, I didn't mean to get you caught up in all this."

Promise shook his head. "That's between you and Tucker. Old lifer like me doesn't get to take a ride in a chauffeured limousine very often to go see a friend."

I laughed. "Guess not."

"Hard out there?" Promise asked.

"Uh huh."

"Heard about JJ. Sorry. How's Liz taking it?"

"She's holding out hope that the police will find him."

Promise nodded. "And you? How are you holding up?"

"Sometimes good, sometimes not so good."

I told Promise more about Ken Tucker and about JJ's disappearance. I must have been speaking in rapid-fire because I saw Promise's head bobbing pretty fast, trying to keep up with me. He made me repeat everything twice. Referring to Ken Tucker, Promise said several times, as if to be certain, "This man asked you to come work for him?"

Promise grew silent. He stared at me, and I thought I heard a hum or a buzzing sound under his breath. Then the sound stopped.

"What's the truth in here?" Promise asked, touching his chest again.

He liked to throw this at me when I got excited and started talking from my head. I paused and closed my eyes for a moment. I focused inward, and noticed a subtle shaking traveling throughout my body. I opened my eyes and cleared my throat. "I'm feeling vulnerable," I said. "Don't know what to do. Remember that story of Faust's bargain with the devil? Tucker will give me the resources to find JJ if I work for him. But I don't know if I can be out on the streets like I used to. The guns. The violence. Don't get me wrong. I haven't lost my touch. I'm just not sure this is the life meant for me." I heard echoes of my conversations with Nora and Liz.

Promise nodded his head. "Now I understand. You think that maybe it's time you graduated from the life you lived before entering prison."

"Something like that," I said.

Promise put his head down in his hands. He appeared to be sleeping. He rose up several minutes later. The intensity of his gaze shook me.

"You can't choose to be against violence," Promise said. "Any more than you can choose to be against death. They're both inevitabilities of life. And all life is bound in an unbroken chain. Life lives on life. It's not moral, not good or bad, not right or wrong. It just is. There's a symbol you find in West African temples, a snake in a circle eating its own tail. The snake represents life growing, then throwing off its dead skin for a new one. But it's eating itself. All life is a continual process of death and rebirth, demise and renewal, destruction and reclamation. Birth happens in pain and violence. Often death does too. Whatever food you put into your mouth was once living before humans used violence to kill it. Even that piece of lettuce in your salad was once alive. Nothing can step outside this cycle."

"But isn't that the problem? When humans resort to violence, it makes us no better than animals."

"Used right, violence supports life. You've got cells in your body called 'killer cells.' And what do they do? They patrol your bloodstream and tissues looking for invaders. And when they find them, they don't take prisoners. Violence is not the problem. How you use it, that's the problem."

"Last night, I found myself with four handguns," I said. "I'd taken them away from several boys, and I left one man seriously hurt."

"You can't escape your destiny. You know that much, don't you? You can only welcome it with your eyes and arms wide open, unafraid of whatever it brings. You can accept your destiny with grace, gratitude, and humility."

"What kind of destiny is that for me to welcome? Acting out violently helped to drive Liz away."

"You ever think that that boy and those men also have to accept their destiny? Liz too. You just happen to be the deliverer of their destiny in that moment. It's not just you on this earth," Promise chuckled. "We're all moving and living in an interconnected web." He spread his fingers out, then interlaced them. "Just like you and me sitting here talking now, or us meeting when you got to prison. We're all deliverers of each other's destiny."

"Like gods dispensing the destinies of others?"

"Nothing like that. S'pose there's plenty of guards in prison; plenty of police and prosecutors outside that think that way. But that's not what I'm sayin'." Promise shook his head.

"I'm sayin' approach every situation, every person, with the same attitude—clear heart, clear mind. You don't know what's gonna happen beforehand. If you think you know, and you like what might happen, then you'll work to make it happen. If you don't like it, you'll work against it taking place. Now you *are* trying to play god. If you don't know and just allow whatever's supposed to happen to happen, then you're lettin' the gods play through you. You understand what I'm sayin', or you just sittin' there noddin' your head like you do?"

"Approach any situation without regard for the outcome. Act without desire. Trust that whatever outcome follows is the one destined."

Promise laughed. "That's what I'm sayin'."

"Acting without desire?" It was my turn to stare at Promise. "I want to find my son unharmed. I want to clear my name of this murder. I—"

"Uh huh." Promise cut me off. "I want to get rich. I want to drive a nice car. I want power. I want to sleep with a beautiful woman. I want . . . I want . . . I want. . . . Why do you think people are in prison?" Promise raised his voice. "Acting on desires leads to prison. Oh, it may not be a prison with bars like the one I'm in, but you'll be bound up inside all the same. Look inside yourself. You're bound up now.

You stay in prison long enough, comes a point when you realize that you won't get what you want. Stay in prison beyond that, you realize the wants themselves are your prison. Did you read the book I gave you?"

"Some."

Promise laughed. "Guess you've been busy, huh? It's all there in that book. Take Shango, the Yoruba god, for example. By the way, did you get that pendant I had made for you?"

I'd forgotten that I had it on. I reached inside my shirt and pulled it out.

Promise's eyes lit up. "Looks good. Had to call in a lot of favors to get it made."

"Thanks," I said.

"Shango's challenge is the same as yours," Promise said. "Shango is the god of thunder; his symbol is a bolt of lightning and that double-headed axe. He was known as a great warrior, but one given to excess on the battlefield because he couldn't control his anger. One day he went too far and killed two of his own generals. When the realization of what he had done struck him, he vowed never to fight again and left for a long exile, deep in the forest.

People went looking for him but all they found was his double-sided axe. The gods found Shango, though, and told him sternly that he had made a wrong choice, for there is no disgrace in being a warrior. The only disgrace, they said, lay in being blinded by anger and wedded to victory. A warrior's greatest battle, the gods said, lay not on the battleground outside, but within one's self. Armed with this insight, Shango went on to be an even greater warrior, known not just for his cunning with the sword, but his compassion and wisdom in dispensing justice. And the gods elevated him into their ranks."

Promise directed his penetrating stare at me. "I don't think you can avoid being back on the streets," he said. "It's only a matter of how. You have Shango's cunning with the axe." Promise touched one side of the pendant dangling from my neck. "Now you have to find his compassion and wisdom in dispensing justice." He touched the other side. "But only you can find Shango's truth inside of yourself."

After Promise and I had talked for a while, the tall guy with the ramrod posture knocked on the door. When I opened it, he handed me two brown bags with white containers. "One order of garlic prawns. One order of Pad Thai chicken. Plenty of rice. Four stars," he said. "Hope you like it spicy." He closed the door. The food was courtesy of Ken Tucker.

I set the boxes in the middle of the table.

"Enough talk," Promise said. "I'm hungry."

I pushed the garlic prawns his way. "Feels like anything we'd eat is simply death warmed over now."

"It is," he said.

He laughed. I did too.

"Then what the hell?" I said. "Let's dig in."

After lunch, Promise and I hugged goodbye. I knew that I'd be seeing him again and I hoped it would be soon.

The tall guy with the straight spine escorted me back upstairs. Charlene waved me into Tucker's office. Tucker was on the phone. He waved me into a seat. When he ended his conversation, he clasped his hands behind his head. He leaned back in his chair and stared at me.

"It's your move," he said.

"Thanks for lunch," I said. "But the answer's still no."

"You're making a mistake," Tucker said. He shook his head.

"Least it's my mistake."

"That matter?"

"Uh huh."

"Why?"

"If things don't work out I'll know who to blame and I won't have to go far to find him."

"You know what Muslims say?"

"What?" I asked.

"The most difficult convert is the most dedicated follower."

"Well then, Salaam Alaikum," I said, getting up and moving toward the door.

Tucker leaned forward and with a sly smile replied, "Walaikum Salaam."

———

SPENDING TIME WITH PROMISE left me feeling hopeful about finding JJ, although we didn't talk much about what I should do. It also left me feeling hopeful about finding a direction in my life after prison. I couldn't say I looked forward to working with Ken Tucker, as Promise seemed to think I should. He never really came out and said as much. But then Promise never told me what to do. He merely pointed out the pitfalls and possibilities of a given path, and left the final decision to me.

When I entered the Innocence Watch office, Brendan looked up from a steaming cup of coffee. "Sorry to hear about your son." He took a delicate sip. "She's a little bitchy today. I don't think it's going well."

"My case?" I asked.

Brendan winced. "I'll let her tell you." He took another sip, then picked up a telephone handset and punched a few numbers. "He's here," he said. "You look great in those clothes. Do they fit well?"

"They do," I said. "I'm amazed that she could pick out a wardrobe for me without even knowing my style."

Brendan nearly choked on his next sip of coffee, then laughed. I narrowed my eyes at him and he winked at me. "She said jockeys." He pointed the coffee cup toward Nora's office door. "I said boxers." He pointed it at himself. "She said cotton. I insisted on silk. Why do you think she's such a knockout in court?" He grinned. "Girlfriend couldn't find her way around Bloomie's with a map."

I winked at Brendan. The guy had good taste.

Nora sat behind her desk in the midst of a heated exchange over the phone. I couldn't take my eyes off of Georgia O'Keeffe's flower as I fell into one of Nora's leather chairs. She slammed the telephone into the cradle. I jumped.

"Damn prosecutor. Kid's only thirteen. He's a suspect in a drive-by and they want to try him in adult court under adult rules. Innocence Watch is interceding on his behalf. Public defenders are so overwhelmed with caseloads they don't have time to do these kids right."

"Someone die?"

"Fifteen-year-old girl and her sixteen-year-old boyfriend. The girl was four months pregnant."

"Is this kid the shooter?"

"I don't know. But he's being charged as an accessory to a triple homicide."

"And you offered?"

"Juvi court, juvi rules. The kid needs a mother and father who'll whip his ass, not a jury that'll throw him in prison with hardened criminals."

"Does he have a mother and a father at home?"

"No."

"Maybe too late, then."

"Give up on a thirteen year old?" Nora said. "No way."

"You sound like a bleeding heart," I said.

"And you, like a hanging judge," she said.

"I suppose I'm not in a charitable mood toward minors after spending time around them last night."

"If it was JJ would you want me to give up?"

"I hope I never have to face that question."

"How about you? Would you have wanted Innocence Watch to give up on your case because you were convicted of murder?"

"You've got a point there, Madame Counselor."

Nora chuckled.

"You've got your claws out today," I said.

"When I go up against the big boys I need more than my claws," she said. "I might need my knife."

Then she laughed as though a comedian had just whispered a joke that only she could hear. I laughed too. We both knew what that comedian said.

"Might need that too," Nora said with a wicked smile. "Why do you think I keep a Georgia O'Keeffe image on the wall?" She hiked her thumb over her shoulder. "It helps to remind me of the source of my power."

I looked at the image again. Scalloped purple, red, and orange leaves burst open in the middle, delicately enfolding each other toward the bottom and top. If I stared long enough I knew I would lose myself inside the flower. I felt blood move in my loins. Maybe from the sparks that flew between Nora and me when we argued. Maybe from Georgia O'Keeffe's erotic flower. Maybe from two years of pent-up desire. I leaned back in Nora's chair. The next time she spoke, she sounded serious.

"What happened this morning?"

I told her about meeting with Curt, Tucker, and Promise.

"You feel like Tucker's playing you?" she asked.

"Uh huh."

"He must really want you to work for him."

"What he really wants are people that he can control."

"Hard to turn down his offer, though."

"Easy if you like looking in the mirror at yourself," I said. "Do we need to talk about my case?"

"Uh huh," Nora said. "But with all that's going on about JJ, it can wait."

"I'm staying put," I pointed down at the floor, "'til I hear from Curt."

"Is he coming by the office?"

"Don't know. Curt's an old fox. He's liable to do anything."

"And you trust him?"

"Like a brother," I said. "What do I need to know?"

"I want to bring you up to speed."

"Shoot."

Nora grimaced at my choice of words. "I'm meeting with the federal prosecutors sometime in the next few days. I want to convince them to drop a retrial. I'll dangle this second lie detector test in front of them, but we're also pursuing a DNA angle just in case they want to play hardball and go for a second trial."

"DNA? From what?"

"The tunnel."

"You're not serious. It's an old concrete access tunnel. The walls are filled with gang graffiti and the homeless sometimes use it."

Nora waved me off. "I know that. But you used it to gain access to the abandoned warehouses overhead. The one where the drug deal went down and the one at the far end of the lot, where NYPD maintained a surreptitious field office. You climbed up from the tunnel into that warehouse. And you said that right before you were shot, you thought you heard someone else climbing up the ladder."

"It wasn't even a ladder. It was just a set of rusting iron rungs. The rust flaked off in my hand."

Nora nodded. "We sent an investigator down to scrape off rust from each set of rungs leading to the five warehouses overhead. He also collected rust flakes from the ground. They're bagged and labeled. From what we can gather, NYPD has stopped using that warehouse to stage undercover drug deals, although they still maintain a field office in an adjacent abandoned warehouse. So we think we've got good samples."

"Even if there was DNA evidence, it would be more than three years old."

"It's one thing I like about this job," Nora said, smiling. "DNA can stay around literally for millions of years. Innocence Watch just secured the freedom of a man who'd been on death row in Illinois for almost fifty years. DNA from a cigarette butt collected at the scene linked the murder to another suspect who'd died years earlier. The tests can run into the tens of thousands of dollars. We're not ready to go there yet but we've got the evidence. Let's see what the feds and the city do first."

I leaned back in my chair. I thought about Promise. He never spoke of the murder he was convicted of fifty years ago. Someday I wanted Innocence Watch to review the evidence in his case.

"There's something else," I said. "Something that never came out in trial. Don't know how important it is. A sound. I think I heard a strange noise right before I was shot."

Nora perked up. "A sound?" She pulled a tape recorder from her drawer and pressed a button.

"One day, Promise and I were sitting with our faces to the sun and our backs against the prison wall. He told me to follow my breathing and his voice. Next thing I knew I was in that . . . well, it was like a half-asleep, half-awake state. Have you ever experienced that?"

"Like a trance. Lying in bed, eyes open, aware of your surroundings but seemingly unable to move your body?"

"Yes, only I was sitting up. Anyway, Promise asked me what I saw, smelled, tasted, felt, and heard in the warehouse and the tunnel that night. I told him about seeing the drug deal, the dank smell of the warehouse and of gunpowder when the shooting started. Then a sound came into my head, a metallic screeching sound. Right after that, I felt the searing heat in my shoulder. Then I passed out. Subway trains do run under the ground near that location. I may have only heard a passing train, but it surprised me that it came to me the way it did. I've thought about it, but I don't know what to make of it."

Nora shrugged. "We'll keep it on file. It's a piece of a puzzle. You never know how it'll fit in."

The intercom buzzer went off.

"Brooklyn D.A.'s on line one," Brendan said.

She looked at me. "May be about you."

"I'm flattered."

I leaned forward in my chair.

"Nora Matthews," she said.

She listened. Her eyes got wide. She tightened her lips and then pursed them. Her jaw muscles flexed. She cast a quick glance my way. She breathed hard and then she shouted into the headset.

"No. You can't do that. His conviction's been overturned on appeal. The federal government has not decided on a retrial. You can't issue an arrest warrant for him now."

THIRTEEN

I HAD A PRETTY good idea where Nora's conversation with the Brooklyn D.A. was heading, and there wasn't much I could do, so I tuned her out and tuned Promise in. I listened to him tell me the story of Shango and then say that I had to find what Shango found inside me. Then Nora slammed the phone down. My time for tuning out had ended.

"Bad?" I asked.

"Bad," she answered. "First the bastard apologized. He'd heard what happened yesterday and thought that maybe someone in his office had jumped the gun and issued a warrant for your arrest once you stepped out of prison. Then he laughed and said, 'That warrant was scheduled for today.' He was calling to arrange for your surrender."

"Uh huh. That's bad. And you offered . . ."

"To accompany you to Brooklyn." Nora sighed. "He'll meet us at the Brooklyn Detention Center at six."

I looked up at her. "I'm not going."

"You have to. I can't protect you if you're out on the streets."

"You can't protect me, period."

"What are you talking about? You're going to take a semiautomatic pistol and go up against the entire New York City police force?"

"No. I'm going after my son."

"You don't even know where JJ is. And the moment this arrest warrant is issued you'll be fair game for every cop in the city." Nora ran her hand through her hair. She shook her head and then put her hand on the telephone. "You want me to call the D.A. back? Maybe we can arrange to postpone the warrant and your surrender until tomorrow."

She pounded the telephone keys, but this time her call lasted only a few seconds. Apparently the Brooklyn D.A. was not easily persuaded. Nora looked glum.

"At least you tried," I said.

"I don't understand what you're doing," she said. "Everyone in this office has worked hard on your case. We can beat anything the D.A. throws at us, I'm sure of that, but not if you gallop off on your own."

"Brendan," I said.

"What?" Nora looked at me, clearly bewildered.

"Not only did he buy my clothes and your clothes, but he also decorated your entire office. He's the one who decided on that Georgia O'Keeffe, isn't he?"

"Yes." She pounded her desk. "You're about to become a fugitive, to put your life at risk, and you're thinking about who bought your clothes and decorated my office?"

"No," I said. "I'm thinking about what it's like to live from inner truths."

"I don't understand," Nora said.

I told Nora about meeting with Promise, and about the story of Shango. I heard myself speaking rapidly, although I wasn't sure I'd connected all the dots. When I looked into Nora's eyes, they'd glazed over.

"I know your son's missing and it's stressful," she said. "But you're facing new criminal charges related to a murder, and I need you grounded, not spinning off into some fantasy about 'living from inner truths.'"

At that moment, Brendan knocked on the door and walked in. "This just came by courier," he said to Nora. "It's marked 'urgent'." He slid a manila envelope across the surface of her desk.

Nora grabbed a stiletto letter-opener off of her desk and took out her frustration on the envelope. She reached inside and pulled out a smaller white envelope. She took one look at the envelope before slapping it down on the desk. "Here," she said. "It's for you."

I opened the envelope, pulling a handwritten note from inside.

"Row at 8. CW," is all that it said.

IT WAS ALMOST FIVE o'clock. Harlem Hospital was on the way to Striver's Row. Curt probably hadn't called Liz. I thought she should know, so I called her. We agreed to meet in the hospital's cafeteria.

At the hospital, I walked through a side door reserved for staff. I knew the guard on duty, a man named Bill. He'd waved me through many times before to meet Liz or to conduct police business. He waved me through today. I'd spent countless hours in this hospital even before I knew Liz. My mother died here. Since then, every time I walked into the hospital I swore I smelled the disinfectant that they used in her room, and it nearly brought me to tears. That odor lingered in her room as she slipped away.

Liz stood to greet me. Her eyes were still red. It looked like she hadn't slept much last night. She had on a long, white lab coat. A stethoscope hung around her neck. I wasn't sure if I should hug her.

She hugged me. My body responded instantly and strongly. I remembered the time she came to bed wearing a white lab coat and a stethoscope, and nothing more.

Liz was nursing a cup of tea. I sat down at the small table with her. I told her about the note from Curt. She lifted her eyes.

"Does he have news about JJ?"

"I hope so."

"The police came by the hospital this morning and told me they were doing everything they could. They said his disappearance might have something to do with drug gangs in Harlem. Is that true?"

"That's what I heard. That's why I met with Curt this morning and asked him to find out all he could."

Liz wiped tears from her eyes. "All the time this child was with me and I couldn't see how much he was hurting. I couldn't see how he was asking for help. I could have gotten him better help. I could have made sure he stayed off the streets. I'm sorry for what I said to you last night. What could you have done these last two years? It's me who's to blame for what happened to JJ."

"Blame doesn't help."

"At least Curt's working on it." She sniffled. "I'll fix pasta."

"He always liked the way you made Italian food."

Liz checked her watch. "My last patient's in fifteen minutes. You wanna wait and we can go home together?"

She blinked her eyes with the words and then lowered her head to the cup. She pulled the teabag up by the string and dunked it several times.

"At least you're here at a time like this," I said.

She raised her head and shook it. "Here? You mean doing what I always said I loved. Bringing new life into the world. Helping women fulfill themselves."

"Uh huh."

"It's not the same anymore," she said. "Seems like nothing's the same." She dunked her teabag again.

"I thought maybe delivering babies was one thing that wouldn't change."

"Delivering babies hasn't changed, but being an obstetrician has." Liz raised her cup to her lips but she set it down without taking a sip. The expression in her eyes wavered between anger and sadness.

A discomforting silence hung in the air between us. I knew Liz was debating if she should say more. Suddenly, she started talking.

"I think more about insurance than I do about episiotomies." She chuckled sarcastically. "My malpractice premium has doubled in three years. I'd have to work eighty-hour weeks just to make what I did two years ago. I won't do it. I'm working too much already. That's one of the reasons I wasn't around for JJ when he needed me. I used to be able to see patients and manage their care. Now I see patients, and some bureaucrat a thousand miles away, who wouldn't know a cervical cap from a cervical spine, tells me how to manage their care. I feel like a managed-care robot. It's not what I became a doctor for."

I touched Liz's hand. "We'll get JJ back," I said.

"Yes," she said. "I need to have JJ back. But it's more than that—" She shook her head and fought back tears. "I've got to see my patient now," she said. She pushed back from the table and got up.

————————

I ALWAYS LIKED THE kitchen of the Striver's Row house. Even with all the remodeling that had occurred over the years, it had the feeling of a nineteenth-century gathering place for a large family. In the middle of the kitchen, pots hung on a rack above a butcher-block preparation table. A large stove protruded from the wall behind the table, and in front of the table, a shiny metallic refrigerator stuck out from the wall. A walk-in pantry sat at one end of the kitchen, and at the other end there was a circular table large enough to seat a family of ten. Next to the table, a door led out to a small patio, then down a few steps into the garden.

I sat at the table. Liz pulled jars and packages from a cupboard. She dumped tomato sauce into a pan, added spices, and stirred the mix. She dipped a large wooden spoon into the saucepan, tasted the sauce, and then adjusted the heat of the burner. She looked over to me. "You went to Claudine's last night?"

"You spoke with her?"

"Yeah."

"I had to. Our son's out there. I won't rest until I find him."

Liz took a seat at the table. "When we were together, every day you left for work I wondered if that was the last time I'd see you alive. And now I don't know if I'll see our son alive."

"I'm not giving up," I said. "I've got to believe that JJ's alive, and I won't give up until I find him."

"I know you won't give up," Liz said. "But the police are doing all they can. You don't need to bring any more trouble on yourself."

"I've got enough trouble already," I said. "What's a little more?" I thought it unwise to mention the arrest warrant now out for me.

Liz took a deep breath. "You're a good man deep down, and I know that. John, I need to tell you something, and it's not easy to say. I started to say it at the hospital, but I couldn't bring myself to do it there."

Whenever Liz used my first name, I knew to hold my breath. And I did.

"I didn't say everything last night about why I want a separation. There's more to it than your anger, more than JJ's attitude as well."

My leg started to tremble. "Are you in love with someone else?"

Liz burst out laughing. And for the first time in longer than I could remember, I caught a glimpse of the dazzling young intern that

I'd met one evening while bringing a shooting victim to the emergency room.

"In love? Hell, no," she said. "I didn't file for a separation because I stopped loving you. You being in prison gave me the time to examine my life, and to ask myself if I was living a life that felt right to me. I'd never asked myself that question before. I'd lived the life my parents wanted, became the doctor my father wanted because he was a doctor and his father was a doctor. I work in the same hospital they did. I became the wife I thought you wanted, and the mother I thought JJ needed.

Somewhere in all of that 'becoming' for others, I lost sight of becoming for myself. I looked into the mirror one day and I didn't like who I saw. I know you want us to be together again. And maybe one day it can happen. But I can't be together with you until I'm first together with me."

"This have something to do with yoga and meditation?"

"Claudine told you I was taking classes with Daya?"

"Uh huh."

"No . . . I don't know . . . maybe. Maybe the yoga and meditation helps keep me calm enough to look at my own painful truths."

I reached for Liz's hand. She began to sob. I stood up and put my arm around her. She allowed it. I was about to pull her closer when the front door chimes went off.

"Must be Curt," I said.

Liz wiped her eyes with her hands, then jumped up and walked out of the kitchen. I lingered by the stove on my way to the front door. The water for the pasta sat in the pot. Liz hadn't turned on the burner underneath it, so I did. I heard more than one male voice at the front door. I craned my neck out of the kitchen. Four cops stood talking to Liz—two in uniforms and two in plain clothes. Curt was not among them.

"Is there a problem?" I shouted down the hall.

Liz turned to me, panic blazing in her eyes.

"John Shannon," a detective bellowed, waving a paper in the air. "You're under arrest."

Just inside the entrance to the kitchen I stood frozen, looking down the hallway at the detective waving the arrest warrant. Our gazes locked, and for a brief instant we had that age-old silent conversation between predator and prey: Will you run? Or will you make the kill easy? Perhaps it was as Promise said, that in a brief instant I welcomed my destiny, as the detective did his. I thought I even saw a smile on the man's face, as though we both knew what came next.

Liz also knew. "John, don't," she pleaded.

But I turned on my heels, blew past the pasta, past the family table, whipped open the door to the patio, and leapt down the steps into the garden. By the time I reached the back fence, I could hear Liz yelling, and the men pushing the heavy wooden table out of the way. They burst out of the patio door. A searchlight splashed over my body.

"He's on foot, headed over the back fence and into the alley," I heard someone yell.

"Shannon! Stop!" another man screamed.

I jumped down from the fence into the alley. My legs buckled and I scrambled to my feet. To my right, a police car turned down the alley. In the cold air, smoke rose from its headlights like a monster's fiery breath. A blue light pulsed as though keeping the heartbeat of the beast. I turned and ran down the alley the other way, until a second police car came screaming around the corner, headed for me.

I climbed over a fence on the other side of the alley. I must have set off a motion detector because brilliant lights flooded the night and a watchdog began barking. A narrow walkway led between the house, whose backyard I'd just entered, and the adjacent home. I could feel my pulse clear into my throat as I squeezed through the tiny space. I checked behind me. The police had already scaled the fence. They were rushing toward the walkway. When I popped through into the next street over, I saw a police car racing down the block from my left. I turned right and headed up the street, when another cruiser turned the corner. These patrol car guys had this pincer maneuver down.

I dashed across the street, not absolutely certain why, but in the back of my mind I remembered that this block of homes shared a common courtyard in the rear. I looked both ways, searching under the orange haze of the streetlamps for a space between adjacent houses. I found none. I ran farther up the block to my right, still looking for a way into the courtyard. I heard brakes squeal, then doors open and slam shut. I turned around and ran back the other way.

An officer knelt with his gun out, ready to take aim. At the last minute, I found an opening and shimmied between two houses, into the courtyard behind them. Adrenaline raced through my body. I breathed hard, sweating profusely even in the chilly air. As I ran along the courtyard, bluish-white lights of televisions flickered in the windows I passed. Then I heard the whump, whump of a helicopter's blade in the distance, headed my way. Someone had pulled out all the stops to bring me in.

I peered down the covered passageways that led from this courtyard into the next street. I knew I'd find a locked gate at the end of nearly every one. I could hear the voices of the police. They'd almost made it through the gap. In a moment, they'd have me trapped. The beating of the helicopter's blades grew louder. Then flashlights played in the darkness of the courtyard. They'd gotten through. Even if I managed to chance upon an unlocked gate, once the helicopter got here I'd easily be spotted from above.

I crouched low and ran. Behind me, a dog barked like a wild animal. "Go get him, boy!" an officer yelled.

They'd also brought in a K-9 Unit.

The animal took off, its feet racing toward me at the speed of destiny. I peeled off my overcoat and hurled it down the next passageway I came to. Then I skipped a couple before taking a chance and turning into one. I heard the dog growl as he attacked my coat.

Ahead of me, I saw the long iron bars of the gate with a padlocked chain around it. I scurried back toward the courtyard. The officers in pursuit came up quickly. I waited until they got to the dog, then I slunk out, pressing my body against the wall of the house, slithering along toward the next opening. I don't know if I was running on adrenaline from fear or disbelief. Maybe both. Had Curt given me up? With nine months left, maybe someone had gotten to him.

The helicopter arrived at the far end of the courtyard. It moved slowly toward me. Its spotlight swept back and forth across the courtyard. I slipped into the next walkway. I ran to the front and shook the gate. It was locked too. I stepped back, at any moment expecting the arrival of the beast that would devour me. I also heard Promise's voice repeating, "Welcome your destiny."

Outside the gate, a car with a blue flashing light zoomed to a stop. A man got out, keys dangling. He thrust a key into the gate, pushed the gate open, and shined a flashlight at me. I shrank further into the shadows.

FOURTEEN

"Irish. It's Al. Big Al," he said in a whisper. "Get into the back of my car and lie down."

I ran from the passageway toward the open car door and then dove onto the floor. Al slammed the door closed, jumped behind the wheel, and took off. His blue light flashed. His siren whooped. He picked up a microphone from the dashboard and his PA system blared with his voice. "Just got a security call," he said. "Can y'all move the barricades for me to get through?"

It must have worked, because the next thing I knew we were speeding along.

"You can sit up now, Irish," Al said, chuckling. "They ain't around here."

I sat up, my heart pounding. "Where's Shorty?" I asked.

"Ain't workin' tonight. Jus' me."

"How'd you know where to come looking for me?" I asked.

Al laughed and then turned a radio on. It cackled and hissed. I listened over a police band to bewildered officers wondering how a trapped suspect had escaped. "Humph," he said. "NYPD treats us like shit. Thinks we're some kinda tin policemen. Hell, we're the first responders, while they're sitting there dunkin' donuts. 'Sides, I spoke with your missus yesterday. Said she had her doubts about you being guilty and all. Told her I thought you was framed right from the beginning."

"Thanks, man. You didn't have to do that," I said. "You may have put yourself in a lot of trouble."

"Hell, man, no trouble helpin' out a brother. Look, Irish, what you want to do now that we're away from the Row?"

I tried to think clearly, but I couldn't. "Drop me at a subway station," I said.

"Eighth Avenue line at 125th Street okay?" Al asked.

"Fine."

"Why they after you now, Irish?"

"'Fraid I'll find out who really killed that agent."

"Make them look like dunkin' donut cops?"

"Uh huh."

The car screeched to a halt near the stairs leading down to the subway.

"Man, give me your ashtray," I said, motioning impatiently with my hand over his shoulder.

"What?"

"Your ashtray," I said. "They have a K-9 Unit. If they think you helped me, they'll have the dog sniff the car for my scent."

I heard a tiny ping of metal and then I heard Al rip the ashtray from the dash.

"Here," he said, handing it to me.

I dumped the ashes and then I smeared them on the seat and the floor. "That should stop Rin Tin Tin," I said. I gave Al a quick locked-thumbs handshake. "I owe you one," I said before bolting out the door and racing down the steps to the subway.

Even after I climbed aboard a southbound *D* train my body still shivered. I closed my eyes and pressed back against the subway seat, taking slow, deep breaths. The train jostled me back and forth as it hurtled along the express tracks. Occasionally, I opened my eyes to the blur of lights and people waiting at local stops.

My thoughts raced as fast as the train. Right now my options were few. I couldn't go to Nora's home or her office. I didn't have Brendan's number, didn't even know his last name. I suppose I could hit the gay bars in the Village and hope that I'd run into him. Forget it. That wasn't a good plan. I thought about riding the subway all night, then showing up at Ken Tucker's door. That idea stuck in my mind until a voice came over the train's PA system.

"Fifty-third and Fifth next," the conductor sang out. "Change for the *E* train to Queens."

We pulled into the station. At the last minute, as the doors of my car were closing, I dashed out and down the stairs to another platform. I hopped on a waiting *E* train and it lurched forward. Moments later, we were headed for Queens. Curt Wilson lived in a neighborhood called St. Albans, which was about as far east as you could go and still be in New York City. It was not only a forty-five minute train ride from here, but also a bus ride after that. It didn't matter. If Curt had betrayed me, he'd have to tell me to my face.

An hour later, I sat at the back of a city bus plodding through the streets of eastern Queens, past block after block of single-family dwellings, settled decades ago by African Americans who could not afford Striver's Row, but had fled the ghettos of Harlem and the Bronx and Brooklyn looking for a haven of tranquility. Many of these families had since gone to the surrounding suburbs, or, like Curt and Dorothy, were waiting for that one last paycheck before moving away from New York.

I reached up and pushed the buzzer. After three more blocks, the bus shuddered to a stop. Its back doors swung open and I stepped into the bitter cold.

The bus pulled away, releasing a cloud of foul-smelling exhaust, and for the first time in a very long time I felt alone, even more alone than when I was in prison. I heard the bus' engine cough and then I lost the sound in the chill of the night.

I had a ten-minute walk to Curt's house. I hunched my shoulders against the cold and headed down the street. Above me an orange sodium light spit and hissed, then finally sputtered out.

I couldn't see any lights on in Curt's two-story brick house. Their SUV was parked in the driveway in front of the garage, which probably meant that Dorothy was home sleeping and Curt was still out in a departmental vehicle. I hated to wake her up, but she'd been a cop's wife for thirty years, and she was accustomed to being wakened at strange hours.

I rang the front doorbell several times, but no one answered. I walked around to the back. The screen door leading into the porch was open, which didn't feel right. I reached for the doorknob into the house. It was open too. A thirty-year veteran of the NYPD does not leave the doors to his home open at midnight.

"Dorothy. Curt," I called out.

No answer. An eerie chill crept over me, like the feeling I got when I was first at a murder scene: that sense of ghosts present, ready to lead me to bodies. Instinctively, I reached for my gun and then realized I'd left all the guns at Nora's. I moved cautiously through the kitchen and into the living room. I saw nothing there. I pulled back a curtain and looked across the street for a parked car, but saw none. I stood at the foot of the staircase, debating whether to walk up. How do you welcome destiny with open arms when you fear those arms will be bloodied?

"Curt? Dorothy?"

I could hear my own voice, which sounded weak and feeble, as though I'd already given up the expectation of an answer. I crept up the flight of stairs, past two open bedroom doors where their children, now grown, once slept. The door to their bedroom was partially closed. I kicked it open. My hand flew to my mouth. I heard my own muffled scream echo inside my head. I pressed my hand harder, holding in my disgust. My stomach heaved. I wanted to vomit. I slumped to the floor, pushed my back against a wall, dropped my head into my hands, and cried. I had seen double murders many times before, but never when the victims were my friends. It sickened me to think that I'd doubted Curt. I squeezed my fist hard and pounded the carpeted floor, trying to bring my emotions under control long enough to examine the grisly scene.

Finally, I stood up and walked toward the bed, where Dorothy lay spread-eagle in a black full-length nightgown with her head on a blood-soaked pillow and her eyes shocked wide open with a dime-sized hole between them. I turned my head away and bit my bottom lip. When I turned back, I saw Curt's feet sticking out from the other side of the bed. I walked toward him and found him crumpled with his back against a chair, his service pistol in his hand, and blood still trickling from a gaping wound to the middle of his chest.

Old reflexes kicked in. I leaned over Curt's lifeless body and carefully slipped my hand into the back pocket of his pants. His wallet was still there. I walked over to the couple's bedroom dresser, took a tissue from a box, and used it to cover my hand as I opened the top drawer. I found Dorothy's jewels, including the diamond necklace I'd helped Curt pick out for their twenty-fifth wedding anniversary. Robbery was not the motive, which meant that in all likelihood their murder had something to do with Curt getting word to me.

I massaged my forehead as I walked back over to Curt. I lifted his gun from his hand and slipped it into my pocket. I patted his pants pockets and worked my fingers into the one with the biggest bulge, pulling out a set of car keys and a slip of paper with them. The receipt showed he'd eaten an early dinner in Little Italy. I knew how much Curt loved Italian food. I hope he'd enjoyed his last meal. I clasped his car keys in my hand. A wave of self-loathing washed over me. I felt like the grave robber of a friend.

I plucked a handful of tissues from the box on the dresser. Nine more months until retirement. That's all he had. The thought brought tears back to my eyes. "Curt," I whispered to his body, "wherever you're on your way to now, buddy, I hope the fishing there is good."

I walked out of the bedroom, running a tissue back and forth along the wooden banister on my way downstairs. I told myself I'd call in the murder from a pay phone when I was a long distance away. Eventually, a crime scene squad would be out here. I might be erasing the prints of the murderer, but I didn't want them connecting me to the crime.

On my way back to the kitchen, I passed the hallway closet. I needed a coat, and Curt and I were roughly the same size. The realization hit me suddenly. I'd left Curt's message about meeting me at Striver's Row in the pocket of the coat I'd thrown to the dog. If they even suspected that Curt had sent it, they'd have a squad car out here soon. I opened the closet door, pulled a dark gray overcoat off a hanger, and found some leather gloves on a shelf above. I slipped on Curt's coat and wiped my prints from the doorknob. Then I hurried through the kitchen, wiping off any surface that I may have touched. I cleaned the doorknobs at the back of the house too. I started to get into the car when I remembered that I'd first tried the front door. I raced up the front stairs and wiped the doorbell. Then I headed for Curt's car.

I backed the SUV out of the driveway, driving slowly down the street. Two blocks away, I checked the rearview mirror. An NYPD squad car turned the corner, moving slowly until it reached Curt's driveway, where it pulled in. I took the next left, then brought the SUV up to speed. I didn't know where I was going, but I needed to get away from St. Albans. Once I was linked to another dead law enforcement officer, every man and woman in the NYPD would be out gunning for me.

I drove twenty minutes into Long Island on the expressway. If NYPD had issued an electronic alert for me, there was a chance it had not yet reached police departments outside of the city. I found a gas station and convenience store off the expressway. I went in and got a fistful of change, then left to find a pay phone. I had to call Nora.

"Hello," she mumbled from somewhere deep in sleep.

I felt a moment's relief upon hearing her voice, and I thought about hanging up. "It's me," I said.

"Where the hell are you?" she asked, instantly sounding as if she was wide awake.

"I can't tell you, and I'm not going to talk long in case there's a wiretap on your phone." My hand started to tremble. "They killed Curt and his wife."

"Who killed them?"

"I don't know. I found their bodies in their home."

"If you turn yourself in I can help you, but if you're on the run I can't."

"I can't turn myself in. I've got to find out what's happening. I'll try to get to Tucker. Maybe he can help."

I hung up. I really had no intention of going to Tucker. Those remarks were only intended for whoever else might be listening, which might buy me a little time.

I tried to shove my leftover change into the pocket of Curt's overcoat, but a wad of papers blocked the way. I pulled them out. Photocopies of credit card receipts. The chef's-hat logo on one of the receipts looked familiar. I unfolded the crumpled piece of paper. The Di Lustro on Mulberry Street in Little Italy. I unfolded a few more. One . . . two . . . three . . . four . . . five . . . six. Six receipts from the Di Lustro.

I jammed my hand into my pants pocket and pulled out the receipt that had fallen from Curt's pocket when I took his car keys. The Di Lustro. That made seven. I jumped into the SUV, turned on the overhead light and looked at the bills more closely. Lunch. Dinner. Sixty-, seventy-, eighty-dollar meals. Two of them over two hundred dollars. And all within the last several weeks. Not on a cop's salary. I don't care how many years he'd been working for the department or how much he liked Italian food. No cop spends this much regularly on a meal.

The name on the receipt was Dr. Michael Castiglione. Curt was working on more than his appetite at the Di Lustro. These photocopied receipts were from an undercover detective working for the Organized Crime Unit. Then I looked closer at the receipts. Underneath the logo was the restaurant's slogan: "Home of the City's Best Gelato." The phrase clicked. That's where Ciccarello had eaten just before paying a visit to Striver's Row. Only Liz, Nora, and I knew about Curt going to Striver's Row. Curt may have told Dorothy, but Nora and I didn't even tell Brendan. Someone had used Curt to find me. Someone who had Curt under surveillance. Someone like Vincent Ciccarello. I checked the dashboard clock. It was already after one a.m., too late for a gelato at the Di Lustro.

I was tired and needed rest. I needed some time to think, to try to piece together all that had happened in the last two days. I needed a safe haven. But I wasn't sure where I'd find one with the NYPD probably out looking for me on double-murder charges now.

I drove east on the expressway for a few hours. Miles Davis blew "Some Day My Love Will Come" on a late night jazz station. That tune was one of my favorites, one of my dad's favorites too. Funny how easy it is to be lulled into a false sense of security. Settling into the plush driver's seat, with only the red hue of the instrument panel staring at me, I drifted back to the days when I curled up in my father's lap listening to Miles.

Miles had turned the Disney classic, featured in *Snow White and the Seven Dwarves*, into a complex but sad lament. All of his sidemen took their turns at solos. Coltrane on sax. Wynton Kelly on the keyboard. Jimmy Cobb on drums. I loved the way they improvised, weaving disparate notes into a mellow sonic tapestry. But it came to an end too soon, and I found my mind still moving to the rhythm of Jimmy's high hats, humming my own improvised tune. And then it dawned on me where I might go.

FIFTEEN

I TURNED AROUND AND drove back toward the city. At nearly five a.m., the first commuters were pulling into park-and-ride stations. That seemed like a good place to leave the car—not the first location police normally checked for stolen vehicles. So I pulled into one, paid for the day, and parked. I purchased a roundtrip ticket to New York City from an automated machine.

Barely a hint of dawn brightened the eastern sky. The Long Island Railroad station was cold and lonely with only a few of us waiting on the concrete platform. Our breaths puffed like tiny steam engines against the surrounding darkness. I popped some change in a dispenser and pulled out a *New York Times*. When the train arrived, I took a window seat, slipped the ticket under a flap above the headrest, and raised the newspaper as a shield.

It took more than an hour for the train to reach Penn Station. When I got off, I grabbed an uptown local for Harlem Hospital. Like clockwork, Liz arrived at the hospital at seven a.m. each day.

I didn't use the staff door. Instead, I walked toward the Emergency Room entrance, where an elderly black woman pushed an elderly black man in a wheelchair into the hospital. I asked if I could help. Before she answered, I pushed him in with her at my side. I left them at the check-in desk, excusing myself to the bathroom.

I peeked out of the bathroom door, and when no one was looking I walked down the hall. In a closet marked "Janitorial," I found a broom and a smock. I slipped into the smock, grabbed the broom, and headed up a staircase to the ob-gyn wing on the fifth floor.

It was almost seven. I waited at the fifth-floor landing, cracking the door and looking down the hallway for Liz. Suddenly, a door opened several floors above me. Footsteps and voices echoed in the concrete stairwell as they traveled closer to me, step by step. Then a door opened below me and I heard several more people headed my way up the stairs. I looked around for a place to go. Nowhere.

I looked out the door and I didn't see Liz, so I reached up and unscrewed the housing for a stairwell light. Then I unscrewed the bulb. I cursed loudly at it as the group traveling down crossed paths with the group traveling up in front of me. Janitors don't rate much attention in a hospital. I screwed the light bulb back in as they passed.

I thought I heard Liz's voice coming down the hallway, but when I looked I saw her walking with another man. I recognized him as her colleague. He was about to enter her private office with her, then at the last minute he changed his mind and walked the other way. Liz placed her key in the door lock. I checked the hallway. It was clear. I bolted from the stairwell as she opened the door, then pushed her into the office and smothered her mouth with my hand. She flailed against me with her fists until I turned her around and placed my finger to my lips. Her eyes were wide with shock. I took my hand from her mouth.

She hissed. "What the hell are you doing here? And why did you attack me like that?"

"I'm sorry," I said. "I couldn't risk you calling out my name."

"What are you doing here?" she asked again.

"Curt and Dorothy have been murdered. I found them dead in their bedroom."

Liz bit her lip and looked at me. "And the police are charging you with double homicide. They came by the house early this morning and told me to call them if I saw you."

"And you believe them? You think I killed my best friend and his wife?"

"No." Liz started crying softly. "But I don't know what to believe anymore. I don't understand what's happening. I don't understand how all this is related to JJ."

"Neither do I."

We sat down on a couch in her office, underneath a poster showing a fetus developing into a baby at each of the thirty-nine weeks inside a woman's womb.

"It's a repeat of what happened after Danny Rodrigues' murder," Liz said, her voice quivering with anger and fear. "Why did you run last night? If you didn't kill Curt and Dorothy, why don't you turn yourself in now?"

"Because I can't trust NYPD and I don't know whom I can trust. Curt was the last person I trusted. Now he's dead."

Liz shook her head. "I can't do this. I can't live my life this way."

"Neither can I. Someone's killed Curt. Someone's got JJ. And someone's out to get me. When Danny Rodrigues was killed, the prosecution made me into an angry man out for revenge. Maybe you were right and I helped them make their case against me. But I'm not seeking vengeance now. I want justice. For Danny. For Curt. For JJ. For me. If I go off half-cocked, I may only make things worse. I can't take that chance with JJ out there. I need time to rest, to think, to figure out what to do next. Just a few hours."

"That's why you came here?" she asked. Her voice became tight and thin with the question.

"Yes. It was the only safe place I could think of."

"The police are out looking for you. And by being here you put the hospital's patients, our staff, and me in danger. You can't stay here. You've got to leave. I'm sorry."

I could feel my anger rising. "It's her feelings that matter, not the facts," I heard Promise's voice in my mind.

"I understand that you're scared," I said. "Please just call Nora for me, and then I'll leave."

"Why don't you call her?" Liz said.

"Because her line is probably tapped and they'll trace the call back here."

"What am I supposed to say?"

"Just ask her if she's seen me."

Liz huffed. She got up from the couch and walked over to her desk.

"Not from your office," I said.

She looked at me askance.

"From a pay phone downstairs."

She checked her watch. "I see gyn patients at eight," she said. "I'll call Liz, but you need to be out of my office by then." She yanked the door open and then slammed it. She tromped down the hall.

A sharp pang of aloneness wracked me. I lay down on Liz's couch and tried to connect the dots. Curt was investigating the Di Lustro restaurant, where Vincent Ciccarello was a customer. Curt sent me a note to meet him at Striver's Row, but instead the police showed up to arrest me. Curt and Dorothy were murdered in their home. JJ's been kidnapped, possibly by feuding drug syndicates.

Maybe the murders and the kidnapping weren't connected. Curt's death could have been a Mob hit. Perhaps he'd gotten too close to something unrelated to JJ's disappearance. Maybe someone had seen the note about Curt meeting me at Striver's Row and realized that they could set me up for a double murder. Or maybe it was all related, and Curt's mob connection to drugs in Harlem had something to do with the Di Lustro and Curt and JJ. Maybe—"

Liz burst back into the office. I sat up. Her eyes were wide, her mouth half open. She looked more frightened and confused than when she left. "You can't leave," she said, speaking fast.

"What?"

"You can't leave. Nora said to tell you, if I saw you, that under no circumstance are you to turn yourself in to the police. She's afraid of what might happen if you do."

"Why? What happened?"

"She said that you called her after you found Curt and Dorothy. It was about twelve thirty a.m."

"That's right."

"Nora checked the arrest warrant issued for you in their double murder. It was issued at twelve midnight."

"I had just gotten to their home by then."

"It was prepared beforehand," Nora said. "That's why she doesn't want you to turn yourself in."

"Someone in NYPD set me up for Curt and Dorothy's murder."

"Who?" Liz asked.

"Maybe Ciccarello. Maybe someone else. Curt said there were others unhappy about my release. Too many 'maybes' in all of this for me."

Liz joined me on the couch. She held my hand and looked me in the eyes. "I'm sorry for what I said earlier. I'm feeling whiplashed by what's happened to JJ, and to you. I'm not handling it well. And on top of it all, I have this nagging sense that I don't belong here." She pointed at the pregnancy poster overhead.

"You're good at what you do," I said.

"But I'm not happy," she said.

"Happiness doesn't come from what you do. Happiness comes from welcoming your destiny with grace, gratitude, and humility."

Liz smiled. "You sound like Daya."

"Who?"

"My yoga teacher."

"I'm just passing along something I learned in jail."

"From whom?"

"Man named Promise."

"Beautiful name."

"Beautiful man."

I checked my watch. "You need to see gyn patients soon."

"I do," Liz said. "And you're the first one."

"Huh?"

"This way please, Mr. Shannon."

Liz donned a white lab coat and snapped a stethoscope around her neck. Then she led me through the back door of her office, into a hall of six numbered exam rooms with plastic chart holders affixed to each door. She opened the first door and switched on the lights. A brown leather examination table with stirrups dominated the small space.

"Lay on your back," she said.

"That mean you're gonna play 'doctor' with me?"

"You wish."

"I do."

"You can rest here as long as you want. I'll put a sign on the door and let my staff know that this room is off-limits to all except me."

"They won't be suspicious?"

"No. We do it routinely with rape and sexual abuse victims. Here," Liz said. "Lay down. I'll adjust the table."

I lay on my back while she swung the stirrups out of the way and then cranked a handle that lengthened the table to fit me. She leaned over to kiss me on the forehead, then she turned to leave.

"No exam, doc?"

Liz whipped around. She pulled a wrapped plastic speculum from her pocket and held it menacingly in one hand. Then she twirled her stethoscope in the other hand as though it was a floozy's long necklace. She had a wicked smile and feigned a thick German accent. "Zo, into vich orifice do you vant this inserted?"

I raised my hands. "Okay, no exam."

"But maybe lunch in a couple of hours," she said, switching off the light as she left the room.

Shortly afterward, I heard paper slipped into the chart holder on the door. Then activity in the hallway picked up. Doors opened and closed. Mostly female voices wafted on the air currents traveling through the ventilation system and underneath the door.

I tried to sleep but couldn't. All the unanswered questions about JJ, Curt, and Danny swirled around my mind as I lay in the darkness. My uncertainty about what role Tucker and Ciccarello and Nicky Brooks played in all this only made the confusion worse. With the police after me, my options seemed few. Promise would say that when you don't know which direction to travel, just pick one and start walking. If it's not the right one you'll find out soon enough.

I must have dozed off because the knock on the door surprised me. Liz walked in, but she didn't turn on the lights.

"Are you awake?" she whispered.

"Was I asleep?"

"Last time I checked you were. I can't stay long but I brought lunch."

"I need it."

She switched on the lights. I sat up. She set a tray of hospital food on the counter next to a jar of Q-Tips.

"I leave here at four p.m. today," she said. "What are you going to do?"

I sighed. "I don't know."

"Can you go to Nora's?"

"No. The police are watching her office, I'm sure."

"And Striver's Row?"

I shook my head. "They've gotta be watching there as well."

Liz touched my shoulder. "I'll be back around three," she said. "I'll help in whatever way I can."

"I'll need a way out of the hospital."

She smiled. "Got that one covered."

"What?" I asked.

"Strictly need-to-know. And you don't need to know right now. You need to figure out where you're going once you leave here." Liz chuckled as she closed the door.

Cold fish, pasty mashed potatoes, rubbery green beans, and sugary applesauce on a Styrofoam tray. I wolfed it down. I could barely remember the last time I'd eaten. I think it was a day ago with Promise.

After lunch I got back to digesting my options. I still had Ken Tucker's card. I suppose I could call him for help. I didn't like that idea. I'd be playing right into his hands. I could visit the Emperor's Club and squeeze Fat Daddy for more information about his drug land feud with the Mob, but the police were apparently watching that place the last time I was there. I could go down to Little Italy and have a gelato at the Di Lustro, but I knew for a fact that the police were watching there too. And that left me feeling that with all the watching the police were doing, maybe it was time for me to start watching the police.

Suddenly, the door flew open and Liz burst in.

"You've got to leave, now," she said.

I looked at the clock on her exam room wall. "It's not three."

Liz waved away what I said. "Nora just left word that the police are on their way here to question me about you." Her words came out breathy and short.

An orderly rolled a gurney into the room behind her.

I pointed to the man. "Who's this?"

"Oh," she said. "You just died, and Derrick is going to take your body down on the special elevator to the morgue. He's a good friend."

Derrick smiled.

"Good plan, doc," I said.

Liz came over to me and touched my knee. "You know where you're going from here?"

"Uh huh."

"Where?"

"Strictly need-to-know. And with the police on their way here, you don't need to know."

"I need to know that you'll be safe."

"I'll do my best."

Liz kissed me on the forehead again.

"Dr. Winstead," Derrick said. "They'll miss me on the third floor if I'm not back soon."

"I'll keep in touch with Nora," Liz said.

"Thanks for what you did," I said.

Liz hurried from the room. Derrick, a big, beefy young man, had me lay on my back on his gurney. Then he covered me with a sheet, tucking it in around my sides and pulling it over my face. He laid a clipboard on my chest. I closed my eyes and tried to breathe shallowly so I would not move the sheet. Derrick wheeled me out through Liz's private office, moving quickly down a hallway. An elevator door swung open. The gurney wheels bounced over the metal threshold. Derrick inserted a key into a lock, turned it, and pushed a button. The elevator dropped without stopping at any other floors.

As the elevator slowed to a halt, Derrick said, "Mr. Winstead, you can get up now." In here, I was known as the doctor's husband.

I didn't bother correcting him. When the elevator doors opened, Derrick pointed to an exit. And I slipped out through the ramp that hearses used to pick up the dead.

———————

I BURIED MY FACE in the evening edition of the *New York Times* as I rode in a train car with a contingent of commuters headed home to their Long Island suburbs. I ate dinner in the small town where I'd left Curt's SUV. It was almost eight when I walked from the restaurant into the cold, clear night. If I had any hope of finding JJ and avoiding arrest for murdering Curt and his wife, then it was time for me to get into the game. Like Ken Tucker, it was time for me to play chess too. I hopped back into the SUV and headed east toward the city.

An hour later, I swung off the expressway and took the Throggs Neck Bridge into the Bronx. Vincent Ciccarello lived in a residential neighborhood near Pelham Bay Park. When I worked Narcotics, every summer he'd have the detectives and their families over for a poolside barbecue. All the cars couldn't fit on his street, so we used a back lot of the park. He showed us a shortcut from there through the trees that ended at his backyard.

Even at this late hour, a few cars were scattered in the parking lot when I pulled in. My headlights caught the rear side window of a late model Chevy. A boy raised his head sheepishly from below the window. The look in his eyes hovered midway between fright and bliss. Apparently, the lot was used for more than overflow parking. I killed my headlights and stepped from the car into the cold. No streetlamps were on in the parking lot and only a crescent moon hung in the sky. I reached back into the SUV, flipped the glove compartment down, and groped for a flashlight, but I found none. I slammed the door shut. I'd have to feel my way through the trees to Ciccarello's house.

Beyond the parking lot, orange sodium streetlamps twinkled through the mesh of denuded branches. I stepped over the curb and into an ankle-deep layer of leaves. I knew the path to Ciccarello's was nearby, but the fallen leaves made it impossible to see. I shuffled through the leaves down a slight embankment and then up a small rise until I reached the edge of trees. I walked just outside of the trees, straining to see a path in the darkness. Suddenly, a dog growled, crashing through the leaves toward me. I turned to run, but too late. It caught me, snared my pants leg in its jaw, and twisted its head back and forth.

I knew better than to engage the animal in a tug of war or try to kick it away. It looked like a Rottweiler. I reached in my pocket for the pistol. I didn't want to shoot the animal, but if it came to that I would. I wrapped my finger around the trigger. With my other hand I tried the signal for "sit" that I'd learned from a guy in the K9 unit, but the dog didn't pay me any attention. I was about to bring my gun up when a voice from the other side of the trees called out, "Hades. Hades." The dog snapped to attention. It let go of my pants and looked up at me as though I didn't realize how lucky I was. Then Hades turned and scampered into the trees, pointing out the path.

I traipsed through the leaves, bumping into trees as I made my way. At the end of the path, I saw the backyards of several homes. I recognized Ciccarello's by the covered pool with a mass of leaves sitting on top. His house was dark. A ten-foot-high fence with a gate guarded the perimeter of the property. Ciccarello had bragged about his high-tech alarm system, with piezoelectric sensors in the fence and a computer that analyzed sensor readings to screen out vibrations from wind, animals, or traffic.

I stripped off my coat and hid it in the bushes. I tucked Curt's 9mm into my belt. Then I scaled the fence.

I knew I'd set off the alarm.

SIXTEEN

I DROPPED INTO A waist-deep pile of leaves on the other side, and the backyard lit up like a stadium at night. I crouched low and looked around. Thankfully, Ciccarello didn't like dogs. A light flashed on inside his house. I burrowed into the leaves beside the back gate, covering my body with them. Thankfully, Ciccarello didn't like yard work either.

I peered out through the leaves.

The back door crashed open. Ciccarello came out, crouching and turning in circles, moving stealthily through his yard with a gun in his hand. He steadily approached the back fence. My heart pounded. I took shallow breaths so the leaf pile wouldn't move. Even though I knew he couldn't see me, I felt naked and exposed.

Ciccarello rattled the back gate, then punched a few numbers into a keypad. There was a buzz, then a click. The backyard lights went off and the gate swung open. He stuck his head and his gun outside. He looked both ways. Apparently satisfied, he grabbed the gate and swung it closed. His hands hovered over the keypad, ready to enter another code, when I erupted from the leaves. He gasped and tried to turn around to face me, but I nailed him in the back with my shoulder, drove him into the gate, and shoved the barrel of my pistol into the back of his head.

"Drop your weapon on the ground," I said.

Ciccarello's pistol crunched through the leaves. His body shivered under my weight. He had on only his pajamas, a bathrobe, and slippers.

"Reach above you and grab hold of the fence with both hands," I said.

Ciccarello coughed. "Shannon? You're a dead man."

I thrust my pistol deeper into his skull and pushed his face into the fence. "I said reach above you and grab hold."

"You push me up against this fence and the sensors will go off." With his mouth mashed into the fence, Ciccarello strained to speak. "I don't enter the code and security guards will be all over this place."

"Bullshit. You didn't rearm the system."

"You're scum," Ciccarello said. "Scum. You killed another cop tonight. Thirty-year veteran. Supposed to be your friend."

I whipped the pistol across the back of his head. Ciccarello held on, but his body drooped lower on the fence.

"We both know that I didn't kill Curtis Wilson."

"That's not what the arrest warrant says, pal." His words came out in a breathy, halting rhythm, probably timed with the pulses of pain he felt.

"You remember quid pro quo?" I said. "You wanted to deal? I'm ready."

"Fuck you. You ain't got nothing to deal with anymore. I'm holding all the cards now."

"You're right. I ain't got nothing; I got something. The last gift from a friend. See, Curt left an insurance policy in case something happened to him. An affidavit that links you with the Mob."

"Bullshit."

"No, not bullshit, Vince. Gelato. Think gelato. Think the Di Lustro Café. Home of the city's best gelato. You remember that Curt worked the OCU. Well, he had the Di Lustro under surveillance, and this affidavit details meetings that took place there and it's got the names of those who attended the meetings. Funny how your name appears more than once. But maybe you were working undercover those nights too."

"You got zip."

"You sure? Think carefully. Your future's on the line here."

Ciccarello squirmed in silence. A moment later he said, "Okay, for grins, let's say this affidavit does exist. How would I get a look at it?"

"For grins, of course, it would cost you a million dollars in small bills."

"Fuck you."

I pushed his face harder into the fence with my gun. "You got it wrong again. You've already done that. This is quid pro quo, remember? Now it's my turn to fuck you. Meet me in Central Park at one thirty in the afternoon tomorrow by the statue of Alice in Wonderland. Have the money in a large shopping bag from Bloomingdale's. I'll be watching from a distance. I see any plainclothes guys and I walk to the nearest newspaper with the affidavit. Now, you're going to catch a cold standing out here in your pajamas."

I reached down to pick up Ciccarello's gun. I slipped it in my pocket. Then I pulled him off the gate and threw him into the pile of leaves. "It's warmer under there," I said. "See you tomorrow."

I ran into the shadows of the woods, stopping to pick up my coat. I couldn't imagine that Ciccarello would follow me into the darkness.

Even if he did call the police from inside his house, I'd be long gone by the time they arrived. But I didn't think he'd do that either. How had Ken Tucker put it? "I don't trust you. What I trust is how you'll respond to the pressures you're put under." That's what I trusted about Ciccarello.

I made it back to the SUV, drove out of the park, and waited on a nearby street. I didn't have to wait long before my trust was rewarded. A white Audi came zooming down Ciccarello's block, headed toward the parkway entrance. Ciccarello took the Hutchinson River Parkway south into the city. I followed behind him at a respectable distance. I wasn't too concerned about losing him. I had a pretty good idea he was headed for a late-night gelato.

Eventually we got on the East River Drive, and then we got off at Canal Street. I took a different route to Little Italy and drove down Mulberry Street. Even at two a.m., multicolored lights hung across the street, remnants of the recent festival of San Gennaro. The Di Lustro, a double storefront restaurant, sat in the middle of the block.

I parked on a side street and walked to the corner of Mulberry. I didn't see Ciccarello's car. Perhaps he'd parked and entered through the back door. Twenty minutes later, a black limousine pulled in front of the Di Lustro and a lone older man got in. The vehicle came down the block toward me. I hurried up the side street, slipped into the entryway of a closed café, and pressed my back against the door. Whoever was riding in that limo was too high up to be of interest.

I walked back to the corner. Two men now stood outside the restaurant. A moment later, Ciccarello stepped out to join them. They engaged in a heated conversation. A late-model black Mercedes came to a halt in front of the trio. A young man hopped out and handed the keys to one of the men arguing with Ciccarello. Ciccarello ducked back into the restaurant. The other two men got into the car. These were my guys. Threaten someone's possessions and they'll usually move to protect them. I hoped these two would do exactly that.

Chess players call this a gambit.

I ran back to the SUV, hopped in, and cranked the motor. The Mercedes flew by and I pulled out after it. It headed east on Canal Street, then north on the East River Drive. I stayed several cars behind. The good thing about following another car this early in the morning is that, with so little other traffic, it's hard to lose sight of your target. The bad thing is that, with so little traffic, it's easy for them to catch sight of you. But Mercedes have distinctive rear lights. I let them pull far ahead of me and kept the taillights in view.

We took the New York State Throughway across the Tappan Zee Bridge. An hour later, the Mercedes exited south of Poughkeepsie. I slowed down more, arriving at the exit in time to see the car take a left at the end of the off-ramp. When I got to the stop sign, I turned my lights off, took the same left, and drove a few blocks before turning them back on. No other cars were on the street. I followed the Mercedes' taillights, keeping the car about one-quarter of a mile ahead, until it disappeared around a curve. I sped up, but when I took the curve I saw only a dark road ahead, so I slowed down again.

I passed through a section of exclusive homes with massive hedges flanking long driveways protected by tall metal gates. I craned my head both ways, looking for the last subtle movements of a gate sliding closed or a line of entryway lights flashing off, anything that would alert me to which driveway the Mercedes turned into. But I saw nothing. A yellow sign up ahead announced that the street ended in a cul-de-sac.

I jammed the heel of my hand into the steering wheel. I played it too cautiously. I let the Mercedes get too far ahead and lost it. Then, as I steered around the circle, I saw to the left of the cul-de-sac sign a depression in the concrete curb. Beyond that, an unpaved dirt road disappeared into the woods. Every instinct I had told me they'd taken this road. I switched off my lights and drove over the curb.

The stars and the crescent moon offered barely enough light to find my way. Branches scraped the sides of the car. At low speed, I bounced along the narrow, winding road, wondering at each turn if I'd meet the Mercedes head-on. After several minutes, the road gained elevation and the woods thinned out. Pieces of earth-moving equipment, looking like oversized mechanical monsters, slid by silently on both sides of the car. As the road leveled off, I saw a faint blush of light before me. Then suddenly the trees fell away like a curtain lifted from a stage. Stretched in the distance, the orange glow of New York City lit the sky, and a few flecks of orange light peppered the darkness between here and there, like fireflies flung far from their luminous nest.

This looked like a construction site or a storage depot for heavy equipment. I pulled the SUV off to the side of the road, tucking it behind a large bulldozer. Before I got out, I worked the action on Curt's 9mm. The ground felt frozen hard under my feet. In the dim light, I made out the silhouette of a large prefabricated building ahead. I squinted. Long thin shafts of hazy green light leaked from edges of the tall doors leading into the building. I crept closer. The Mercedes sat parked, its engine fan still whining. A green light also shone through a door pane on the side of the building, illuminating two figures standing outside. I moved to the other side of the building, looking for a window. I strained to understand the muffled voices coming through the structure's metal walls, but all I could discern was shouting.

Suddenly, an engine roared to life inside. The large doors squealed as they rolled open. I threw myself up against the metal wall, inching my way back to the front corner of the building, which shuddered as the vehicle rumbled out. The white delivery van shimmered eerily under the fluorescent light. It rolled slowly over the building's threshold. The doors squealed again. I squinted, trying to read the license plate number before they closed. But I forgot all about the license plate when I saw what was in the van's rear window.

I wanted to cry out, but I couldn't. I wanted to run after the van, but I stayed in place, afraid I would be seen. I watched from the shadows of the building as the dwindling light caught JJ's face bouncing in the van's rear window. His eyes were turned down. One eye looked puffy and half-shut. He had a gash across his cheek. Then the garage doors slammed shut. The light cut off. And the van hobbled into the night.

I ran along the edge of the road leading from the garage. I thought about shooting out the tires. I could only clearly see the taillights in the dark. And I didn't want to take a chance with JJ inside. The van bounced along the twisted dirt road. I ran faster. JJ stared out the window with sullen eyes, but I don't think he saw me. The van slowed as it rolled through a large rut. I was so close that I could almost reach out and touch the rear fender. Then the engine revved and a puff of smoke blew from the tailpipe. Already breathing hard, I sucked in a lungful of exhaust and coughed violently.

My body forced me to stop running in order to catch my breath. When I looked up again I saw JJ staring at me, his eyes wide, filled with tears. The van had slipped beyond my reach. JJ pressed his fingers three times on the window, and I thought I saw him mouth the words "I love you," as he'd done when he visited me in prison.

Still coughing, I turned and stumbled back toward the SUV. With only one road to the freeway, it wasn't too late to follow the van. Then the realization hit me hard: I'd forgotten to memorize the van's license plate number. I pounded my fist into my thigh. Suddenly, I saw a pair of headlights dancing along the road ahead. I dove into the bushes, crashing headlong into briers as the Mercedes bounced by.

When the car passed, I picked myself up and raced toward the SUV. I grabbed the door handle, ready to yank it open, but a pair of beefy hands grabbed me by my shoulder and waist, jerked me backward, and then rocketed me headfirst into the door.

The window shattered as my forehead thumped off the glass. My body caromed back from the impact. I fought through the crushing pain to keep my eyes from closing. I held on to an image of JJ's face and his fingers pressed against the window as I slid down to the ground. I tried to reach behind me for my gun, but now two men were on top of me and I had little fight left. They spun me over and ripped the gun from my waistband. Then they stood me up, stripped my coat off, wrenched my arms behind my back, and bound my wrists with several turns of tape.

"Walk back to the building. You try to be a fuckin' hero, I put a fuckin' bullet in your head. Capiche?" The man who spoke cracked the butt of his pistol between my shoulder blades. I moaned and arched back from the blow. Then he shoved me toward the large metal building. I don't know what was worse, the pain in my body or the real-life nightmare of watching JJ slip away just beyond my reach.

Stepping into the building, I blinked. The sharp fluorescent lights intensified the throbbing pain in my forehead. Dump trucks, cement mixers, and heavy equipment filled the cavernous space. The men marched me past long metal racks that held stacks of framing timber, prefabricated roofs, doors, and windows. They pushed me into a corner at the back of the building, then told me to turn around. My feet crunched over glass as I did.

"Who sent you?" the older of the pair said. "You a cop?"

I said nothing. He rifled through my pockets and found my wallet.

"John Shannon," he said. "Fucking mick name for a black guy. Go figure that."

His partner looked to be in his early thirties, a thin pretty-boy sporting a black leather jacket and slicked-back black hair. He held a gun on me. "Must've followed you here," the younger man said. "What you think, you're some kinda ghetto gumshoe?" He yucked at his choice of words.

"No," I said, barely managing to speak. "But I think you're some kinda plebeian punk."

His jaw flexed. He lunged at me, hammering me in my midsection with a punch. The pain shot deep into the core of my body. I doubled over, pushed myself back against the wall, and struggled for a breath.

"Tony, what's that?" he asked.

"What's what?" the older man said.

"Plee-bee . . . whatever the fucking word was he used."

"How the hell am I s'pposed to know? What's that?" Tony asked, pointing to the glass on the ground.

"Tall black kid mouths off like this one did." He pointed to me. "Then he comes at me. I mean, I've got a gun and the kid comes at me swingin'. He pushed me into a window and it broke."

Tony laughed. "Kid got you, huh, Sal?"

"Like hell he did. I hit him so hard he flew back across the room. Probably gave him a shiner, but on a black kid how the hell would you be able to tell?"

"Okay, so now we know you can handle a kid."

"Fuck you."

Tony laughed.

"Look, sweep away the glass, tape this guy's ankles, then have him sit in the corner," Tony said. "I gotta make a call to find out what to do with him."

Tony held a gun on me while Sal kicked away some glass.

"What was that word?" Sal asked.

"Plebeian," I murmured.

"Well, plebeian this," he said. Another explosion from Sal's fist rocked my gut. Before I found my breath again, Sal had taped my ankles, kicked my legs out, and shoved me to the ground.

Promise was fond of saying that pain is like a Chinese rope trick. The more you fight against it, the worse it becomes. "Just watch it and it will change," he'd say. I tried to bring my mind to the fire in my belly, tried not to quell it, just observe it. The muscles around my ribs relaxed and I sucked in a breath. It seemed to work until the hammer inside my skull began to pound. I found my mind bouncing back and forth between my head and my gut. I tried even harder not to fight the pain but to watch it moving in and through me as if I were standing in the middle of a rushing stream. While trying, I noticed a new pain knifing me in the back of my thigh, only this pain came from outside my body not within. Sal had pushed me down onto a sharp fragment of glass that poked into my leg.

Sal pulled a chair from a nearby table, turned it around, sat in it backward, and then rested his gun on the chair back.

Tony burst into the building. "You're not gonna fuckin' believe this," he said. He held his cell phone in one hand, waving it, pointing to it. "I just stepped outside to make a call on this guy. Guess what we gotta do? Call the State Patrol. There's a murder warrant out for him. He used to be cop. He just got released for whacking one cop, then tonight he whacked another cop and his wife."

"No way," Sal said.

"Can you believe that? You and me, Sal. We gotta be good citizens and call 911 on this guy." Both men laughed.

With my arms bound behind me, I inched my body forward until I sat on the piece of glass.

Sal turned to me. "You whacked two cops? Maybe you're one of them plee-bees, or whatever that word is too," he said.

I glared at him without speaking while I dug my heels into the concrete floor and pushed myself back against the wall.

Sal laughed. "At least we don't have to worry about what to do with your body."

I slid my fingers under my butt, stretching them toward the glass. My middle finger found a jagged edge. I pushed my hand farther under me, trying to wrap my finger around the fragment, but I jammed it into the glass. The sharp edge sliced through my fingertip, and I clenched my teeth to stem the pain.

"Sal," Tony said, "as much as I can't believe this, I'm steppin' outside to call the police."

"Yeah," Sal said. He turned to me. "What was that word?" he asked.

"Plebeian," I said. I scooted forward slightly then pushed back against the wall as I spoke. I stretched my fingers under me again. This time I hooked the piece of glass and worked it between my index and middle finger. It wasn't larger than a quarter. I stretched out one wrist and bent the other to bring my fingers to the tape.

Tony walked back in.

"State Patrol said they'd be here in fifteen. I told them no problem. Don't rush. We have the situation under control. He thanked me. Can you believe that? A cop thanked me."

I didn't have much time. I rocked the edge of the glass against the tape, and as I did it cut into my fingers. Blood trickled from the cuts, warm and sticky-wet, but I didn't stop. I closed my eyes, pretending to be asleep, hoping to hide the gusts of pain that buffeted me as I worked the glass against the tape. I thought I'd nicked at least a few edges, though I couldn't really tell.

"Hey." Sal kicked my feet. I didn't open my eyes. He kicked me again. I rocked the glass harder against the tape with his kick.

"Hey." He kicked me again, and I sawed furiously with the small sharp fragment, finally opening my eyes.

"What does that mean? Plebeian? Sounds like a damn astrological sign or something."

I rolled my eyes at Sal, and then I closed them.

"Hey. I'm talkin' to you."

I waited for his kick. When it came, I pressed hard against the tape with the glass. I bit my tongue. My fingers were numb from the cuts. I tugged against the tape. I thought I felt a slit in it lengthen.

"I wanna know what that word means," Sal said.

"Look it up in the dictionary," I said.

"Fuckin' wise guy."

Sal kicked my feet repeatedly and I pretended to grimace. I stretched my wrists apart with all my strength, hoping Sal's kicks would mask the sound of the tape tearing.

"You know how to use a dictionary?" I managed to say amidst the onslaught.

It only enraged Sal further, and he turned his feet to my ribs. Still, I strained against the tape with each kick until I tore one side of the tape through completely. Tony stepped in not a minute too soon.

"Hey, Sal. Back off. The police'll be here soon. Let them take care of him. Less work for us, ya know what I mean?"

Sal went to his chair. My body was one throbbing mass of pain. I still had tape binding the backside of my wrists, and I worked the glass maniacally to remove it.

When I got the tape off, I whispered, "Sal, want to know what plebeian means?" I motioned with my head for him to come closer. He stood up and walked toward me. When he bent down I lunged at him, hooking my arm around his neck. I grabbed the wrist with the gun. His eyes flared open.

"Tony!" he yelled.

Tony came running toward us with his gun drawn.

SEVENTEEN

I JERKED SAL AROUND and down so he sat in my lap, facing forward. He struggled under my one-armed chokehold. Sal was losing strength, but he still gripped his gun, so I raised his right arm, wrapped my finger around his trigger finger, and fired at Tony. I heard Tony sigh. His large body crumpled into a heap. I yanked the gun from Sal's hand and threw it on the floor. Then I caught him in a two-armed chokehold.

"This is for hitting me." I flexed my arms sharply. His body jerked. He clutched my forearms, trying desperately to peel them away.

"And this is for hitting my son." I flexed my arms again and held them there, squeezing even tighter. Sal gurgled once, his arms flailed at me, and then he stopped moving altogether.

"Plebeian," I said. I threw his limp body off me. "It means common or vulgar." I tore the remaining tape from around my ankles. I pushed my bleeding hands against the wall, using them as crutches to help me stand. I took Curt's pistol from Sal, and then I staggered toward the door.

MY CHEST TIGHTENED AS I thought about what had just happened. I'd been so close to my son that I could have almost reached out and touched him. A deep pain struck me, sending shivers shooting through my body. I grabbed the steering wheel tightly with both hands to steady myself. I'd let him slip away. But I couldn't let that stop me now.

I'd driven at least a mile beyond the cul-de-sac when I saw a fleet of patrol cars racing toward me. Their sirens blared. Their headlights flashed. And their red beacons pulsed. The convoy screamed by. I sped up. It wouldn't take them long to realize what had happened. I got back on the highway and looked east, where a swath of reddish-orange light brightened the sky.

Early morning traffic on both sides of the roadway moved slowly, as though an accident had happened up ahead. Rounding a curve a few miles down the road, I understood why. A line of flashing lights blocked both sides of the highway. State troopers checked each vehicle moving through a roadblock.

I whipped the SUV right and squeezed between two cars. The driver behind me laid on his horn. I pulled over to the shoulder, stuffed Curt's pistol into my belt, and barreled out of the car. Maybe I had twenty minutes of lead-time before a driver pulled up to the roadblock and reported a black guy on foot, running from his abandoned car—maybe less time if someone placed a cell phone call.

Up ahead, a highway sign read "State Park Next Exit." I scurried down the side of the highway onto a surface street. I jogged in the general direction of the park. My eyes must have been as big as saucers. I felt like I had several cups of espresso in me, like I was in the middle of an iron-man triathlon. I kept jogging, afraid that if I stopped I'd collapse and never get up again.

After running about a mile, I came to a small sign for the state park; the sign had an arrow that pointed toward a tree-lined road and what looked like a back entrance. I followed a well-worn roadside walking trail to a log guardhouse with two long, thin, yellow, metal poles lowered across the park entrance and exit. Chains locked down the poles, and a sign in the window of the small guardhouse read "Park Closed for the Season." I slipped under a metal pole and shuffled through a layer of leaves into the park. I looked behind me. No cars headed my way, and in this respite from the danger and the chase I sucked in a crisp breath of air.

"Difficult," a wooden sign cautioned. Underneath the yellow stick figure of a hiker, I read the words "Lookout 3.0 mi." Early morning chilly air penetrated my clothes. Smoke drifted upward as I blew a warm breath into my cold hands. The beginning of the trail rose sharply along a ridge cut into the side of the hill. After a bridge across a small stream, the trail cut into the trees then switched back several times as it wound its way further uphill.

Rounding the corner of a switchback, I heard something crashing through the leaves. I froze with my hand on my pistol. Then I laughed to myself. Up ahead I saw two people in brightly colored spandex running suits headed toward me. I pulled my sweater down over the pistol handle. A man and woman jogged passed, nodding, puffing smoke with each breath. I continued walking, then turned around and found them looking back at me curiously.

Halfway up the trail, I rested and caught my breath while sitting on a small bench fashioned from split logs. When I rose to leave, I heard the blades of a helicopter beating the air not far away. Someone had reported seeing me, or perhaps it had taken this long for the police to run a check on the SUV's plates. From the sound of the helicopter, it was flying in a standard search pattern of ever-tighter circles. I felt like a deer being hunted. It would be easier if I simply walked back down and turned myself in. I was tired of running, tired of fighting. I was just tired and ready to give up, if only for the rest.

But something inside of me wanted to make it to the end of a trail marked "Difficult," as useless a goal as that seemed right now. So I kept going.

I neared a clearing and waited for the helicopter to dip out of sight before I ran for the cover of trees on the other side. After several more switchbacks through the woods, a rocky trail led up to a log building with a boarded door. Again, I waited for the helicopter to disappear before dashing to the building. I put my shoulder to the door and splintered the planks nailed across it. I tumbled inside the visitor center.

Knotty pine covered the ceiling and walls. Through a window I saw two pay-per-view binoculars on a small porch outside. I broke through the door to the binoculars and rummaged through my pockets to find a quarter. The blinders on the scope vanished when I slipped the coin into the slot. I pointed it down at the park's main entrance.

At least twenty police cruisers lined the parking lot. Sitting off to one side, a large white van had big black letters on the sides reading "SWAT team." I raised the binoculars beyond the park and the police. Sunlight sparkled over the placid waters of the Hudson. Suddenly my time was up and the binoculars went blank.

I heard the helicopter coming around for another pass, and I slipped back inside the building. This time the pilot hovered directly overhead. A loudspeaker blared.

"John Shannon. Drop any weapons you have and exit the building with your hands on top of your head."

I looked out the front door and around the sides of the building. The SWAT team hadn't arrived yet. The chopper's bullhorn blasted away again.

"John Shannon, if you don't exit the building we will be forced to come in after you."

Somewhere in a command center, probably in the parking lot down below, a captain dressed in a uniform and a trooper's tall hat argued with the head of the SWAT team, dressed in camouflage and a baseball cap, to see how much time they would give me to surrender peacefully.

In prison, we called this "the check-mate decision." Men would bet on how long a cornered inmate would hold out before surrendering to the guards, or whether he'd go to the bitter end and then survive the inevitable onslaught. Maybe the time had come to welcome my destiny.

A telephone rang, startling me. I guess the captain had won the first round. I debated whether to pick it up, but I found the phone behind a small counter and answered.

"Shannon," I said.

"Bill Garmin here." The voice on the other end sounded surprised. "New York State Patrol Hostage Negotiations."

I laughed. "Mr. Garmin, it's just me up here."

"Sorry," he said. "I'm used to hostage situations."

He sounded like an older man, perhaps a psychologist who worked with the New York State Police.

"Look, help me out here. Will you? You were once a cop. You know the drill. I want this to end peacefully, so nobody gets hurt. We've got the park surrounded, a chopper overhead, and enough firepower on the way up to blow that wooden building off the hill. I don't care what you're carrying, you don't stand a chance, and I think you know that. So for everyone's sake, please, lay down your weapons and step outside with your hands over your head."

"What's the ETA on the SWAT team?" I asked.

"Ten minutes," he said.

"Call me back in five." I hung up.

I stepped back outside to the binoculars and slipped another quarter in. The helicopter hovered overhead. I didn't bother looking down at the parking lot. I turned the binoculars toward the Hudson River and south to New York City. I couldn't see the city, but I imagined Nora arguing a case in front of a judge, Liz bent over a patient, and JJ locked away somewhere. Then I turned the eyepiece northwest, envisioning Promise's face among the clouds.

"What would you do, old man?"

The telephone rang and I walked back in.

"Times up. SWAT team'll be there in five."

"Okay. I'll come in, but I have one request before I do."

"There's not much room for negotiation, or much time," Garmin said. "But try me."

"I want to make one call from here."

"One call?"

"Uh huh."

"Hold on," Garmin said.

I heard muffled voices at the other end of the call, as though Bill Garmin had placed his hand over the receiver.

"You've got two minutes," he said.

I pulled out my wallet and thumbed through it until I found Ken Tucker's card. I dialed the cell phone number marked "Private." After four rings, I heard a click and then Tucker's voice, but it was his answering service. I hung up. Out the window, men in camouflage fell to the ground around the building, aiming sniper rifles with telescopic scopes my way. The telephone rang again. The time to welcome my destiny had arrived.

"Shannon," the voice said. "What the hell are you doing in the visitor center of a New York State Park that's closed for the season?" Ken Tucker had called back.

187

"I'm ready to talk," I said.

I heard a long pause.

"You got company up there with you?" Tucker asked.

"You mean the guys with baseball caps on backward looking down the scopes of sniper rifles?"

"You smartass bastard. I gave you a chance before. Now what the hell do you want me to do?" He hung up.

"John Shannon," a man on a bullhorn outside bellowed. "You have two minutes to throw your weapons outside the door and exit with your hands over your head."

I felt destiny's hand slowly tightening around my throat. A minute later, the telephone rang. I took my time picking it up.

"Bill Garmin here again. Who the hell are you?" I heard the incredulity in his voice.

"Why?" I asked. "What's happening?"

"You tell me. Our orders are to keep you right where you are until a chopper from New York City arrives to take you away."

I breathed deep. "SWAT team know that?"

"They do now."

Garmin hung up. Overhead the thumping of the State Patrol's helicopter blades slowly faded away. I peered out the window. The SWAT team had lowered their eyes from their sights and turned their caps forward. I slumped to the floor with my back up against the wall and buried my head in my knees.

I must have dozed off because the front door rattled so hard that it catapulted me awake. It sounded like a tornado had touched down. I jumped to my feet thinking the SWAT team had decided to take matters into their own hands, but I realized that another helicopter had landed outside the building.

Someone pounded on the door. "John Shannon," the voice yelled. "Sir, my name is agent Parks. I'm from the Office of Municipal Security, and I've been instructed to escort you back to New York City. Sir, I need to know that you will comply with my orders."

I peered out the window before replying; after all, this could also have been an elaborate ruse. The SWAT team had their caps turned backward now and their sniper rifles pointed at the door. A blue and white helicopter sat fifty yards away with both rotors turning, kicking up leaves and dust. It had no identification on the fuselage other than its registration letters and numbers. The agent at the door was dressed in a suit and tie, but over that he wore a Kevlar vest. His dark-brown hair blew wildly in the wash of the helicopter's blades. He banged at the door again.

"John Shannon, I need to know that you will comply with my orders."

I stood silently behind the door. I don't know what took me so long to reply. Perhaps the absurdity of all that had happened in the past two days had just begun to settle in, or perhaps I found it hard to believe that a powerful man like Ken Tucker would intervene on my behalf. Maybe I was simply questioning destiny one more time before opening my arms to her.

I cracked the door. "Agent Parks," I called out. "What do you need me to do?"

"Sir, first I need you to kick every weapon in your possession out the door."

I put the 9mm in the crack of the doorway and nudged it out with my foot. A gloved hand reached from the side of the door and the weapon disappeared.

"Sir, next I need you to exit with your hands on top of your head."

I kicked the door further open, interlaced my fingers, and placed both hands on top of my head. The moment I stepped across the threshold, two men sprung at me from either side. One grabbed my right arm, the other my left. They spun me around and threw me up against the log wall, then jerked my arms behind my back and snapped handcuffs around my wrists.

"This way, sir," Parks said. He cupped my right elbow in his palm and led me toward the helicopter.

We all ducked low under the helicopter's blades. The pilot swung open the door. The agent on my left held the front seat forward. Parks and I climbed in the rear. The other agent hopped in the front. They fastened my seatbelt while we rose.

I looked down at the SWAT team. Most of them had dropped to one knee with the butts of their rifles planted on the ground. They looked up at the helicopter with expressions suggesting they'd just witnessed an alien abduction.

———

THE HELICOPTER ROCKED GENTLY back and forth, floating through a blue sky south toward New York City. It reminded me of being on a boat out in the open ocean, with that sense of spaciousness and endless possibility.

Out the window, in the distance, the Statute of Liberty saluted the sky with freedom's torch. We banked left and swung around the tip of Manhattan and over to the east side. Near the Southside Seaport, the pilot hovered above a large white circle on the ground before setting the craft down gently. Once the rotors whined to a stop, he popped open the front door. The agents and I piled out. A black limousine pulled up to the landing pad and its back door swung partially open. Parks escorted me to the limo. He pulled the back door open farther, pushed my shoulders down, and shoved me inside. Then he slammed the door closed.

"Shannon," Ken Tucker said from the shadows at the other end of the seat. He faced straight ahead. "I run an intelligence agency, not a baby-sitting service." He leaned forward and rapped his knuckles on the glass partition in front of us. The driver nodded and the limo pulled away. "Only big boys work for me," Tucker said, still not facing me.

We headed up the Eastside Drive, and Tucker remained silent. So did I. What was there for me to say? Simply placing the call to him meant I had answered "yes" to his Faustian bargain. The driver took the 14th Street exit, and we drove slowly past a huge electrical utility complex.

Tucker knocked on the partition again. "There," he said to the driver. He pointed to a secluded spot that overlooked the river, next to a fenced-in gray box with thick wires running into it and a sign that read "Danger: High Voltage." The driver stopped the car. My hands were still locked in cuffs. A line of sweat broke out across my brow, and with it the thought that this would be a perfect place to dump a body.

"You're on my watch now," Tucker said. "You fuck up this time, I throw you to the wolves."

Finally, Tucker turned to face me. Above his neat suit and fur-lined overcoat, contained fury burned in his eyes. I felt a sudden explosion in my solar plexus. A searing pain shot through my body. I doubled over and looked down to see Tucker's gloved knuckles buried into my mid-section. I tried to find a breath but I couldn't. Pain radiated from my belly outward. Bent over my knees, I thought I would vomit. I felt Tucker reach behind me and slip a key into my handcuffs. Then I heard the car door open.

Tucker lifted my chin. I fought for a breath. "Big boys clean up their own mess," he said. I felt his foot on my side. The next thing I knew I shot out the door and fell onto the pavement, gasping, coughing.

"You got twenty-four hours to clean up your mess," Tucker shouted.

He slammed the door closed. I watched his limo pull away and I collapsed onto the ground, mouth open, struggling for air. Then I heard the brakes of the limo screech. I looked up. It shot back at me, but I was too weak to move out of the way. The rear wheels stopped within a few feet of my head. The back door flew open.

"Shannon."

My body tensed. I craned my neck up and saw Tucker's gloved hand emerge with the 9mm pointed at me. He tossed the gun and it hit me in the leg. I groped on the ground for it.

"Twenty-four hours. That's all the time you have," he said, before closing the door and zooming away.

EIGHTEEN

LAYING ON THE ASPHALT, I felt even more like a minor chess piece saved from jeopardy, only to await the other side's next move. It did surprise me that Tucker plucked me from the jaws of a lion without asking for anything in return. He was after someone but he didn't know who. He sensed I was getting close. That's why he kept me in play. It wasn't only my mess to clean up. He also had me cleaning up his.

Any way I cut it, the first mess I needed to clean up was myself. A rest, a shower, a meal, and a change of clothes, in any order, sounded good. I stumbled down the stairs of the nearest subway station and found a phone booth. I called Nora's office even though I suspected her lines were tapped. Brendan answered.

"Hi lover, is that you?" I said, embellishing my falsetto with a lilt and a slight lisp. "Brendan, sweetie, I can't wait to see you tonight," I crooned.

Silence gathered at the other end. Finally, Brendan jumped in. "I thought I told you not to call me at work," he hissed. "Don't you know Girlfriend does not like me socializing on her time?"

"I wanted to remind you to pick up my dress," I said.

I let my hand slap the air gracefully as I'd seen Brendan do. It helped me stay in character.

"You promised to dress me and make me up before we go out tonight," I said.

"Marty," Brendan said.

"Marlene," I said, objecting with high-pitched indignation.

"Honey, I didn't dress you yet. Besides, I already have the dress and I left it at Conrad's last night. You do remember where he lives, don't you?" Brendan didn't wait for my reply. "1339 Prospect Avenue. Listen, I'll take off work early and meet you there at four."

"Okay," I said.

"And Marlene," Brendan added. "I can't wait to see you, either, honey."

"Ta ta," I said.

"Ta ta," Brendan said.

I didn't know if that performance rated an Oscar, but I hoped it fooled whoever was listening long enough for me to get a change of clothes and a shower. I checked my watch. It was already after three, so I paid my fare and caught the subway to Brooklyn.

A moment after walking up the stairs at Prospect Avenue, two men came up from behind me. They grabbed my elbows. I pulled away, turned quickly to my left, and crouched slightly.

The men looked surprised. "Honey," one of them said, "Brendan told us you needed a ride."

They ushered me to a waiting car. The three of us crammed into the back seat. I sat between one tall man and one short one. The moment the door shut, the driver sped off.

"See that?" the short man on my right said. "Brendan's been holding out. He didn't tell me you were tall, bald, and good-looking." Both men laughed.

The car turned off Prospect Avenue and a cold wave hit me. I wriggled free from between my two escorts. "Hey," I said, grabbing the driver's shoulder. "This isn't the way to 1339 Prospect."

"And manly too," the tall one said. "Are you sure you're taken?"

"I'm Conrad," the shorter man on my right said. "Brendan's mother lives at 1339 Prospect. Brendan lives at 32 Park Place in the Slope."

The car pulled up to Brendan's brownstone. It reminded me of a smaller version of our Striver's Row home. Conrad and the other man walked me through an iron gate and into the bottom floor of the brownstone. Conrad pointed to a wrought-iron staircase that spiraled up one floor. "Up there," he said. "The bedroom's on the first floor. Just knock on the door." Both men giggled then disappeared out the front door.

So far, my esteem for Brendan had risen to unparalleled heights, although I questioned my readiness for what I might find behind his bedroom door. I walked up the staircase, marveling at his taste in home décor. The brownstone had parquet wooden floors and one wall of completely exposed red brick. I stepped from the staircase into the living room, where a large nude sculpture of a man's torso from the waist down, done in white marble, sat in the middle of the floor. Small track lighting overhead illuminated the torso and the paintings that adorned his wall.

I walked through the living room toward the back of the house and knocked on the door I assumed to be his bedroom. "Brendan," I said.

No answer.

I pushed the door open.

"Hi," Nora said. She was sitting atop the bed, smiling. "Come." She held out her hand.

Nora moved to the edge of the bed. I sat beside her.

"I called Brendan. How did you get here?"

"After you called, he burst into my office. We stripped out of our clothes. Then he dressed as me and I dressed as him. He took the subway to my apartment while I took a taxi here. Maybe they'll figure out what happened, but at least we have a little time."

Nora pulled away from me and frowned. "You need a shower," she said. She handed me a bag with clean clothes and pointed to the bathroom door.

I came out dressed in a new pair of silk boxers and a tee shirt. Nora hadn't moved. I sat next to her again and I gave her the short version of Pelham Bay Park, Little Italy, and upstate New York. When I told her how close I'd come to JJ and how he'd said "I love you" with his fingers, she started to cry.

"It's Ciccarello," I said. "But I can't prove it. At least not yet. I haven't slept in thirty-six hours. I need an hour or two of rest. Then I've got a visit to make. It's a good thing Brendan lives in Brooklyn. I won't have to travel far."

"Lie down on your stomach," Nora said. She patted the bed behind us.

I looked at her funny.

"Nothing kinky," she said.

"Shucks," I said.

"Brendan's not only my wardrobe consultant and interior decorator—he also gives one hell of a massage. I've learned some great moves from him."

"And you're sure this doesn't cross professional boundaries?"

"I'll submit a bill to Innocence Watch for my services."

"It's my innocence I'm concerned about here, counselor."

Nora smiled. "Lay down." She patted the bed again and laughed. "I promise not to touch your innocence."

Nora's fingers seemed to melt into my flesh. The last thing I remember is mumbling something about how wonderful her hands felt after two years of not being touched.

I BOLTED UPRIGHT, A flutter in my chest, certain that it was morning and that I'd slept through the night. I whipped my head around to check the clock. The lighted red numerals floating in the darkness next to the bed read "8:00 p.m." Then I heard dishes rattling outside the bedroom. I flopped back down, my inner turbulence subsiding. I closed my eyes and took some deep breaths, conjuring Promise's voice in my head.

"Let your breath relax your body," I heard him say. "Take yourself back to the construction site in upstate New York. Tell me when you're there."

I slowly followed my inhalations and exhalations with my mind, as Promise had taught me. I felt myself slipping into a half-asleep, half-awake state. I saw myself parking Curt's SUV and walking toward the large metal building. "I'm there," I said to an imaginary Promise.

My body jerked hard as the squeal of the metal doors rolled through my mind. This time the white van seemed to bolt out of the garage directly into my face. I threw my head to one side to move out of its way. Then I saw JJ's face. My chest heaved and my legs twitched as I re-experienced running down the cold, hard road after the van.

"JJ," I heard myself shouting.

The van's red taillights loomed in the darkness of my mind like the eyes of a nocturnal predator.

"No!" I heard myself yell as the van pulled away. In my mind, I saw JJ flexing his fingers against the glass.

A flash of light from the middle of the van's rear brightened the imaginary scene. I saw the words "Empire State" in small letters on the license plate. I squeezed my eyes closed even harder. I saw JJ's fingers pressed against the glass. In my mind, I counted them several times, the way I remembered counting his tiny fingers and toes over and over in the moments after he was born.

"No!" I cried. My body writhed in the bed as the van disappeared into the dark corners of my memory. "No." I couldn't tell if I was really yelling or just imagining it. My body shook.

"John."

I heard another voice calling to me through my inner chaos and confusion.

"John."

I felt my body being rocked. White light flashed in my eyes. I sucked in a breath and sprung up. Nora was standing over me, her hand still on the bed-lamp switch.

"You were having a nightmare," she said.

Still half asleep, I looked into her eyes, trying to make out if she was real or a dream. I closed my eyes briefly. Once again, I saw JJ's fingers on the glass. I counted them. "Five," I mumbled. I threw my head back against the wall. "Five. The license plate had three fives in it."

My eyes flashed open. Nora stared at me as though I were a madman. And I felt half mad, spinning over in bed, jerking open a nightstand drawer. I fumbled for paper and a pen or pencil, anything to record the fleeting images that hung on by slender tendrils in my mind. I found an envelope and a chewed yellow pencil.

Like trying to remember a dream upon waking, I raced against memories that were wearing off fast. I scribbled three fives and tried to match their order with what remained of the license plate in my mind. New York State license plates have letters and numbers, but all I could recall was a five at the beginning of the van's plates, and two more fives somewhere toward the end.

I finally looked up at Nora. "Not a nightmare," I said. "I was trying to recall the license plate of the van that drove off with JJ, but I only got a partial."

"You need to eat," Nora said. She placed her hand on my shoulder. "I warmed some of Brendan's leftovers for us."

A few minutes later, I got out of bed and I dressed. Brendan had dark-brown pants, a cream-colored shirt, and a tan sweater for me to wear. He'd left baked Alaskan halibut, asparagus, and broiled potatoes for me to eat. I sat at the dining room table with Nora. Brendan's leftovers tasted as good as a restaurant's freshly prepared main course.

"You said you had a visit to make. Where?" Nora asked.

"The partial plate number from the van . . . I need to run it."

"But you got it from a dream."

"I got it from a trance. Something Promise taught me how to do."

"Still it's next to nothing to go on."

"Right now, it's all I have linking me to my son."

"Even if you're right, and you did get a partial, how can you trace it?"

"From the field office."

"The one in the abandoned warehouse near where the drug deal went down?"

"Uh huh. I can run the plate from there."

Nora gasped. "You haven't been in that tunnel since you and Rodrigues were shot."

"I know, but I damn sure can't walk into a police station and ask them to run the plates."

"And you're sure you want to do this?"

"I don't have another choice."

BRENDAN INSISTED THAT I match, so I donned a brown suede jacket that he'd bought for me. He even left Nora the keys to his car. I swung into the passenger's seat, and, finally, the thought of re-entering the tunnel seized me. A subtle vibration began in my chest. I took a deep breath and watched. When an image of JJ came to me, the vibration settled down.

I'd need a flashlight. I popped the lid on the glove compartment and laughed. Brendan had one there. A real boy scout. I laughed again, and it helped to ease my fear.

Nora remained silent as she drove.

"It has to be this way," I said.

"What?"

"I have to believe that JJ's still alive, and I have to try to find him before something happens. I have to discover the link between his disappearance and Curt's murder. I'm sure it's Ciccarello. Now I have to prove it."

"I'm scared," Nora said. "Scared that events will mushroom beyond control. Scared they already have."

"I'm scared too. But I don't know what else to do," I said.

Nora stopped the car at the water's edge. From across the river, the bright lights of Manhattan shimmied and fluttered in elongated, swirling patterns, broken apart then pieced together by the ever-moving current. I thought about Promise. I don't know if what I was about to do qualified as pushing the river. It felt like a last-ditch attempt at swimming upstream.

I got out and then stuck my head back in the car. I leaned over to kiss Nora on the cheek. I tasted a salty wetness there. I walked down to the water, then turned back to see the red taillights of Brendan's car fading away. I kicked a beer can out of my way. I picked up a rock and tossed it in the water. A river cannot look back upon itself. Try as I might, each step I took felt like a step back in time.

A few fenced-in, waterside condos, under construction my last time here, now stood within a hundred yards of the tunnel's entrance. It wouldn't be long before all the vacant lots and warehouses had given way to urban development. Harlem wasn't the only part of the city changing.

Ahead I saw the opening. I hesitated. The entrance reminded me of the large open concrete barrels on the playgrounds of my childhood. I pulled out the flashlight and patted my 9mm. The flashlight backlit a cloud of smoke rising from my nose and mouth. I stood outside the tunnel and shined my light along the walls, lined with graffiti like a tattooed arm. Then I pointed the flashlight down the center of the tunnel. The light seemed to disappear into the blackness.

I ducked inside the tunnel. Each footstep traveled before me, sounding into the darkness then echoing back. I once looked at civil engineering plans from the early 1900s. They showed a network of tunnels, not all leading into buildings, though no one knew how much of the network had actually been built. In order not to get lost, I always counted the exits leading from this tunnel. Tonight, the magic number was five.

I passed the warehouse that was too close to the condos, and then the one that was structurally unsound. The stench of urine grew. An eerie chill passed over me as I reached the third exit. Up above me was where Danny Rodrigues had died. I paused and shined the flashlight along the walls until I found the iron rungs leading up. I banged my fist against the concrete wall. If only this tunnel could talk. If only it could tell me what really happened that night. Or maybe the thick walls could suddenly turn translucent and a shimmering motion picture could magically appear like a crystal ball, revealing all, like who came up these stairs from beneath me that night, and what was that strange sound I later recalled. I pushed forward.

I wondered if the fourth building was still a crack house. It seemed such an irony to let it operate as we labored to remove drugs from the streets. But having a crack house as a neighbor provided realistic cover for our operation.

A familiar comfort came with reaching the fifth exit. I held the flashlight in my mouth and found the iron rungs leading up. At the top of the rungs, my head bumped against the bottom of a circular hatch. I held on to a rung with one hand while I illuminated the combination lock that secured the hatch from unwanted intruders. 5-2-2-7-2. I punched the numbers into the small keypad on the lock—"crack" spelled backward, in honor of the neighbors. A green light came on. The combination had not been changed. I put out the flashlight and lifted the hatch. Its rusted hinges groaned.

Moonlight and the glow of the city filtered in through fractured glass skylights and windows. I moved quickly over the aged concrete floors that were crumbling and turning to dust. I walked past tall, rusting, metal support beams. A dank odor infused the air. Against the far wall, a metal staircase led to a line of offices arranged along catwalks on each floor. A dim light shone through the opaque glass of a door on the second landing. I tiptoed up the steps, but they creaked under my weight. I slipped my fingers around the handle of my gun.

I moved along the catwalk. Outside the lighted office, I paused and listened. I squeezed the pistol. The crosshatched pattern on its handle pressed into my palm. Sweat oozing from my pores moistened the grip. I worked my hand around the metal doorknob and tried to turn it. It didn't budge. I leaned back against the railing and raised a foot. My heel slammed into the door, shattering the glass pane and bursting it open.

I found myself standing with my gun pointed at two men I did not know. They sat inside a windowless room, dwarfed by banks of electronic equipment. Both men were young and white. Both were dressed in jeans and a sweatshirt. Their faces blanched. Their gazes fixed on me. They had their pistols tucked into shoulder holsters. Both men reached for their guns.

NINETEEN

"Don't!" I yelled.

"Man, we don't have any cash or dope here," one said.

"Asshole." I wanted to slap him with my pistol. "Both of you bring your guns out slowly with two fingers and place them on the floor over there, away from the chairs. Do it now."

I watched their faces turn from pale white to beet red as they pinched the handles of their weapons, lifted them out of their holsters, and placed them on the floor. I moved closer to the weapons, keeping my gun pointed at the men as I stooped down to collect them. I looked into both men's eyes. The guy with the sandy blonde hair avoided my glance, while the dark-haired one with a crew cut returned a cold, steely gaze. His jaw twitched, and I knew he was watching my every movement for the slightest misstep. Cowboys always stick out.

When I reached down to scoop the second weapon off the floor, Cowboy sprung from his chair at me. He would have made an easy target to shoot, but as he rose from his seat, I took a step to one side, grabbed the back of his neck, brought my knee into his gut, then slammed the butt of my pistol into the base of his neck. He went down and stayed down, but his sidekick leapt from his seat toward the pistols. He had his hand on a gun, ready to sweep it off the floor. I stood over him with the barrel of my 9mm pressed against the side of his head.

"Don't do it. I could have killed Cowboy easily if I wanted to," I said. I pointed to the man sprawled on the floor. "All I came for is some information. You give it to me, and I'll be gone."

"We're a listening post, that's all," the man said in a shaky voice. His arm quivered as he moved it back from the gun. "You can't come in here and hold us at gunpoint. We don't have any information."

I crouched to pick up the weapon. "You've got a computer on that desk," I motioned with my gun. "That computer is connected to the department's central database. You seem like the brains of this team. So here's what I want you to do."

I walked over to a locker where we used to hang coats. I swung the metal door open, and out of the corner of my eye I saw the same centerfold taped to the door that had been there the last time I opened the locker. I kept my eye and my gun on both men as I reached up with one hand and groped around the shelf above the coat rack until I found a pair of handcuffs there.

Sidekick's eyes and nostrils flared.

I smiled. "Didn't know these were here, did you?"

"Who the hell are you?" Sidekick asked.

"You must be new to the unit," I said. I tossed the cuffs to him. "Turn your friend over and cuff his hands behind his back. Then come sit down in front of this computer."

Sidekick followed orders.

"What do you need to use the department's computer for?" he asked.

"Sit," I said. "Then open the license plate verification database and run this partial plate."

I plucked a pencil from Sidekick's shirt pocket and scribbled the portion of the van's license plate that I remembered.

"What's this?" he asked. "That's not a license plate number. It's just a bunch of fives."

"Run a partial plate lookup," I said. "The plate had a five at the beginning and two fives near the end."

"Yeah. A lot of good that will do," he said. "You remember any of the letters? New York State plates have letters and numbers."

"No, I don't remember any letters, but it was a white van, late model, maybe a Dodge or a Ford."

"Hell, could be thousands."

"Then we'll be here a long time. Now run it." I motioned toward the screen with the gun.

Sidekick grabbed the mouse, clicked it several times, and a search request box appeared on the screen. He typed in the information I gave him. A tiny hourglass appeared onscreen, sand falling from one chamber to the other before it flipped over and continued emptying itself. I didn't need a reminder that time was running out. Then the screen flickered once before it overflowed with responses. A message at the top said that 1,123 entries in New York State satisfied the search criteria.

"Sort it by county," I said.

Sidekick clicked over a header column marked "County" and the screen rearranged itself.

"I saw it in Duchess County. Look up all the records there."

"Fifty-seven," Sidekick said. "Mostly minivans and SUV's."

"No. It wasn't a minivan or an SUV. It was full-sized."

"Why are you after the van, anyway, if I may ask?"

"Someone kidnapped my son. I saw them driving away in a van with this partial."

"So why didn't you go to the police?"

"I did," I said. I swept my hand around the room.

I looked at the plate numbers that Sidekick had highlighted. They all had letters before the numbers, and somehow none of them looked right.

"You sure it was an upstate plate?" Sidekick asked.

"No," I said. "Look up all the city boroughs, Westchester and Rockland counties."

"Great," Sidekick said after a few clicks. "There are 592 possibilities. Now what do you want to do?"

I scanned the list, trying to match the fives with the pattern that I'd retrieved from my mind. Something seemed wrong about all the letters. None of entries struck a chord. I slapped the desk with the barrel of the pistol. Sidekick jumped.

"What plates don't have many letters?" I asked.

"Commercial and special issue," he said.

Sidekick pounded the desk. I jumped.

"I know who you are," he blurted out, pointing his finger at me. "You're . . . you're John Shannon."

"Bring up the commercial and special issue plates," I said.

"Twenty commercial, thirteen special," he said. "You killed that . . . er . . . I mean you were convicted of killing a DEA agent down here."

"It's nice to know I haven't been forgotten," I said.

I looked over the list, but nothing jumped out at me. As I scanned it again, the electricity dropped, dimming the lights. The computer screen flashed. The wiring in these antiquated buildings was atrocious. I don't know if the burst of light triggered my memory or reenacted the experience I'd had in Brendan's bed, but without conscious effort, I found myself staring at a number toward the bottom of the screen.

"T5392551." It was a special issue plate. "This one," I said. "Who's it belong to?"

Sidekick clicked on the entry and then laughed. "You must be psychic," he said sarcastically. "You chose a van registered to the NYPD motor pool. Looks to me like the kind used in special operations like transporting high-risk prisoners. The kind that'll be taking you away soon."

"No," I said. "That can't be. It was a Mob van."

"Look for yourself," Sidekick said, pointing to the screen.

"Can you find out who requested that van?"

"Probably," Sidekick said. "Let's see what I can come up with."

His politeness and eagerness to help surprised me. Sidekick worked at the keyboard while I looked over the equipment in the room. My gaze fell on three switches, marked "Tunnel," "Warehouse," and "Office." Only the office switch was on. Then it clicked. "Son, you're gonna make a great officer someday. Unlike Cowboy, you'll use your brains, not your brawn." I toggled the switch with the barrel of my gun, and a green light above the switch turned to red.

Sidekick looked up at me with a pained grin. "We're just a listening post," he said.

"You left the microphone on in here. It picked up everything we said?"

He nodded.

"Where's it transmit to?"

"Intelligence Unit somewhere in Manhattan."

In just a short while this warehouse would be crawling with police. I kept my gun on Sidekick and walked over to the doorway. I glanced outside, and through the fractured glass windows above the truck doors that led into the warehouse, I saw a kaleidoscope of lights headed this way. None flashed. I supposed they were trying to sneak up. I grabbed my gun with both hands and pointed it at Sidekick. He raised his hands chest-high.

"I don't want any trouble," he said.

"How sensitive are the mics in the tunnel?" I asked.

"Very," he said.

"Switch it on."

He didn't move fast. I knew he was stalling for time, so I rushed over and hit the tunnel switch with my gun. I found a large black knob and twirled it. The speakers in the room crackled and hissed with static, but nothing more. The tunnel was clear.

"You stay in here with Cowboy," I said, backing quickly toward the doorway. "If you come out, I will shoot you."

I raced down the stairs two at a time. By the time I reached the ground floor, I could see headlights just outside the warehouse.

"Hey, Shannon, you cop-killing bastard," I heard Cowboy shout from above. Sidekick must have also discovered the keys in the closet. I stopped behind one of the metal support beams. A shot rang out, pinging above my head and sending a shower of sparks raining down. Then I heard a swarm of officers barge through the front door.

"He's headed for the tunnel," Cowboy shouted.

A floodlight shattered the darkness and caught me as I found the first iron rung down into the tunnel. A bullet crashed off the top of the hatch as I slid down a few steps. I reached up and yanked the hatch down, then I locked the hatch and jumped to the bottom of the tunnel, running back toward the river. But I saw light playing in the darkness ahead. Someone had entered the tunnel.

I turned back toward the field office. I passed the iron rungs, where I heard fingers working the keys to the combination lock. I bet Cowboy itched to be the first one down. I peered farther back into the tunnel, then over my shoulder at the flashlights gaining on me. I heard the hatch above swing open. In all the times I'd been down here, I'd never traveled beyond this exit, but heading into the darkness was my only way now. I switched off my flashlight, stuffed it into my pocket, and spread my hands to either side of the tunnel wall. I ran, feeling my way as best I could.

The tunnel amplified sound, making it easy to hear the pursuit but hard to locate them. Someone ordered Cowboy and Sidekick out of the tunnel. That surprised me. Footsteps and voices echoed, at times sounding ahead of me, then suddenly behind me. Powerful searchlights cut through the darkness. Reflecting off the tunnel wall at just the right angle, the searchlights provided a moment's illumination into the depths of this nightmare.

I couldn't move fast in the darkness. I didn't want to turn on my flashlight. I felt along the walls for exits as I ran, but I found none. Suddenly, a voice I recognized resounded through the darkness. It seemed to come at me from every direction, riveting me in place.

"I told you, Irish," Nicky Brooks said. He laughed fiendishly. "Told you, man. Fat Daddy would have his turn with you soon. Think you a bad cop, don't you? Do some Rambo shit on my turf, then come bustin' in my place and embarrassing me in front of my people. Then go do some more Rambo shit in the Bronx, Little Italy, and upstate. You don't know who you messin' wit. You messin' wit me. Nicky Brooks. Your worst nightmare." His voice reached a fever pitch, then it dropped off to a cackle. "Think you bad? Let's see how bad you are, Irish. Yeah, man, let's see how bad you are now." His voice trailed off.

Thin shafts of light crisscrossed in the darkness behind me. I heard Brooks whispering to whoever was with him. I kept moving farther back into the tunnel, trying to understand what was happening. I'm at Nicky Brook's place, next minute the police stage an unannounced raid? Then I'm at a remote undercover field office, next minute Nicky Brooks is coming after me? He knows about my visit to Ciccarello's house, about me going to the Di Lustro, about me finding the warehouse upstate where JJ was held. My heart pounded.

"Nicky," I said. My voice echoed down the tunnel and traveled back to wrap around me. "So you're in bed with the Mob."

Brooks laughed. "Irish, Irish, Irish." His voice dropped lower each time he called out my name. "Maybe they should call you Snoop Doggy Dog wit all the sniffing 'round you do. 'Cept you done sniffed some shit that's way over your head now, my man."

I could feel him swagger as he talked. I wanted to rip the tongue out of his mouth. Instead, I kept moving back in the tunnel.

"What? You make a deal with the Mafia? They make you their token black? Put you in charge of Harlem?"

"Fat Daddy's nobody's token. You understand that?" Brooks' voice rose. "A lot's changed since you been in prison, Holmes. It's a new day in Harlem. Era of mergers and acquisitions, you know? Competition's out. Consolidation's in. See, Irish, they wanted back into Harlem, and I owned the territory, so I proposed a merger. Together we're—what do they call that?—an e-co-nom-ic trading block. We get better prices from Mexico and Colombia on our raw materials. We can even extend our business ventures overseas, buying from Afghanistan and selling in Uzbekistan. Damn, man, you know, it's the era of globalization and free trade. All that NAFTA shit." Brooks chuckled. "From fried chicken in Harlem to vanilla gelato in Little Italy. From rock cocaine to powder. We're a full-service corporation. Multinational and all. We value diversity." His laugh echoed around me.

I strained to see in the darkness ahead, but only Danny Rodrigues' face flashed before me. Suddenly, a lot of things began to make sense. I didn't know if I would get out of this tunnel alive, but at least I'd have the satisfaction of knowing the truth.

I called over my shoulder to Brooks. "You set up that deal to kill Rodrigues and me. When I turned up alive in a hospital, you saw a way of framing me for Danny's murder. You must have had someone working inside of NYPD. Someone like Vincent Ciccarello."

"Least you smart, Irish," Brooks said. "I'll give you that much, you smart . . . but not smart enough. Thought we had you put away for at least twenty-five years, then that little bitch lawyer got you out. Can't let you com-pro-mise our en-ter-prise."

A burst of automatic weapon fire ripped through the tunnel. Flashes of light exploded around me. I turned around and backed down the tunnel now, looking for fleeting shadows or shimmering silhouettes. Sweat streamed over my face.

"Yeah, my man," Brooks said. "You ain't smart enough. You or that tired old man who called himself a cop."

"You killed Curtis Wilson and his wife, didn't you?"

"If he hadn't been snooping 'round like you, he coulda gone into retirement 'fore we had to retire him."

"You're an animal. You don't deserve to walk the streets."

"Too bad there's nothing you can do about it," Brooks said.

I went down on my knee and raised my gun toward the lights behind me. In the darkness of the tunnel, an image of Curt and Dorothy, murdered in their bedroom, appeared before me. I could wait, and probably take out one or two of the men coming after me. But with no place to hide, I'd be an easy target, and I had no guarantee of getting Brooks.

"Mad, Irish? Mad that we killed your buddy and his wife? That make you mad, Irish?" Brooks laughed over and over again, his voice reverberating in my ear like a constant drip of water on the forehead of a prisoner, driving him insane.

I stood up. "You had JJ kidnapped too," I said. I started moving back down the tunnel. My guess was that if I kept talking, Brooks would send some men ahead of him toward my voice. Maybe I could pick them off one at a time.

"Had to give you something to occupy your time. Get you off the streets. You lookin' 'round so much would screw things up for us. Make you mad that I kidnapped your son? They say if you die with anger and rage on your mind, it's a more painful death. Guess you're gonna find out, Irish. It's really tragic. You dyin' with your son locked up in a warehouse overhead. So close, yet so far away."

I moved a little faster, groping along the tunnel walls for a ladder or a passageway out. I felt none.

"Irish, since this is true confession time, you wanna know something else?" Brooks said. His echo had changed. Up ahead it came back clipped and flat, while it rolled and reverberated in the direction of his voice. He laughed. "Pretty soon, this tunnel comes to an end with no way out."

I didn't want to turn on my flashlight. When I rounded the next corner, a flash of reflected light from behind me revealed a straight section of the tunnel with no apparent exits. Graffiti on the far wall read "Dead End." A skull-and-crossbones had been painted on each side. When Brooks rounded this corner, I would be trapped. But I kept moving ahead.

"You're mine now, Irish," Brooks said.

I heard the footsteps of Nicky Brooks and his men moving closer. Then I heard a different sound. It reminded me of a large rusted screw squealing as its threads were forced through tightly mated grooves. I also heard hinges squeaking. From the helter-skelter way the tunnel toyed with sound, I couldn't locate where these new sounds came from.

Perhaps someone had found another warehouse from which to drop down into the tunnel. The voices drew closer. I kept moving back, away from their lights, when suddenly huge arms reached out of the darkness, grabbed me by my shoulders, and dragged me over a threshold.

A door clunked shut behind me.

TWENTY

WHOEVER HAD HOLD OF me threw me up against a wall, so startling me that I felt electricity, not blood, flow through my veins. One hand crushed my shoulder, while another hand reached beside me and twisted a large wheel. He must have been a massive man because I felt hot air from his breath above my head. An unbearable stench suffocated me. I thrust my hand into my pocket for my gun, but a match flickered on and I looked up into the eyes of a black giant holding a finger delicately to his lips.

"Shhh," he whispered. The sound rolled forth from his mouth like waves crashing ashore.

The match sputtered out.

I could still hear voices outside.

"Nicky, the man's gone," someone outside said.

"No." Brooks' voice echoed through the tunnel outside. "Muthafucka can't just up and disappear. . . . You let him get away," he yelled at the men. "Now go find him."

I heard a sharp metallic crack, followed by a ringing echo. It sounded like Brooks had smashed a handgun into the tunnel wall.

"Check every exit back to the river. Maybe Irish climbed into a warehouse that we passed by."

The angry voices faded away.

I felt the giant's hand still on my shoulder. "Who are you?" I asked.

No reply.

"Where is this place?"

Still no reply.

His hands left my body. His breath pulled away. A moment later I heard a hiss, and then another tiny flame broke the darkness. Finally, a candle sent out a wavering yellow light.

The big man kneeled by the small flame. The dancing light cast ominous shadows over his face. Thick, dark spirals of dirty, matted hair sprung from his head. He let a scraggly beard grow. The candle revealed his jaundiced eyes. Globs of dirt caked his dark skin. He wore a frayed green jacket with a faded name patch that looked like military issue. I'd always heard that the homeless haunted this tunnel, but I'd never met them down here. I turned away from him and stared at the large turn screw attached to the door. It reminded me of something I might find on a ship.

The big man grunted and stood up. He lumbered over and nudged me out of the way. In the dim light, I saw him put two hands on the turn screw and pull it toward him as one might pull a lover closer. I'd seen no handle on the other side, no way for the world outside to enter his domain unless he allowed it. He locked down the door with a turn of the big screw.

"Thank you," I said.

The big man did not reply.

He walked back to the candle. He picked it up and held it gently in front of him as though initiating a ritual. We were in a ten-foot-by-ten-foot room, with rusting iron pipes running through the earthen walls and overhead. In one corner a neatly stacked pile of cardboard sat about four inches high and as long as the big man was tall. The tips of rags poked out from holes in a plastic garbage bag lying on top of the cardboard, about the right size for the big man's pillow. A foul smell filled my nostrils again, and I wondered what the big man used as a toilet.

I pointed up. "Is there another way into the warehouses up above?"

He looked at me as if he didn't understand my words.

"My son," I said. I put my arm to the side of my body, palm down, then brought both arms to my chest, rocking them like a baby. "My son is being held in one of the warehouses up above. Is there another way into them?"

But Big Man only contemplated the candle.

I put my ear to the door, listening for the sound of Nicky Brooks and the men with him in the tunnel. I was ready to go back the way I'd come, when Big Man put a gentle hand on my shoulder.

He brought his index finger to his lips. "Shhh," he whispered again.

He turned around. The candle lit an opening dug into the wall behind him. Without a word, he squeezed his body through, then poked the hand with the candle back inside, lighting my way.

I went through the hole, and on the other side the stench nauseated me. I turned on my flashlight and saw a dripping pipe overhead and a fetid pool of dark liquid collecting the drip. The odor came from a leaking sewer line that belonged to those of us living in the world above.

Big Man stopped in the next small room we entered. He rummaged through his pockets, emerging with a hypodermic needle. It glimmered in the candlelight. I waited for him to take out the white powder, water, and mixing spoon to heat the concoction above his candle before rolling up his sleeve. I wondered if he popped his vein with a belt tightened around his arm before injecting himself. He reached back into his coat pocket, pulling out two more needles, but he threw them all on the ground, smashed them with his heel, and swept them with his foot into a corner. When I shined my flashlight there, I saw a mound of shattered needles.

Big Man slipped out of the room. I scanned it with my flashlight. This room had the feel of an altar. On the wall in front of the needles a crinkled photograph of a young boy hung inside a broken picture frame. And on the wall to the right of that, Big Man had tacked two newspaper pages, now fading yellow and brown. I looked closer. One of the headlines read "Desert Storm Veteran Shoots Drug Dealer Who Killed Son." The other read "Convicted Veteran Escapes from Psychiatric Facility." I turned to leave, but Big Man stared at me from behind his candle.

He raised his finger to his lips. "Shhh."

Then he stepped from the room again. I followed Big Man through a labyrinth of small rooms and passageways. At one point, I heard a distant rumble. Big Man heard it too. He stopped and pressed himself against one wall as the rumble grew louder. The walls began to vibrate and shake, the sound thundering now. I threw myself against a wall so I would not stumble. It felt like an earthquake moved through my body, then slowly the shaking tapered off as the subway passed. Big Man pushed off from the wall and we continued our underground journey.

Ahead of me, I heard Big Man grunt. He threw his shoulder into a large door, which groaned and then swung open under his weight. He stepped down, and I followed him. We now stood in a huge tunnel with railroad ties under our feet but no rails on either side. I guessed that he'd led me into a deserted spur of the city's subway system. We walked for at least another twenty minutes before Big Man hopped up onto the platform of an abandoned station. I climbed up too, and stood there looking back from where we'd come.

I trailed Big Man down the platform. My flashlight beam bounced off the white tile walls, long ago faded to yellow. We passed the old wooden turnstiles leading onto the station, walking to the far end. Big Man jumped back down onto a surface where tracks once lay and trains once ran. I switched off my flashlight. Big Man's candle barely illuminated the way. He never broke stride or turned around. It seemed he knew the route so well that he walked it from memory, not from sight.

Promise used to walk like this in prison. He'd close his eyes and navigate blindly from his cell to the mess hall to the yard. He said that the echoes of his footsteps spoke to him. Big Man turned to his left, heaving his body, it seemed, into the subway wall. The wall appeared to open up and swallow him whole. When I reached him a moment later, I realized he'd simply shoved another hidden door open and stepped through.

"Shhh," he hissed.

I pulled out my flashlight as I walked through the doorway. He pushed me ahead of him. Ahead of me, I saw a rusted iron stairway leading up. In the distance, I heard a train rounding a turn. The echo of metal grating on metal reminded me of my prison cell opening and the turn screw to Big Man's door.

And then I remembered.

I'd heard the sound that night in the warehouse, echoing up from the bowels of the tunnel moments before the bullet exploded into my chest. It's the sound I recalled one day with Promise in the prison yard.

"You were there," I said.

I whipped around. I searched for Big Man with my flashlight, but he'd already disappeared back into the darkness.

I felt a tug to go after him. It gave me strange comfort knowing that he lived in his own world underground; morbid hope that even in this city I might find a place to hide forever if I needed. Promise, I'm sure, would call him an ancestral spirit living in the subterranean world of the dead, who occasionally surfaced to aid or play tricks on the living.

I climbed the staircase. Thick planks of wood covered the opening on top. Someone had fashioned an exit large enough for a person to fit through. I squeezed out. I looked behind me. Big Man had led me to a deserted lot about one-half mile from the warehouses, facing the rear of the buildings. I picked my way through the rubble field of trash and junked automobiles, walking over crushed red bricks and concrete chunks that probably came from the demolished buildings and homes that once stood here. Now I had to determine which warehouse JJ was in.

I ruled out the one farthest to my right because it held the field office. I also ruled out the one farthest to my left because it afforded people living in the condos a view. And I didn't think they'd use the one where the drug deal went bad.

One hundred yards away, two figures walked back and forth along the rear of the crack house building. They appeared to be armed, holding weapons at their sides. I crouched low behind a pile of rubbish, and a pack of rats scurried away. Two orange dots moved against the dark background of the building. I pulled my gun from behind my back. Smokers made easy targets. Then I circled wide to my left and came up along the side of the building.

The guards walked in a haphazard fashion. I pressed my body close to the edge of the building and waited several minutes before one drifted my way. I took a breath and held it. The lighted orange tip of his cigarette appeared first. I hooked his neck with my arm and whipped him around the corner. I jammed my forearm into his throat and pushed him up against the building, then I jabbed my pistol into his gut. His head drooped lazily to one side, and a thin line of drool oozed from a corner of his mouth.

"Hey, mannn." He slurred his words. His body undulated back and forth. "You want some rockkkk?"

I let go of his throat, and he raised a small rock cocaine pipe toward me. I pushed him aside and didn't bother with the other addict. That left building number two, the one the architects had declared structurally unsound.

I crept past the warehouse where Danny Rodrigues was killed. On the back of the second building, a metal stairway led to a door about two stories up. It looked like an old fire exit. The stairway swayed as I climbed it. Metal pins once bolted into the concrete had rusted away. I picked my way up carefully. A few steps were missing. Rust had fused the lock on the heavy door at the top of the stairs. I pulled on the door handle, but it broke off in my hand. I'd have to find another way in.

I started to walk back down the stairs, but the entire staircase pulled partially away from the rear of the building. It groaned, and then began to sway drastically. Only a few pins held it tenuously in place. I quickened my pace, but halfway down, the staircase made a loud scraping noise as the remaining few pins pulled away from the concrete. The staircase began to fall from the building.

The heavy structure toppled over in what seemed like slow motion. I turned in the direction of the fall and placed one foot on the railing. I waited until the structure was about twenty feet off the ground, and then I pushed off. I jumped as the staircase crashed to the ground.

I landed among the broken bits of brick and concrete in the vacant lot. My knees buckled after the fall, and I hit one on the sharp edge of a brick. It sent pain shooting up and down my leg, but I bit my lip and hobbled behind a nearby heap of refuse. More rats scattered. I peeked from behind the trash and slowly lifted my gun. Four armed men were inspecting the damage. Each was carrying a semiautomatic pistol.

"Damn building's so old it's falling apart," I heard one man say. "But just to be on the safe side, Devon, Oz, you two stay back here. Shoot anything that moves, including the rats."

The man who spoke and one other man walked back around to the front.

I slipped my gun into my belt. Using the downed staircase for cover, I slithered and crawled toward the side of the building, but as I moved, I pushed off on a loose piece of brick and it clattered against the downed staircase. The two men whipped out flashlights. I pressed my body to the ground. A rat crawled by my face. Its eyes gleamed red from the men's flashlights. It stopped and stared at me, as if to ask what the hell I was doing crawling around its turf, then it scampered away. A moment later two shots rang out, hitting close by in front of the staircase. My body stiffened. I heard a tiny squeal.

"I think I got that damn rat," one of the men said.

"Oh great black hunter," the other man replied. Both men started laughing.

I crawled farther along the fallen staircase, which provided me with cover until I reached the corner of the building. Then I tiptoed toward the front with my gun drawn. Peeking around the corner, I saw the man who'd given orders to the others. He stood guard next to the only doorway into the dilapidated structure. A cigarette hung from his mouth. Next to him, the remains of a loading dock rose above the ground, and on the other side of the loading dock the second guard patrolled.

I glided around the corner, leaned my back into the wall, and slipped closer to the first guard. He turned and saw me, but I hit him with two quick blows, first an elbow to his Adam's apple so he couldn't speak, then a smash to the side of his head with the handle of my gun, which knocked him unconscious. His cigarette fell to the ground. I dragged him around the corner. His partner heard the noise.

"Hey man, you okay?" his partner said.

I said nothing, standing just around the corner on the side of the building. A flashlight popped on and the other man ran toward me. Before he realized what happened, I stepped from the shadows, elbowed him in the throat, and then ran him into the wall of the building.

I slipped inside.

Dim light filtering through the windows revealed a building rotting from the inside out. A spider's web of cracks fractured the floor. Denuded of concrete, the tall steel uprights supporting the high ceiling had rusted through to the point that they looked moth-eaten. A thick buildup of pigeon droppings covered several uprights. Whole chunks of the inside walls no longer existed, exposing the underlying metal latticework like a body stripped of skin.

I stepped over pools of standing water. A chorus of tiny chirps and whistles played in the background. I guessed that now the building was as much a home to animals as it ever was to men. Toward the rear of the building, I spotted the hatch leading down to the tunnel. It was sprung open. I stood over it. Lights and the voices of men filtered up from below. If JJ was here, I'd have to find him quickly.

At the rear of the warehouse, pale light shone from an opening in the middle of the wall. I walked toward it. It wasn't a doorway but the top of a stairway leading down. The voices of the men in the tunnel grew louder. Their feet scraped across the iron rungs of the ladder as they climbed up into the warehouse. I hurried to the staircase. I took a few steps down and then crouched in the shadows of the stairwell. I peered back over the top step. The men shined their flashlights my way. I ducked lower. I heard them walking in my direction. They were about thirty yards away. I held my breath and clutched my pistol.

Suddenly, the door to the warehouse burst open and a man ran in screaming, "Nicky, come quick. Latrelle and Cosmo have been hit."

"Irish," Brooks uttered in a low guttural voice. "He's here." Brooks and his posse spun around on their heels and headed toward the door.

A damp chill climbed up the stairway. Thin blue light filled a doorway at the bottom. The old wooden stairs creaked as I walked down.

"Nicky, that you?" A man called out from beyond the door.

I took a few more steps and then froze with my back pressed against the wall. A moment later, the barrel of a gun protruded from around the corner. The man behind the gun obviously never had police training. When you're clearing out an area through a doorway, or around a corner, you don't advertise your presence by sticking your gun out ahead of yourself. Instead, you make one swift move with your body and gun as a single unit, and then trust your instincts to respond to what you face. Hopefully, you also have someone watching your back. What this man didn't know was about to get him hurt.

I grabbed the wrist with the gun and twisted it down sharply, then I planted my shoulder into the wall and yanked him through the doorway. I threw him into the wall on the other side of the stairwell. I slammed his bent wrist against the wall and heard his bones pop, but before he could yell out, I grabbed his throat and threw his head back. It hit the wall with a crack, and he melted into the ground.

I entered the underground room with better form. I crouched, stiff-armed my gun in front of me, then spun through the doorway. A small propane lamp sat on the floor. I didn't see anyone else. The lamp illuminated large, rusting meat hooks dangling from the ceiling by rusting chains. The light cast even larger shadows of the hooks on the walls. I took out my flashlight and shined it beyond the glow of the lamp. Like looking from one mirror into another, as far as I could see, meat hooks lined the room and receded into the darkness. This must have been the cold storage area of a meatpacking plant. I walked over to the row of wooden doors on my left. Some were closed, but others opened onto what appeared to be smaller rooms framed in wood—perhaps once refrigerated areas.

The first door had a new chain and padlock around it. I shined my light down the row. None of the others had chains. I thought about running back to the man at the bottom of the staircase and rifling through his pockets for a key, but I didn't think I'd have enough time. I knocked three times on the door with the barrel of my gun. I didn't hear anything from the other side. I had to chance it.

I stepped back and fired my gun. Even though the bullet took a chunk out of the lock, it still held fast. Now I heard footsteps running across the floor upstairs. I aimed at the lock again and fired. This time I broke it off. But the footsteps had reached the staircase. I kicked the door in and shined my light into the room. Four boys sat back-to-back in a circle, shivering in the darkness, with heavy tape around their wrists and ankles and across their mouths. I didn't see JJ.

I raced into the room, my heart pounding, and spun the boys around. I sighed. JJ was facing away from me, but I didn't have time to rejoice. I stripped the tape from the boys' mouths, scooped a sharp concrete fragment from the ground, and slashed the tape binding their ankles.

"Dad?" JJ shouted.

My chest swelled with the sound of his voice. I wanted to hug him and to scold him, but I couldn't stop to do either right now. I pulled the boys to their feet and pushed them toward the door. Like prisoners of war released from captivity, they shuffled rather than walked. I shepherded them through the doorway when two bullets whizzed by my ear, lodging in the wooden door and sending a tiny shower of sawdust into my face.

I pushed the boys to the ground and dove on top of them. Then I spun around. Brooks and his men stood just inside the doorway at the bottom of the stairs, craning their necks around and under the meat hooks. They shined their flashlights our way, trying to get a clear line of sight. I took aim at the propane canister beneath the neon lamp and pulled the trigger. When the bullet hit, a small explosion lit the room and a cry went up from the men. I lifted my body from the boys.

"Keep down, and follow me," I whispered. I crouched low and felt along the row of smaller rooms until I got to one with the door open. I turned to JJ and squeezed his shoulder. "Son, regardless of what happens, I want you to keep these boys in this room and remain absolutely silent." I nudged them into the room.

I wanted to lead Brooks away from the boys. I didn't dare turn on my flashlight, and I was afraid that if I stood, I'd walk into an old meat hook. Flashlights played over my head as I crawled underneath the hooks. Well away from the boys, I reached up and found a hook in the darkness. I pulled it back and sent it crashing into another, then I scurried off on my hands and knees.

"There," Brooks called out.

Flashlight beams whipped toward the swinging hooks. The men fired several shots, some hitting meat hooks and sounding them like mournful chimes.

"Irish," Brooks said. "Ain't no way out this time, my man. Better you come out now, make it easy on yourself and your kid."

I sent more hooks flying into each other and then hurriedly crawled out of the way. Another volley of bullets followed, another round of chimes played. I counted six flashlight beams in all, coming at me from different directions in the cavernous room. The men had fanned out among the meat hooks. If I fired my gun at the flashlights, I might hit one man, but I'd certainly give away my location, so I kept crawling away from the lights.

Suddenly, my shoulder rammed into an upright beam made of wood, not steel. The beam groaned and I heard several cracks before concrete pieces pelted me. I covered my head and rolled out of the way. Flashlight beams converged in my direction. Shots followed, sending more meat hooks ringing. I moved away quickly on all fours until I ran into a wall. The time to play cat and mouse had come to an end.

I fixed on the flashlight beam farthest to my right. I shimmied along the wall until I'd positioned myself just to one side of the person walking toward me. I reached up for a meat hook, pulled it back, and held it, waiting. When the light was six feet away, I let the hook go. A man yelped. I dove in his direction, wrestled him to the ground, and with a quick blow from the handle of my pistol, put him out. Then I switched off his flashlight. The other flashlights played toward me and I scrambled away from them.

"Irish," Brooks called out. "You can't escape us all."

I moved back toward the boys, trying to stay away from the lights. I searched for another upright beam, and when I found it, I rammed my shoulder into it and spun out of the way. The dry, rotted wood crackled, sending down more concrete from above. Flashlights and bullets came at me. I kept moving until I found the next beam in line.

I hit that one with my shoulder and dodged another downpour of concrete. More flashlights and gunfire followed.

I kept thwacking at the upright beams until my shoulders ached. I'm sure my skin was chafed raw. When I finally got to a beam near the room where I'd left the boys, I struck it several times with my shoulder. This one seemed sturdier than the others. I hit the beam again, the edge digging painfully into my flesh. Shots followed, and a bank of blinding bright lights pointed my way.

Brooks laughed. "Got your ass now."

I slammed my shoulder into the upright again as more bullets whined around me, ringing the meat hooks, making dull thuds as they dove into the beam. The upright started to move. I gritted my teeth, backed up slightly, and came at it with all the strength I had left in my body, plowing my shoulder into it, driving with my feet planted into the ground.

It gave way from above, falling with a crash. The bullets stopped, but nothing else happened. Then a shower of dust sprinkled me. I turned and dove into the room with the boys, gathering them under my body.

An instant later, large concrete pieces began to fall as the upper floor started to collapse. I heard Brooks and the men screaming, sending the meat hooks crashing into each other as they raced to escape. Then suddenly an avalanche of concrete and dust rained down, leaving me huddled in the darkness with the trembling bodies of the boys under me. I covered my head as best I could. A few ceiling pieces bounced into the room, hitting me in the back, but the frame of the small room protected us from the worst of the collapse.

I tried to take a deep breath, but I coughed from the dust. "Is everyone okay?" I asked. I sat up, but I couldn't see.

"Yes," four tired, scared voices said in unison.

"We've got to get out of here before the entire building collapses."

I searched for my flashlight and my pistol. I couldn't find either one. I must have left them near the beam I knocked free. So I groped toward the door. A pile of concrete rubble blocked our exit. I turned back. Straight up seemed the best way out.

"There's concrete between us and the floor above. I need each of you to dig with your hands as fast as you can. The first to break through, yell."

Pieces of concrete clacked as the boys and I shoveled them out of the way. The jagged fragments cut into my flesh.

"Here," JJ yelled. "I broke through."

A blast of fresh air swooshed into the room.

"Everyone go to JJ's voice," I said.

I moved back and let the other boys get through first.

"I can get out. Dad, I can get out," JJ yelled.

"Climb up on the concrete as high as you can, but please be careful, son. Check your footing as you go."

I heard JJ scrambling up the pile of rubble, then I heard him call out again.

"There's some people up here to help us," he said.

"Good. When you get out, help the other boys too."

I followed behind the last boy, clambering up the concrete mound. I stuck my head above the ceiling and saw a crater in the floor of the warehouse. Then I looked up at the man helping the boys, and a shudder rippled through my body.

Vincent Ciccarello aimed his gun at me.

TWENTY-ONE

"Get out," Ciccarello said.

He waved me up from the crater with a flick of his gun. I pushed myself up and over the lip of the concrete. Two other men held JJ and the boys at gunpoint not far away. When JJ saw me, he broke into a run.

"You leave my dad alone," he yelled.

Ciccarello turned his gun on JJ. "Stop right there," he said.

I moved toward Ciccarello, ready to jump in front of his gun. He turned his gun back on me, but looked over to JJ. "First I'll shoot your dad, and then I'll shoot you," he said.

With wide, teary eyes, JJ froze in place. I swallowed hard.

"Get these kids outta here," Ciccarello said to the men behind him. "And leave me alone with Shannon."

One by one, the men handcuffed the other boys, throwing them on the ground facedown. Then they went after JJ.

"No!" he screamed, kicking at the man who grabbed him. "No! That's my dad! He rescued me! No!" he yelled. "You can't take him!"

But the man handcuffed him and dragged him off, throwing him on the ground with the others.

Ciccarello laughed. "Your son's as crazy as you. Too bad—"

He hadn't finished his sentence when suddenly the door to the warehouse flew open. Cowboy and Sidekick blew in with their flashlights blazing and their guns drawn. They scanned the scene.

Ciccarello's jaw flexed. He barked at the two men. "I thought I told you to stay at your post. I've apprehended the suspect, and we have everything under control."

Cowboy raised his flashlight in one hand, his gun in the other, and pointed both my way.

"Vincent Ciccarello," he said, his voice booming through the warehouse. "You're under arrest for conspiracy in the murders of Drug Enforcement Agent Daniel Rodrigues, and New York Police Detective Curtis Wilson and his wife."

"You sons of bitches," Ciccarello said, turning his gun toward Cowboy.

I dove at his feet, sending him sprawling to the ground. His gun fell from his hand, and I kicked it away. The other men with Ciccarello ran for cover, firing on Sidekick and Cowboy as they did. I scrambled for the boys, gathering them together, pulling them back toward the crater as the men exchanged fire. Ciccarello had disappeared from the spot where I'd tackled him, but he wasn't my first concern. One by one I lowered the boys down onto the pile of rubble. I told the boys, who were still in handcuffs, to lie flat on their backs with their heads down, staying out of the line of fire.

When I turned back toward the gunfight, I noticed Ciccarello's men hunkered down behind two steel beams. Cowboy and Sidekick crouched on the other side of the remnants of a conveyor belt. I didn't have a gun to help. I searched on the ground for the one that had fallen from Ciccarello's hand, but I didn't see it either.

A moment later, sirens wailed in the distance. Red lights pulsed onto the walls of the warehouse. The men with Ciccarello yelled their surrender, stepping out with their hands in the air.

"Ciccarello climbed down into the tunnel," Cowboy shouted to me.

He and Sidekick raced to the other two men. They spun them around and handcuffed them, then they forced them to lie on the ground.

I plucked the boys from the crater. "Get the keys and uncuff them," I said to Sidekick.

Cowboy ran over to me. He was breathing rapidly. "Pretty smart thing you did, turning on the microphone in the tunnel and locking it on 'record.' We heard that guy's entire confession." He smiled. "Even got it on tape. Ciccarello headed down into the tunnel. You going after him?"

"I need your flashlight," I said.

He handed it to me and then put his hand on my shoulder. "Detective Shannon," Cowboy said, "you'll also need my gun." He passed me his weapon, handle first.

"Thanks," I said.

Cowboy gave me a crisp two-fingered salute.

———————

I RAN TOWARD THE hatch, climbing a few steps down, then jumping the rest of the way. I looked both ways at the bottom of the tunnel. Ciccarello's heavy labored breaths reverberated in the darkness, as if the tunnel itself were breathing. The echoes of his footsteps reached me, sounding clipped from the direction of the river, full from farther back in the tunnel. I also saw a faint light glowing from that direction. I didn't bother switching on my flashlight. I didn't need the light. I knew my way. I'd been deeper into the darkness of this tunnel than Ciccarello would ever go.

"It's over, Vincent," I called out.

Ciccarello wheezed trying to take a deep breath, then he fired a shot even though I was a long way from him. I didn't hurry. Only one way led from this tunnel in the direction Ciccarello ran. And I didn't believe that two huge dark arms would reach out for him tonight.

I had my gun drawn, dangling at my side. Walking back in the tunnel, I remembered Promise telling me the story of Theseus slaying the Minotaur. Theseus navigated his way to the center of a complex labyrinth, where he met and bested a Minotaur that had been placed there. Those who had tried before him had lost their way, but Theseus cleverly trailed a string behind him. So after slaying the beast, he followed the thread back out.

"Yes," Promise said. "Find the beast at the center of the labyrinth, which is yourself, and best that beast. But do not lose yourself in the process, or think that the only victory lies in slaying the monster. Emerge from the labyrinth with greater wisdom and insight than when you went in. That's the true victory; a victory over one's self."

"There's nothing to be gained by holding out," I yelled to Ciccarello. "It's over, and now you have to face the destiny that you've created."

He fired two more shots in my direction. They whined, biting into the concrete tunnel wall, and those whines tumbled over each other, echoing again and again like the wailings of a banshee.

I followed the pale glow from Ciccarello's flashlight, but when I rounded the next curve, his flashlight flickered several times before dying out. I heard him mutter low before throwing it against the ground. We both walked in utter darkness. I didn't need to feel the walls this time. I realized that by listening to the sound of my own footsteps, I could tell if I was walking in the center of the tunnel or off to one side.

Ciccarello's breathing grew louder. I placed him about one hundred yards away. We hadn't traveled far enough for him to be at the end of the tunnel. I cupped my hands over my mouth and shouted down the tunnel. I wanted my echo to wrap around him. "It's over, Vincent." My voice traveled along the tunnel, rolling off the walls.

Ciccarello gasped, then he started firing haphazardly in all directions. Blue-white flashes momentarily lit the tunnel. Bullets chattered against the concrete. It sounded like some ricocheted of the walls before diving into the ground. Ciccarello had become disoriented in the total darkness. He emptied his weapon until only the sound of metallic clicks remained, then he yelled at the top of his lungs and threw his gun against the tunnel wall.

I walked straight for him. I don't think he even realized I was there. I smelled the mixture of tobacco and cologne coming off the man. I grabbed his arm and he swung at me in the darkness. I twisted his arm behind him and high up his back, driving him to the ground. I put my knee on his neck and leaned my body into him. He strained and wheezed pathetically beneath me, and I realized that if I jerked his head back, I could snap his neck in two.

Holding Ciccarello there, I recalled sitting across from Promise the other day. I remembered his words: "You have Shango's cunning with the axe. Now you have to find his compassion and wisdom in dispensing justice. But only you can find Shango's truth inside of yourself."

I jerked Ciccarello to his feet and pushed him in the darkness back toward the warehouse. Shango and Theseus and Promise would be honored tonight.

We hadn't walked long when the sound of a metal screw turning and a door opening squealed in the darkness behind us.

"Thank you," I called out.

I imagined Big Man raising a finger to his lips. "Shhh."

OUTSIDE, IT LOOKED LIKE a circus had arrived. Police cars, fire trucks, and emergency service vehicles parked haphazardly over the vacant lot. Red and blue lights whirled. A bright spotlight blazed in my face. I blinked in the blinding light and covered my eyes with a hand. An officer took Ciccarello from me, handcuffed him, read him his rights, and then tossed him in the back of a squad car.

JJ and the other boys gathered around an EMT truck, sipping from steaming cups. When JJ saw me, he came swaggering my way.

"That was pretty cool what you did for me and my homeys," he said.

He held out his hand for a high-five. I didn't slap his hand. I could have slapped his face. Instead, I grabbed him by the shoulders. "Son, I want you to go back and bring your homeys over here. I need to talk to the four of you."

JJ strolled back to the group. He had a few words with the boys, and then they all walked my way. Their bodies bobbed and weaved in sync with each other. Their baggy pants fluttered like sails.

"Man, you a cool dude," one said.

"You aww-right," another said.

I pulled JJ into me and turned him so he faced the group. The top of his head nearly reached my chin.

"Here's how it goes down," I said. "You put this out on the street. Anyone messes with my boy, answers to me."

I felt JJ standing taller with the words. I spun him around. "Son, I catch you messing around with anyone in a gang, and you'll have to answer to me as well." His body slumped. "Everyone understand that?"

The boys nodded their heads and shuffled their feet in place. They started to leave.

"I'm not through yet," I said.

I stopped a medic walking by and asked for a pencil and paper. I handed them to JJ and pushed him forward.

"JJ's gonna get your four-one-one. Your street name, your real name, address, and phone number. In a few days, a lady named Claudine is gonna give you a call. Whatever she tells you to do, you will do. If I hear otherwise, I know where you hang, and you'll have to answer to me."

I heard grumbling. From JJ too. I scanned the list he returned with. Poonie was really Charles Simmons. Tank's name was Jamal Williams. And Snoop was born Edwin Perkins III. I was pretty sure that Claudine would welcome the challenge. The other boys dispersed. I looked JJ in the eyes.

"Son, I love you. You mean everything to me. Thinking of you helped me make it through the darkest hours of being in prison. But if I ever catch you hanging with gangbangers again, there'll be hell to pay. Do you hear me?"

JJ looked down. "Yeah," he muttered.

I picked up his chin and squeezed it hard.

"Do you hear me, son?"

His body stiffened. "Yes, sir," he said.

I let go.

Suddenly he burst out crying. "I was scared," JJ said. "I was scared no one would ever find me. But you did."

"I was scared too," I said. "I was scared for me and for you."

He hugged me tighter, buried his head in my chest, and cried. My eyes were wet. After a while, we walked with our arms around each other toward the street. A few stretchers passed us, some with sheets pulled all the way up, others with heads showing and tubes running to bags held high in the air. I believe I saw Nicky Brooks delivered alive to an ambulance. When we got to the street, a limousine sat with its engine idling. The back door sprung open.

"Need a ride?" Ken Tucker said. "His mom is waiting at City Hall."

We slipped into the back seat. JJ sat in the middle. Before the driver had even pulled away, JJ keeled over and fell asleep. With my son's head resting in my lap, I believe I better understood that old man in Henry Tanner's *The Banjo Lesson*. What you find of value inside yourself shines that much brighter when you pass it along to a coming generation. I hope JJ would not soon forget this lesson.

The sky behind us lightened as we crossed the Brooklyn Bridge. Tucker said nothing for the entire trip. We entered the underground garage at City Hall, stopping in the same place where Art and Babyface had left me. I saw Nora's car parked several spaces away. I saw Liz's white Volvo too. I woke up JJ and pointed to Liz, already out of her car and waving.

"Mom!" he shouted. He whipped off his seatbelt, climbed over me, bounded out the door, and raced to her.

Tucker slid a black shutter over the partition, isolating us from his driver.

"Got a minute?" he asked.

"Only if you don't tie my hands and take a swing at me."

"Old man like me needs a handicap," he said.

"Right," I said.

"So it was Ciccarello," Tucker said.

"Ciccarello and Brooks and the Mob operating as a joint venture around the world now. Danny Rodrigues was closing in on them from the Colombian side. And I was closing in on them from Brooks' side, though I didn't know it at the time. They needed to get rid of us, and I guess they thought they could stage a twofer. Kill Rodrigues and kill me at the same time. When it turned out that I wasn't dead, only injured, they tried to make it look like I shot Rodrigues."

"I knew I had you figured right," Tucker said. He reached for an envelope stuck in the seat pocket ahead of him. "Got something for you."

He pulled out a leather wallet and flashed a badge at me. It read "Special Agent—Office of Municipal Security—New York City."

"Take as much time off as you need before coming into work."

"Sorry, I can't."

A pained look stormed onto his face. "What?" he yelled. "Don't fuck with me, Shannon." He snapped the wallet closed and wagged his finger in my face. "I saved your ass the other day, or did you already forget?" His face had turned red.

"You want me to work for you? Okay. I need the work. But on *my* terms, not yours." I pointed my finger at him. "You got work, you call me. If I want it, I'll take it. I stopped working for anyone but myself when I left the force. Check," I said. I pretended to lift a chess piece and move it through the air. "Your move."

We locked gazes, dueling with our wills in a contest of "chicken." At first, I forced my determination on him, staring hard without flinching. Then I remembered: Not the eyes of a raging bull about to run into a matador's sword, but the eyes of a man steady within himself, who takes control by projecting quiet strength. I softened my gaze.

A moment later Tucker said, "An independent contractor?"

"Uh huh."

"Maybe I underestimated you, Shannon." He stuck out his hand, and I took it. "But that won't happen again." He grinned. "You didn't ask about pay."

"You in this just for the money?"

"It's fair pay, that's all," Tucker said, though he never did answer my question. "An independent." He mused. "Damn good move." He nodded his head. "I like how you play the game. I'll call you soon."

I opened the door and got out, walking toward Liz's car. Tucker's limo started for the exit. A moment later, it backed alongside me. His rear window whined as it slid down.

"You gonna use 'Irish'?" he asked.

"For what?"

"Code name. All OMS agents need one."

"Nope." I shook my head. "I'm not 'Irish' anymore."

"Well, have one by the next time we talk." He rolled up his window, but before his limo pulled away I knocked on the glass. The window lowered again.

"Got one," I said.

"What?" Tucker asked.

"Shango."

"Shango?" He paused for a moment.

"African god of thunder and lightning," I said.

Tucker smiled. "I like it," he said, rolling up his window as the limo pulled away.

I smiled to myself. Promise would like it too.

When I got to Liz's car, I could see JJ slumped down in the passenger's seat, asleep again. Liz pushed open her door and jumped out. She gave me a huge embrace and a long kiss that left a bittersweet taste in my mouth. Then she pulled back slightly, her arms still around me. She had tears in her eyes.

"Thanks for finding our son and bringing him back safely," she said. "He'll always be our son, and I'll always love that we had him together. He needs you. Just come to the house when you can; you don't have to call. You look hungry and tired. You want to go for breakfast?"

"Maybe some other time," I said. "Maybe after you've found answers to what you're looking for within yourself."

Liz smiled weakly. She hugged me and kissed me on the cheek this time. Then she slipped back into her car and drove off with JJ.

I walked over to Nora's car and leaned against the driver's door. Nora's head rested on the steering wheel, buried in her hands. She peeked at me and then lowered the window.

"Are you okay?" I asked.

"Uh huh," Nora said softly. When she lifted her head, her eyes were red.

"You don't look okay," I said.

"I was scared," Nora said, wiping her eyes. "Scared you wouldn't come back."

"From what?"

"Everything."

"At times I was scared too," I said.

"Of what?" she asked.

"That I wouldn't be able to accept my destiny with grace, gratitude, and humility."

"But you did."

"Sometimes," I said. "And when I couldn't, I just kicked destiny's ass."

Nora laughed. "The Justice Department won't seek a retrial. Brooklyn D.A.'s case will fold now as well. Means you can get a P.I. license if you want. Are you going to work for him?" Nora asked. She nodded in the direction that Tucker's limo had driven.

"Nope."

She smiled. "That mean you'll come to work for Innocence Watch?"

"Nope."

"Hey, buddy, no free lunch. You want to stay on my couch, I have to charge you rent. You need to find a job."

She stuck her hand through the window and jabbed me in the ribs. I flinched.

"Ouch, you're hurt," she said.

"Not bad."

"You want a home-cooked breakfast and a massage?"

"Depends on who's doing the home cooking."

"Brendan made crepes for us at his house."

"Brendan's a damn good cook. You're a damn good masseuse." I thought about it for a moment. "Maybe some other time," I said. "I need to walk right now."

Nora smiled in a way that made me think she understood. I walked out of the garage, and then headed east to watch the sun rise over the river and the city. I needed to finish walking my long mile, and that's something I could only do by myself.

ACKNOWLEDGMENTS

Joel Gotler, for his suggestion and enthusiasm. Natasha Kern, my agent, for her encouragement and determination. Whatcom County Chief Deputy Prosecutor, Mac Setter, for his consultation and advice. Barbara Sjoholm, for her wisdom and guidance.

Read on for an excerpt from the
next Shango Mystery by Clyde W. Ford

Deuce's Wild

Coming soon from Midnight Ink

Nothing says "starting over" like sitting alone in an empty apartment. But here I sat on a borrowed couch in the middle of bare wooden floors and naked white walls. Looking out the living room window, the one-bedroom apartment, which was in a newly renovated brownstone, had a view of other newly renovated brownstones across the street. And, if I craned my neck and strained hard, I could see a sliver of northern Central Park just a few blocks down from my building. Light green coated the trees. Spring had arrived in the city.

Nora Matthews helped me land this apartment, which had a long waiting list. She had a client, who had a friend, who knew someone, who worked for a man, whose son did this remodel and others in Harlem. So, after slipping an associate of the man two hundred fifty dollars for the man to give to his son, I found myself promoted to the head of the list.

A few assignments with Ken Tucker and a couple of investigations for Nora's legal agency left me with enough for a month's rent, a month's security deposit, an agency fee, a key fee, a utility deposit, a cable TV installation fee, and a telephone deposit. After that, I had barely enough to buy a few pieces of furniture and a television. The television sat on top of the upturned box it came in. But the furniture wouldn't be delivered for a week, which left me camping out in the wilderness of my living room.

The downstairs doorbell went off. I flinched. The ring tone on the high-tech system played a computerized version of "Stars and Stripes Forever," and I fully expected a band of tiny toy soldiers to emerge from underneath the couch and march across the living room floor. I went over to the small monitor sitting next to the front door and fumbled with a few buttons until the screen flashed on.

"Meow. Meow."

A cat's face stared at me from the screen, then a high-pitched, contrived voice coming from behind the cat said, "We just stopped by to say hello."

It was Nora and Madame Meow. I found the right button to push and let Nora in. "Stars and Stripes" played again. I cringed. The instruction manual for the security system said that you could use a home computer to download other ring tones from the Internet. I smiled. JJ, now fourteen, was coming over later to spend two weeks with me, and bringing his laptop, I'm sure. John Philip Sousa's days were numbered.

I opened the door before Nora got there so John Philip wouldn't get going again. She turned the corner from the staircase with a wrapped package in one hand and Madame Meow's leash in the other. Nora had on jeans and a fitted sweater that was the same white as Madame Meow's fur.

"Hi," she said, strolling in. "A housewarming gift for you." She handed me the package.

I closed the door behind her and she let Madame Meow off the leash. The cat took one look at me, sniffed the air, then, claws skidding over wood, raced around the living room and disappeared down the hall.

"Apparently she's not waiting for the cook's tour," I said.

"Well, I am," Nora said.

She reached out her arms, giving me a big hug and a little kiss, setting off a tiny spasm of longing.

"It's only been one day, and already I miss coming home to an apartment where someone else lives," I said.

Nora looked around. "Welcome to sex . . . I mean single life . . . in the city," she smiled, ". . . where, unlike it is on television, you spend a lot of time alone." She sat on the couch and pointed to the package. "Open it."

I peeled off the wrapping paper to reveal a boxed bottle of California merlot—expensive, but one that both Nora and I liked.

"Would you like a glass now?" I asked.

She waved me off. "No, I've got to go. I need to pack. Tomorrow I leave for a week-long public defenders' conference in Phoenix. Let's celebrate when I return."

"That's good," I said. "Because I only have paper cups. What do public defenders confer about for a whole week anyway?"

"You know the joke about lawyers going away to a conference?"

I winced and shook my head. "No."

"All bar exams take place during happy hour. Cross-examination's done behind closed doors. *Habeas corpus* has a new meaning. And married or single, whatever lawyer you end up with will still bill you for their time at three hundred dollars an hour."

"Habeas corpus?" I asked.

She smiled. "Show me the body," Nora said. "In Latin."

"I see . . . drinking and sex," I said.

"For some," she said. "For most of us it's a time to commiserate about the sorry state of affairs for the protection of civil liberties in the 'land of liberty.'"

The doorbell rang. Nora grimaced. "Stars and Stripes?" she said. "Oh, that's precious."

From somewhere down the hall, Madame Meow meowed as though the sound caused her great pain. I shrugged and pointed to the wall. "New high-tech security system."

"Yuck. Change the ring tone," Nora said, "or the Madame will never come back."

"Hey, Dad," JJ's voice came over the speaker. He waved into the monitor. Elizabeth, my soon-to-be ex-wife, stood somberly behind him. I buzzed them in.

"Liz and JJ are here," I said to Nora.

Nora sucked in a breath. "I was just about to leave anyway."

"Hell, Liz wanted to go through with the separation and divorce. If she can't handle seeing me with a friend, what will she do when I'm with a lover?"

John Philip beat me to the front door, and Madame Meow let me know of her displeasure. JJ "hi-fied" me as he sauntered in, dropping his bags on the floor. He glanced around the living room. "Cool," he said.

When Madame Meow came bounding down the hall, JJ went after her. The two were old friends, and she jumped up into his arms. Liz wouldn't cross the threshold uninvited. It seemed formal, but I invited her in, and she handed me a wrapped package about the same size as Nora's. Wine, apparently, was the housewarming gift of choice. Liz had on a pair of jeans too, though she wore a thin leather jacket over a vibrant yellow blouse. I don't think Liz registered Nora's presence at first.

"Hello, Elizabeth," Nora said.

Liz did a double take. "Sorry, John. I didn't mean to disturb anything."

The two eyed each other. JJ looked up from Madame Meow and stared back and forth warily between his mother and Nora. Nora stood and gathered Madame Meow from JJ's arms.

"Nothing to disturb," Nora said. "I was just leaving."

I opened the door and Nora slid sideways past Liz. She waved to me as she walked down the hall, raising one of Madame Meow's paws to wave as well. I closed the door and stepped back inside my apartment, where the tension was thick enough to cut with a knife. It'd been this way ever since Liz decided she needed to "find herself," and the only way she could do it, she said, was without me.

"I'm sorry," Liz said. "I should have called first. It won't happen again. I—"

I put a hand on her shoulder. She stiffened to my touch, so I pulled back.

"You don't need to apologize," I said. "Nora just stopped by to bring me a bottle of wine."

"Oh." Liz wrinkled her face. "So did I." She pointed to the package in my arms.

———————

I WALKED WITH JJ to the Dubois School, then I caught a subway downtown to City Hall. When I pushed through the doors of the Office of Municipal Security, I heard a familiar, deep, female voice sing out, "Good morning, John." I turned to see Charlene Jordan, Ken Tucker's secretary, smiling. She was wearing a fuzzy charcoal sweater with a string of pearls gleaming from around her neck and one pearl hanging from each earlobe.

"Congratulations. I heard you just moved into your new place," she said. Then she reached under her desk, emerging with a long, wrapped box. She handed it to me and winked. "I hope you don't drink it alone."

"Thanks," I said. I took the wine from her. "It's a pleasure to walk into the office and see you at your desk."

She smiled and fixed her gaze softly on me. I knew the look. It seemed to say that if I asked to see her outside of Ken Tucker's office, it would be all right. And I would have asked, if she didn't work for Ken Tucker. Business and that kind of pleasure are a combustible mix in my book.

"You can go right in," Charlene said. "He's expecting you."

I set the wrapped present on her desk. "Thanks again," I said. "I'll take this when I leave."

I knocked on Tucker's door, but there was no answer. I turned back to Charlene, who waved me in with a few quick backside flips of her hand.

Tucker held a telephone to his face with one hand, and with the other he pointed to one of two empty leather chairs in front of his desk. Behind him, out of his wide picture window, a blue sky reigned, sunlight glinted from the windows of Wall Street skyscrapers, and in the distance, the Verrazano Bridge snaked its way across the narrows from Brooklyn to Staten Island. A package wrapped in silver foil stood like a miniature skyscraper in the middle of Tucker's desk.

Tucker hung up, then sighed. "Washington," he said. "Glad I'm out of the agency, working here and not there."

I imagined Ken Tucker's closet organized in rows of blue, gray, and black suits. Some with pinstripes, some without. He wore a dark gray suit, without pinstripes, and a maroon tie today. He pushed the wrapped silver package toward me.

"Before I forget," he said. "It's a housewarming gift for you."

"Thanks," I said. I set the package in my lap and laughed to myself. Forget a bed and bureau. At the rate I was going, what I needed most was a wine rack.

Tucker's expression turned serious, and the already deep lines cutting across his forehead deepened more. "I just got off the phone with Homeland Security," he said. "We got tagged with a terrorist investigation. Seems some rap artist who lives here in the city decided to embark on his own diplomatic mission. Visited a number of Arab countries. Maybe even met with some terrorist groups. The State Department's furious because he asked them for permission, and when they denied it, he went anyway. The Justice Department has him on a terrorist watch list. We need to do a threat assessment on him."

"A threat assessment," I chuckled. "That include his music and lyrics, as well?"

Tucker failed to laugh. He picked up a sheet of paper from his desk. "Guy's name is Edgar Koontz, makes his home on the Upper West Side."

"Edgar Koontz? And you say he's a rap artist?" I shook my head. "Not with a name like that."

The lines crossing Tucker's forehead deepened even more. "Edgar Koontz," he said, as though barking an order. "A.k.a. Deuce F, who just changed his name to Yousef al-Salaam. And guess what, Shannon?" A sly smile swept over his face. He pointed. "Deuce's wild . . . he's your case."

───────────

THE NEXT MORNING WE stopped by the house to pick up clothes and JJ's schoolbooks. Since I wasn't sure who'd taken shots at us, and how much they knew about JJ, I decided it was best for us to stay at Nora's until she returned from her conference.

I'd just left JJ at school and started walking back to my apartment when my cell phone rang. The slow, controlled cadence and low rumble of Ken Tucker's voice added up to one thing: anger. I showered, changed clothes, and jumped on a downtown subway.

Charlene sat facing her computer. She swung around as I entered Tucker's office, and the smile on her face wilted.

"He's not in a good mood."

I managed a smile. "So what else is new?"

I knocked on Tucker's door.

"Yeah," a muffled voice came through the thick oak.

Tucker, sitting behind his desk, was tapping his palm with the blunt end of a silver stiletto letter opener. He put down the letter opener, propped his elbows on his desk, and leaned forward. All of his movements were slow, deliberate, calculated. The consummate chess player, studying, then making a move. I slid into a leather chair in front of his desk. He eyed me until I settled in.

"FBI called me yesterday," Tucker said. "I like Bill Jenkins. We've worked together in the past. Don't mind his temper. It flares quickly and it's a weakness, but I still like him."

He picked up the letter opener and studied it, then he raised his head.

"NYPD called me this morning. I don't like Art McCluskey." He paused and tapped his palm a few times with the letter opener. "It's not that I don't like him. Let's say I don't like when he calls me about the agents who work for me."

Tucker pointed at me with the business end of the letter opener.

"A hip-hop club trashed. An undercover investigation compromised. An unconscious man in Central Park. Your fingerprints on his gun. What the hell is all this about?"

I stared back across Tucker's desk. "Yousef al-Salaam," I said.

Tucker's jaw flexed. The letter opener hit his palm a few more times.

"Deuce F? Deuce F is a corpse, or have you forgotten that? You're investigating his death?"

"I am."

"For a client?"

"Yes."

"Who, may I ask?"

"My son."

Tucker's jaw flexed again. "You're kidding."

"No."

"Why?"

"JJ doesn't believe that al-Salaam was killed in a hip-hop feud."

"So you're destroying property and leaving people lying half-dead in Central Park to prove something your son probably heard on MTV?"

"Guy in the park came after me unsolicited."

"Hell, you've already stirred up a hornet's nest . . . no wonder someone came after you." Tucker shook his head. "Look, I run a security and intelligence agency, not a gumshoe squad, and certainly not a goddamn teenage rumor mill." He pointed the letter opener at me again. "What you do on your own time is your business. But understand this: As far as I'm concerned, you're officially off the investigation of Deuce F. So if you get into trouble with the bureau or with the NYPD from here out, don't expect a helping hand from me."

"That it?" I asked.

"Yeah," Tucker said.

I got up to leave, but the moment I grabbed the doorknob, Tucker called out in a low, slow rumble. "Are you sure you want to get involved in this just for your son's sake?"

I turned around and leaned my back against the door.

"The way I see it, I'm involved now whether I like it or not. Someone didn't like it when I started asking questions. They came after me and JJ with their claws out. I don't suspect they'll stop unless I stop them."

"Watch your six," Tucker said.

I could feel my six pressed into the back of his door. I shook my head, stepped away from the door, and pointed at Tucker.

"I'm touched," I said. "You sound concerned. Or is it that you want someone investigating al-Salaam's death, only you don't want the investigation connected to you? What's that called again?" I snapped my fingers. "Plausible—"

"Deniability," Tucker said. He pinched the letter opener between both index fingers. Then he spun around in his chair and looked out the window. A layer of orange-brown smog blanketed the city.

I pivoted, yanked the door open, and pulled it closed hard behind me as I walked out.

Noted mythologist, trained psychologist, and sought-after public speaker, **Clyde Ford** is a native New Yorker who now lives north of Seattle. He is the author of both nonfiction and fiction, including *Hero with an African Face* and *Red Herring*. Clyde has been a featured guest on *The Oprah Winfrey Show*, NPR, and many other television and radio programs nationwide.